Black Velvet Band

Teresa K. Lehr

This book is a work of fictive history.

For the most part, the relationships between and among the characters
and the descriptions of institutional and community events are based
on thoroughly researched facts.
(See Chronology of Real-time Events)

Characters' words and interactions are products of the author's imagination.

Cover snapshot courtesy of the
Rochester Medical Museum and Archives, Rochester, N.Y.

ISBN:
ISBN-13:978-197922371
ISBN-10: 1979922373
:

DEDICATION

To those women who have filled for me the roles of the sister I never had — confidants, mentors, companions in adventure and consolers in distress— and who have laughed with me and at my somewhat unusual sense of humor. What blessings they have been for me!

And especially to Sue, who demonstrated to hundreds of us that courage and caring about others can be an antidote to cancer . . .
. . . at least for awhile.

.

CONTENTS

Prologue

During the second decade of the twentieth century the temperance and the women's suffrage movements and the European military conflict followed parallel trajectories in the United States. The two movements had been initiated and promoted throughout much of the previous century; America's union with allied nations in a battle against aggressors in Europe was of more recent vintage. The leaders in each of those crusades, both the heroes and the villains, have been clearly identified and their known roles thoroughly recorded.

Suddenly, however, in the fall of 1918, the deadliest health crisis in recorded human history spread like a toxic blanket over this already tumultuous period, making it, in effect, a kind of "perfect storm." How the Spanish influenza pandemic may have influenced each of these events is the subject of *Black Velvet Band*, a fictive history account that places real characters in their actual historic contexts.

The setting – a training school for nurses in one of several general hospitals located in a major American city – is representative of similar institutions in other metropolitan areas. The nurse trainees in this story have been inspired by letters written by student Alice Denny to her sister Bess. They are the classmates Alice writes about most often. Facts about the hospital administrators and the city officials appear in existing archival records: meeting minutes, patient inventories, and annual reports. Most of the events portrayed in the hospital and in city neighborhoods have been gleaned from contemporaneous newspaper accounts.

Black Velvet Band fails to uncover a human villain in its examination of 1917 and 1918. But it does reveal historic individuals who, through their foresight, intuition, and selfless actions, may be considered authentic, if unheralded, heroes of the period.

Chapter 1

ROCHESTER GENERAL HOSPITAL AND NURSES HOME, ROCHESTER, N. Y.

Courtesy of the Rochester Medical Museum and Archives, Rochester, NY.

January 9, 1917

Dear Ruth [Alice's niece]:
    This card doesn't show the house I have a room in nor all of the hospital buildings. I'll try and write a letter…but I'm too busy for more now. My love and best wishes to you all, and do write often.

        Lovingly, Aunt Alice

"Here, let me help you with that."

A man's arm reached from behind Alice Denny and took the suitcase from her, allowing her to grasp the railing with both hands for balance. She lifted her boots from the street slush and ascended the three stairs into the warmth of the trolley. She deposited her coins in the glassed-in fare box. They clinked as they rolled down the chute and joined their counterparts at the bottom.

"Thank you, sir," she said, turning toward the young man and retrieving the suitcase that he held out. He was nattily dressed, she noticed. Under the heavy tweed overcoat peeked the lapels of a navy suit jacket and a royal blue bow tie. *Probably a clerk in the men's department at Sibley's or the National downtown*, she guessed. She noticed his eyes. They matched the tie exactly.

Holding the bulky suitcase in front of her, she moved down the aisle toward the back of the streetcar. Passengers' winter coat sleeves narrowed her passage. She didn't want to nudge anyone. It might disturb the quiet. This early in the morning, her fellow travelers were probably contemplating their coming day as she was, not yet alert to its possibilities – or its perils .

She would be joining Rochester's working class for the second time this cold, overcast day. Her first foray into employment a couple of years back had been a physical disaster. Every day she came home with a screaming headache and her back practically shouted out loud for the relief of a soft mattress. Being a stenographer in an office was definitely not for her. The job hadn't been physically demanding, but being always at the beck and call of business men challenged her mental endurance.

1917: a new year and a new life. Last year, Alice Denny would have still been in bed at this hour, snuggled warmly under the down comforter in her own fashionable bedroom. Tonight, she knew, she would be in a Spartan dormitory room, vying for closet and dresser space with a roommate from God knew where.

The bell dinged three times, and the streetcar jumped forward before she reached an empty spot on her right. Dropping the suitcase, she grabbed the seatback handles on either side of the aisle to steady herself. Again, the young man rescued her from behind, steadying her. As soon as she was seated securely, he lifted the suitcase to the rack above. "There. I'll get it down for you just before we reach Main Street, Miss, if you're going that far."

Thank you again," she repeated automatically, and then joined her fellow travelers gazing into the shadowy pre-dawn scene outside. Back on the sidewalk shapeless forms moved on stilts, hunched over against the wind, their heads bowed toward the icy sidewalks.

For the past year, Alice had been aware that challenges were coming, but she had successfully avoided thinking about them through the holidays. The parties, the presents, the carol singing had distracted all of the family from the reality that was lurking ahead.

The fortunes of the Denny family had begun to change two and a half years ago, when her father William died suddenly, at age 59. William had provided well for his family. A skilled machinist, the patriarch had worked his way up to a supervisory position at the Graves elevator factory, Rochester's home-grown competitor to the huge Otis Company. The family had moved to a two-story residence at 916 South Avenue on a block where William purchased a cluster of cottages. For several years the rents they brought in augmented his ample salary. And to insure the family's financial security, he had invested heavily in a growing Buffalo concern which manufactured chicken incubators.

After the South Avenue move, Sarah, Alice's mother, settled easily into her higher social tier. She was content with the anonymity that being the wife of a middle-class head of household brought. Her husband's death eclipsed that world somewhat. Collecting rents and directing property maintenance was an increasing worry. And Alice's health issues were adding to her burden.

Will Denny, Alice's brother, was more than a decade older than she was. He had established his own career, married and moved to Buffalo, and begun to raise a family. He lived a separate life now. The family did travel to Rochester for major holidays, making the return trip at the end of the day. But he rarely contacted his mother and his siblings by letter or by telephone between visits.

Alice's older sister Bess had broken away from their mother's middle-class matron model. After taking courses in stenography, she had secured a job as a secretary in an office downtown. Being in the business world was stimulating for Bess. It broadened the young woman's world and introduced her to her future husband Floyd Green, a lawyer. Following their wedding, they moved to Hornell, New York, and began raising a family.

Four years apart in age, the sisters had always been close, but Alice was more like her mother, content with their busy social visits, active in church projects, keeping abreast of fashions, staying close to home, and associating with friends whose values and lives were very much like her own. However, she knew she would have to find a way to support herself some day. At age 25, she was going back to school to learn skills she would need to work for a salary, perhaps for the rest of her life. A nurses training school offered a young woman free room and board as well as a place to practice her new knowledge and skills.

The streetcar bell dinged once, and the motorman yelled out, "Court Street!" The passenger sitting in the window seat next to Alice buttoned his overcoat, straightened his fedora, and stood. "Excuse me."

Alice moved her legs into the aisle to give him room to pass. Then she slid into the vacated seat as new passengers made their way toward her. She squeezed tightly into the seatback as a very heavy woman approached. The newcomer plumped down in the adjoining seat just as the trolley bell rang three times and the car lurched forward. She heaved a huge carpet bag on to her lap and sighed heavily.

"Thanks, Dearie," she said, her tone clearly conveying an urge to begin a neighborly conversation. "Sure is cold enough out there. Thought I'd freeze for sure." The woman leaned forward, inspecting Alice's stylish overcoat and hat and her leather gloves and matching shoulder bag and boots. "Isn't it a little early to go shopping, Missus? Stores don't open 'til ten."

"I'm not on a shopping trip," Alice stated curtly. She turned her head abruptly toward the window, shutting off the woman's impulse for a friendly chat. A fog had condensed on the inside of the glass, and Alice swept it away with her gloved hand. The darkness outside had lifted a bit; the stilted, amorphous shapes on the sidewalk were now oval blobs moving quickly on identifiable legs. Sleet began to hit and then drizzle down outside the pane, which steamed up again, spoiling her view. She refocused on her own reflected image.

Her lovely feathered hat, she observed, would have to be stored until she was set free from the regimen of the nursing school, as would her fur-collared overcoat and hand-tailored dress. She would have to put away the purse, gloves, and boots she'd found to match the suitcase as well.

Of all of the ensemble, she regretted most giving up the boots. True, they were not very comfortable, but they hugged her ankles like a second skin, giving her narrow feet the appearance pictured in most of this year's ladies' magazines. So many of her friends had admired the boots with envy. The training school, she knew, would make her wear ugly, but serviceable, shoes.

She laughed to herself. Just yesterday, her hairdresser had coifed her locks to perfection so that Alice would make a fine first impression. The hairdo would have to go, she was sure. She had never seen a nurse, or even a picture of one, who didn't wear her tresses in a tight bun at the back or on the very top of her head. On her first day off, she promised herself, she would make an appointment to have the mahogany brown waves shorn so that she wouldn't need to fuss getting dressed for work. That might allow her to stay in her warm bed a few minutes longer.

The bell dinged twice and the motorman yelled, "Main Street!" Her seat companion heaved herself into a standing position and moved quickly forward, shouldering past the people ahead. Passengers from the back of the motorcar filled the aisle, so Alice waited. Arriving at her seat from behind, the young man stopped just behind her and retrieved the suitcase from the rack above. "You go on ahead," he directed. "I'll carry it off the car for you."

She edged in front of him and followed the line out, stepping down gingerly onto the slushy island between the trolley tracks and the traffic lanes. The young man handed her the suitcase, tipped his homburg, and wished her a pleasant day. Once again, she yelled, "Thank you," to his retreating form, more in politeness than with sincere gratitude. After all, wasn't that what young men were for? To help damsels in their time of distress? Alice couldn't remember any time in her life that had been more stressful than today was going to be.

The noise of the street at this early hour surprised her. A continuous line of trolleys, the tethers on their roofs *zapp*ing and flashing momentary clarity to the scene, rumbled east and west in the center of the broad thoroughfare. Cars beeped impatiently as they edged past clopping horses drawing wagons at the curbs. Hack men punctuated the cacophony with friendly hails and shouted epithets not fit for a gentle woman's ears.

The odors assaulted her nostrils: exhaust fumes spiraling upward from automobile pipes, offal deposited by the horses as they plodded along, bacon and sausage aromas emanating from breakfast eateries. This early morning downtown was a world she had never before experienced. Being taxied in a comfortable, heated sedan around noontime was pleasanter, and far less stimulating to the senses.

The young woman negotiated her way between a boxy, red Pierce Arrow and a horse-drawn hay wagon. She kept her eyes on the brick pavement, gingerly stepping across trickles of melting snow and around steaming piles of fresh manure, all the while avoiding icy patches. With relief, she reached the northeast corner of the St. Paul/East Main intersection without slipping in the mire. But her boots were a mess. Where and when could she find some saddle soap, and who could she get to polish them? She searched the sidewalk crowd to the east; no bootblacks were in sight.

A trolley approached bearing a "West Main to Genesee" sign, its musical dinging a contrast to the other loud and angry noises. She searched in her shoulder bag for the fare for this trolley. There was no helpful young man riding on this conveyance, though, only factory workmen wearing caps, their crowns shoved forward and, their visors concealing the wearers' eyes. Struggling with the suitcase, she ascended the three steps and deposited the coins. Luckily, a man in a front seat, a bit less sullen-looking than the others, offered her his place and moved toward the back of the car. There was room enough, she found, to store the suitcase between her feet and the back of the motorman's stool.

As the trolley door closed and the familiar three dings pealed, Alice settled into her seat. She would have to keep alert for the Reynolds Street stop where she would get off and (*sigh!*) begin her new life.

Mary Keith, RN, Superintendent of the General Hospital, reached the bottom of the stairs and entered the subterranean tunnel, her brown skirt swishing around her ankles. She was rushed as usual, and frowning. She paused at a classroom door, pulled at the starched white cuffs peeking out from her jacket sleeves and checked to make sure the stand-up collar of her blouse was actually standing up. Here, the excited chatter of women's voices was unmistakable. It was loud enough to wake the dead – or in this case, the sick.

She winced as she opened the door; the noise was just short of deafening. Most of the new probation class were seated in wooden chair-desks that filled the room in tidy rows. Recalling her own student experience, she knew the girls had arrived at the hospital as strangers, quiet and shy, many of them away from home for the first time. But the china cups of hot tea being served from a table against one wall were melting their reticence, and clusters of two or three of them were beginning to explore each other's backgrounds. The soprano voices, amplified by the concrete walls and high ceiling, had risen to a crescendo.

This would be her thirtieth, bi-annual class-welcome speech. Health problems last year had hinted that perhaps she might not be delivering it many more times. Each of the past fifteen years had brought her at least one major challenge. So far this year her main concern was the perennial one for all of the city's general hospitals – St. Mary's, the Homeopathic, the Hahnemann, and the General – finances. Income from well-to-do patients in the private rooms plus the paying patients in the wards wasn't even close to equaling the hospitals' expenses. Charitable donations had steadily diminished since 1909 when Mr. Eastman's generous gift had made the General the city's health-care flagship. It was becoming nearly impossible for the institution to fulfill its pledge: to care for all seriously ill patients who sought admission, including the indigent.

Fighting an urge to quiet the hubbub, she approached Eunice Smith RN, Principal of the hospital's training school for nurses, who was seated at a small table to the left of the tea service. The school's director was registering a few young women who had entered the room tardy.

Eunice will put an immediate stop to that behavior, Miss Keith thought. The Principal stood and straightened the skirt of her white uniform as Mary approached.

"How does this group impress you, Miss Smith?"

"Enthusiastic! — And <u>very</u> young," the younger administrator said, eyeing a group of four girls who were moving their desks out of the neat rows to include others in their conversations. "This class will be like the others, I would guess. I'd hoped that the national situation would attract a soberer crowd. But these seem a little more agitated – actually excited."

Principal Smith stood, placed her pencil in the registration book, and closed it. "Well, they're all here," she said, smoothing a tawny lock that had worked itself free. She nodded to her assistant, Alice Gilman RN, who then began to clear the silver service and china from the table. "Let me introduce you to the probationers, and we can begin."

"I'll just make a few remarks, and then I'll turn the meeting back to you and leave. As usual, I have a very busy day ahead."

"I understand. Glad I'm not walking in your shoes."

The Principal moved to the front of the gathering. "Ladies!" Her voice had an edge to it that commanded attention. "It's time to get started!"

A few shushes from the probationers in the front seats put a damper on the noise, and it slowly abated until only a couple of girls whispered in the back. Finally –blessed silence.

"I'm honored to introduce you to Miss Mary Keith, Registered Nurse and Superintendent of this proud institution."

Miss Keith took over. "Thank you, Miss Smith," she said. For this first meeting with probationers, she always used a motherly tone, one that would not betray her realistic concerns about members of the audience. During the next three months, she knew, up to a third of these hopeful young women would be dismissed, judged as not possessing the qualities that registered nursing required.

"Welcome to General Hospital's Training School for Nurses," she began her usual speech. "Each of you has been conditionally accepted to Rochester's oldest nurse training school and second oldest hospital." She began her usual "tour of the room" delivery, walking up one aisle and down the next, gesturing broadly to keep her audience's attention.

"When we admitted our first few patients in 1864, this institution, known then as City Hospital, was a single building. The staff consisted of only two doctors-in-training, one resident intern, who also served as the apothecary, and two nurses who had learned their skills at the bedsides of sick family members and neighbors. This institution's goal then was to help the city's impoverished sick to regain their health. If it could."

A few of the probationers' eyes were glazing over, she noticed, and toward the middle of the assembly one young woman's eyelids were already closed. *The past bores them*, she thought. *So I'd better bring them up to the present fast.*

"Today this campus is a complex of a dozen buildings. Twenty-two senior physicians and thirty-eight junior medical staff diagnose and treat as many as 250 suffering men, women, and children from all social levels every day. In addition, we employ five interns, a resident physician, and a pharmacy specialist, not to mention the cooking and laundering staff, the ambulance drivers, and the workmen who do heavy chores and maintenance."

A murmur of interest began to spread through the gathering. "Each year this school graduates more than thirty young women, professionally trained and fully prepared to serve in one of the very few careers available for women. When you complete your courses and practical work, you will have a variety of current paths to choose from and the brand new fields in health care that are developing as I speak."

A listener in the back row raised her hand.

"Yes, Miss….?"

"Alice Denny, Miss Keith. Good morning."

"Good morning, Miss Denny. What would you like to know?"

"Are the wages good? After I graduate, will I be able to live on my own? Or should I start looking for a husband to take care of me for the rest of my adult years and old age?" A couple of the listeners giggled. The flush that rose in their cheeks suggested that they had been wondering the same thing.

"Registered nurses in private duty can demand the prevailing rate of $25 per week. The nurses on this hospital's staff don't receive that much, but they live in our buildings, dine in our cafeteria, and use our laundry services as part of their compensation. Factories are paying industrial nurses quite handsomely to keep their workforces healthy and on the job. Hospital-trained nurses are needed in the schools, in neighborhood settlement houses, and in the offices of private physicians.

"I can't speak for the other employers, but I believe that registered nurses make more than female teachers and certainly more than female stenographers do. And hospital-trained nurses can move up in their field, like Miss Smith and I have, as administrators, where their salaries will reflect added responsibilities. Does that answer your question?"

"Yes, thank you, Miss Keith."

"Now, since I need to earn _my_ salary by superintending this institution, I will turn your orientation back to Miss Smith, your Principal. I'm sure I'll see you in the halls of the General in the next three months. I'll know by your dresses that you're probationers, but you'll need to remind me of your names.

"Thank you, Miss Keith," the younger administrator said as her superior left the room. Then she turned to the assembly. "We're going to go easy with you to day, ladies, so that you can get oriented to your new home. Tomorrow you'll begin at 7:00 a.m. with inspection of person and dress." She eyed the pair of the probationers who had arrived late. "No one will be tardy. And everyone will have her hair combed up away from her collar. Do not have your hair cut; it is a proud sign of your womanhood. And everyone will be wearing a corset." The expected complaining whispers spread through the room.

"I see you've all brought suitcases. I sincerely hope that each of them holds the required three blue gingham dresses, at least six long aprons, under garments, two laundry bags, and a pair of high-ankled, low-heeled boots with broad toes. During every twelve hours of duty, you'll be doing a lot of standing and walking, and you'll probably need to change your apron more than once a day."

Several of the listeners shuffled their feet and looked at each other, frowning.

"When you are officially admitted to the school, you will share rooms in the Nurses' Home. But that building can accommodate only about eighty nurses, even with beds placed in every available alcove. Today, as probationers, you will be assigned rooms in one of the four buildings we maintain on the campus to house the overflow staff."

The whispers built into murmurs.

"Let me remind you," the Principal continued, "that even though you have the most heart-felt impulse to help the sick, you are not nurses yet. In fact, for the next three months, you will not even be pupil nurses. Any misconduct or inefficiency or moral or physical unfitness for work will be cause for your immediate dismissal."

Another hand shot up, this time on the far right of the assembly. The Principal nodded to the inquirer. "Florence Austin here, Miss Smith," the probationer identified herself. "Do you mean that if we get sick we can be dismissed?"

"No. If you get sick you'll get a free bed in one of our special wards and have the best care we're capable of giving you. Your services are valuable to the hospital, and quite frankly, we need you here and healthy. If you have a short-term illness, the days of class and duty hours you miss will have to be made up at the end of your training. But if your illness incapacitates you permanently, we will have to give your spot to another candidate."

"In three-months' time, when you have passed your examinations and you have shown a commitment to the patients and demonstrated the stamina to withstand the demands that being a nursing pupil requires, you may be formally admitted into the General's Training School for Nurses. Then you will have two and a half more years of demonstrations, studies, and work with the patients before graduating as hospital-trained nurses. If you pass the New York State board exam, you will be officially licensed as Registered Nurses."

Miss Smith reached for the tumbler of water that her assistant had left on the tea table. During the address she noticed that her audience was beginning to sit up straight, most of their expressions shifting from disappointment to determination. After a couple of swallows, she walked to the door and opened it. "Members of this year's graduating class will now assign roommates and conduct you to your dormitory rooms. Good luck. I hope to see all of you when you've successfully completed your probation."

Thirty young women gathered their topcoats and suitcases and filed out into the hallway. They were silent.

After showing two other pairs of probationers where their third-floor rooms were, the Senior tour guide opened the door labeled "Miss Denny - Miss Whitely." Alice entered first and looked around. Two beds flanked the single window in the wall opposite the door. Chips in the white enamel paint suggested that the metal bed frames had seen service in the wards during the previous century, before having been retired. A pillow, linens, and a gray blanket were stacked at the foot of each bed. Faint light from an overcast sky filtered through a single window.

"You'll be sharing the bathroom down the hall with the four other probationers on this floor," the Senior explained, yanking the chain dangling from a hooded ceiling light fixture. Electrification was obviously a recent addition; a couple of gas light sconces were the only wall decorations. "A warning: if you're not used to wearing a corset, it's time to adjust to one." Alice's new roommate groaned as the senior pivoted and left them alone.

"Which bed would you like? —Is it Mabel?" Alice asked.

"No. My name's Norma. I'll take the one on the right, I guess. It looks about as uncomfortable as the other one." She slid her suitcase across the dark brown linoleum toward the bed, leaving skid marks on its polish. Then she removed her coat and hat, threw them, and then herself, onto the bed. It squeaked in protest. "Mattress is thin. I can feel the springs right through it. But I'm bushed. I could sleep for a whole day." She lifted her booted feet to the top of the bedding pile and closed her eyes.

Her roommate had pronounced "about," "aboot," unconsciously identifying herself as a Canadian, Alice noticed. She also noticed the white marks made by the suitcase. *Housekeeping in this room is going to be difficult,* she thought, *especially through the rest of the winter and muddy spring. Wonder how often they'll inspect our rooms.* She looked down at her own leather boots, now stained with the dried mire she'd walked through earlier that morning.

"You'd better not get too comfortable," she admonished her roommate. "It's almost noon, and we need to get into our probation dresses and walk all the way over to the nurses' residence for lunch. It'll take time to get our hair up into that bun Miss Smith warned us about."

"I'd best get used to a tighter schedule," Norma replied. "And tighter underwear." She pronounced it "shed-yule," confirming the Canadian impression. "I wonder where we can get an extra sheet to cover the window. I must have privacy when I change clothes, even three floors up." She draped one of her own bed sheets across the empty curtain rod.

Both probationers got busy making their beds and unpacking their suitcases, becoming acquainted as they worked. They divided the drawers in the single dresser along the left wall and chose different halves of a scarred, wooden chifferobe that stood against the right wall. Two mirrors, one long and the other short, attached to this chest were losing their silver backings around the edges. A couple of small tables, each with a straight-backed chair, completed the room's furnishings.

"You're from Canada, aren't you," Alice observed. "I can tell from your accent."

"I don't have an accent; you do." Norma giggled.

"What made you apply here in the States?" Alice asked, carefully folding her undergarments and putting them in a drawer. "You're so far away from home. There must be nurses' training schools in Canada."

Norma sat up abruptly. "There are. In Toronto and Montreal and Hamilton. But they all have long waiting lists. I couldn't wait."

"How about Buffalo? That would be closer. I'd never want to be that far away from home."

"Why? Where are you from? Where's your sense of adventure?"

"I was born here, and I've lived here all my life. My home's about half an hour into the city by streetcar."

"Buffalo's schools are all filled up, partly with Canadian girls who want to get into the excitement like me. Remember, Canada joined the Brits in the war back in '14. Besides, my Aunt Edith graduated from this school in 1900. She thought it gave outstanding training, and now she's the housekeeper in the nurses' residence here. So I have an advantage."

She paused and looked at Alice, her eyes imploring. "My high school grades weren't all that good, though. I may need some help." Hearing no reply, Norma stuffed her under garments in one of the dresser drawers.

Alice quickly changed the subject. "So you really want to become a nurse?"

"It's been my dream since I was thirteen! And last summer told me I had to do it."

"What happened last summer?"

"I got a job as an attendant at Muskoka Sanatorium taking care of TB patients. At first I thought it was just drudgery, but when I saw patients actually getting healthy again, I was thrilled that I could help them recover." Again she paused. "Helping others makes one feel good about herself."

"Tuberculosis is terribly contagious, isn't it? I'd never want to get near someone with it."

Norma took the price tags off a brand new corset and fought her way into it. "Here, can you lace me up?" She turned her back to her roommate. "I didn't get it, though. When you take the right precautions, you don't get consumption." The Canadian grunted as Alice tugged at the corset strings. "Don't you want to be a nurse?"

"No, not really. I have to. Or find something else to do with my life."

Alice slid a shirtwaist over her head and viewed herself in the long chifferobe mirror. Carefully, she lifted an apron bib over the bun she had balanced precariously at the top of her head. Now she'd look just like all the other probationers. She sighed. Hand-tailored suits and fashionable hats and matching gloves, purse, and shoes would have to become just a memory. She might have avoided the regret if she'd become a teacher or a telephone operator, the other career options for women in 1917, but they wouldn't have given her three years' worth of free room and board.

"I need to learn a trade, to be able to earn a living. Didn't make it as a stenographer. It seemed wisest to come here where I can live free while I learn skills to support myself. That is, <u>if</u> I make it through probation and <u>if</u> I'm accepted into the school."

Norma stood in front of the smaller mirror, brushing her hair into an upsweep. "But it's such an adventure for a woman. Imagine! Sailing to Europe! Helping to save our brave Tommies! Even being assigned to an army training camp would be better than staying on a boring farm."

Alice talked to her roommate's reflection in the mirror. "How old are you Norma?"

"Eighteen. I graduated from high school last spring."

"That explains it."

"Explains what?"

"Oh, nothing." Alice glanced at the time piece that hung from a black velvet ribbon around her neck. "It's almost time. Let's go." She stored the little clock with its tiny red cross in the breast pocket of her dress and patted it. It was the only heirloom she'd brought with her. Aunt Anna had

worn it all through her own nurses training and career. She had left it to
Alice when she died.

"How old are you?"

"Twenty-five."

"I knew you were older. It's splendid that you live in Rochester. You
can show me around the city when we have time off."

Both women put their coats on, Alice pulled the light chain, and they
entered the hallway. "I don't think so, Norma. I have family responsibilities
that will keep me busy whenever we have our half days off. Momma's not
well, you know. She needs me. There'll be other local probationers that I'm
sure will be able to tour the city with you."

Norma frowned as she closed the door behind them. "Oh," she said,
no longer with enthusiasm.

The rapping at her apartment door was insistent, and Mary Keith
reluctantly dog-eared her place in a fascinating article in this month's
Harper's, "My Trip to the Front," by Mrs. Vanderbilt. The author, a
millionaire's wife, had organized the American ambulance service in France
when the European war broke out there. Mary admired the woman so
much, but she also envied her. She wished she was twenty years younger
and could serve in a battlefield hospital, especially now. But her age and her
expertise anchored her stateside. She needed to pilot this hospital ship
through the ocean of its patients' health issues, but threatened by waves of
insolvency.

The visitor, she knew, would be Eunice Smith. Mary had asked the
school's Principal to stop by for an informal chat. She needed to keep her
finger on the pulse of every vein and artery of the organism that was her
hospital. The training school was tantamount to the institution's aorta;
without the probationers, the pupils in training, and the graduate head
nurses and instructors who made up the staff, the institution wouldn't just
sicken; it would die. Physicians performed their magic and went home at
night, but the resident nursing complement ensured that the magic
continued to work.

Her friend, now dressed in a colorful shirtwaist, entered the suite that,
with its floor-to-ceiling bookcases, looked for all the world like a library. A
colorful carpet was the only hint that this was a living room, not just a
library reading room. A couple of comfortable chairs and side tables with
shaded lamps invited repose and meditation.

Once again, Mary noted how much she and Eunice looked like sisters.
Their hairdos, parted in the middle and now flowing to their shoulders in

graceful waves, were identical except for the coloring. The younger woman's tawny waves contrasted with the hospital Superintendent's silvery mane. The women were nearly identical in height and weight as well. Even without the obligatory corsets, neither of them had lost her hour-glass silhouette.

"Here, Eunie," Mary invited, removing the afternoon edition of the *Union and Advertiser* from the other comfortable chair in the room, "sit down and relax. Can I get you some tea?"

"No, thank you. I just got back from my half day off. Alice Gilman and I saw a delightful comedy at the Regent and stopped for tea at the Powers on our way back."

"I'm glad you enjoyed yourselves." The older woman put the newspaper on one of the side tables and took the second upholstered chair. "I was thinking that it's been a couple of weeks since I welcomed this semester's probationers. How are they doing?"

"As usual. The world situation has sobered the young ladies somewhat. Most of them seem anxious to have their time pass quickly so that they can begin practice before the war's over. Emptying bed pans, passing out food trays, taking temps, and giving backrubs is pretty dull stuff compared to the lives of the overseas nurses they're reading about. They're pretty keen on the bandaging class, but anatomy and physiology bores them to tears, as usual."

"How about the pupils in the school?"

"As you would expect, the Seniors are finding it hard to wait 'til graduation in May. The underclassmen aren't being distracted by the world events as much, and they're performing well."

"And your staff?"

Miss Smith deliberated before answering. "You know, a week ago I would have said they're all being their efficient selves, happy in their work and focused on preparing responsible and caring young women to advance our profession. That was when the headlines said that Germany was about to agree to peace terms."

She leaned over, picked up the newspaper from the table next to Mary, and read the lead headline aloud: "Today it's: 'German Raider Has 3 Submarines in the South Atlantic.'" She dropped the paper into her lap. "Civilians are dying on torpedoed ocean liners, and we're all waiting for the other shoe to drop. If America enters the war, the demand for trained nurses will explode." After a pause, she admitted, "We're all on edge. Should we volunteer or stay safe here?"

"What's the prevailing mood?" the Superintendent probed.

The Principal folded the newspaper, replaced it on the table, and brushed back a lock that kept falling in front of her eye. "Well, there's a rumor that Dr. Swan is looking for volunteers to form a Base Hospital unit.

If he's successful and the government needs us, our head nurses will find volunteering hard to resist. It does sound heroic, doesn't it? Crossing the ocean and saving the sight and hearing and limbs – and lives – of hundreds of courageous American soldiers?"

"I have to admit that it does, Eunice. If I were only a couple of decades younger…."

"Not knowing is the hard part, especially for the Canadian probationers. They're anxious to finish their training so they can help their countrymen –they call them 'Tommies'– who are already on the front. Speaking of Canadians, I separated the two probationers from Ontario so that they aren't roommates. In fact, they're not even on the same dormitory floor. And I've assigned them a couple of the more mature Probies as roommates. I'm hoping they won't be as standoffish as last year's Canadian pupils were, looking down on Americans because we've remained neutral. "

The younger woman stood up. "Sorry, but I can't stay longer, Mary. I've got to monitor the pupils that are on night duty. Generally, they're reliable, but on occasion one will nod off. And, of course, the one on duty tonight in the men's ward may need help with the man who was admitted this afternoon with DTs."

Mary accompanied her visitor to the door and bid her good night. Sighing, she returned to her chair and found her place again in the *Harper*'s article. It was a relief to be able to escape from her own mundane problems into the life-and-death world of the War in Europe.

Dear [Sister] Bess,
…. [We] were told tonight that we'd soon have bandaging exam, so pray for me as I haven't had Mama here to practice on. Miss Scarry and the other heads will watch, and we are to be able to do any bandage they ask for and we've had so many I fear I'll be confused.
                    With Love to You All,
                    ALICE

Chapter 2

Dear Bess,
....Rumors were that Miss Scarry and
Miss Gilman were to leave [with Base
Hospital 19] *but I hardly think it's true....*
Our demonstrations last week were
enemas though we haven't given any
yet. Our first ones are given under Miss
Scarry's eye. Hope she won't be as nasty
as usual...."

"NO! Not that way!"

Margaret Scarry, R. N. realized that she had shouted the words. She'd been concentrating more on the bandaging than on the student she was teaching. A perfectionist who had entered nurses training with the dedication of a religious sister, she intended to make it her life's work. But in the three years she'd been a member of the teaching staff of General's nursing school, she was beginning to question whether she could stand another year of this.

The instructor didn't care that the Probationers called her "Scary Scarry" behind her back. She had no patience with them when they first arrived. *Most of them are still teenagers, giddy and irresponsible. They have no appreciation for the knowledge and precision that the profession requires. The Canadians are worse than the Americans. They're either too eager to go help their Tommies in France without learning what they need to know, or they fall in "love" with any man in a uniform.*

Probationer Whitely's chin was trembling, and her eyes threatened to let loose a flood of tears. Not a good thing for an idealistic young woman in the first weeks of class. The instructor untied the botched bandage and moderated her voice. "It goes like this." Establishing eye contact with everyone except the weepy Miss Whitely, she demonstrated in slow motion on Alice Denny, who was role playing as a patient with a sprained ankle. "The first crossover is behind the ankle, not in front of it. That will limit movement of the ankle, which helps the muscles regain their strength." The instructor dreaded having to move on to splints and compresses and tourniquets.

As much as she disliked the Canadian girls, she shared something in common with them. She yearned to use her skills in a battlefield hospital in Europe or in one of the army training camps that were opening on this continent. Last week she had made an appointment with Miss Sophia Palmer, RN, nurses' recruiter for the local district of the American Red Cross.

Nurse Scarry had prepared her arguments like ammunition, ready to shoot down, or at least wound, the profession's attitude about selfless service. She would start with her personal objections. Then she would bring out the big gun, Miss Palmer's own activism and political lobbying.

The sixty-four year old career woman seemed delighted when Margaret entered her office and stated her purpose. "Yes, the military is desperate for nurses to help in the French Army hospitals, and your hospital experience would be welcome. However, you are needed at the General, Margaret, so I can't advocate your joining the Base Hospital that Dr. Swan is organizing."

The younger woman sat uncomfortably in the straight chair she had been offered, anticipating her superior's next argument. She was sure it would begin with the word 'But.'" Before that happened, though, she would fire a barrage of her reasons.

"It's not just the girls who think of my classes as an interruption to their social lives, Miss Palmer. The older ones are nearly as bad. There's this one girl who's a year older than I am. I catch her frowning at me all the time I'm lecturing, like she knows more than I do; she's <u>very</u> condescending to her instructors, especially to me. And she keeps aloof from the other probationers. She's smart enough, but she doesn't offer to help the younger girls who are struggling. Her home is here in the city, and she spends her free time either going there or studying or writing letters. Every half day she's not on duty, she gets all dressed up and disappears."

Miss Palmer spent a moment clearing a space on the paper-strewn desk and then leaned toward the nursing instructor, looking directly into her eyes. "Have you talked to Principal Smith? I would think that she might intervene if there was a severe morale problem among the students."

Nurse Scarry recoiled into the chair's back. She spread her arms wide, palms up; her voice pleading this time. "I did go to her. Miss Smith said that she doesn't want to interfere. It's up to Miss Reid and me to gain the respect of the Probationers." She looked down at her lap, avoiding the recruiter's intense gaze.

Recovering her composure, the younger woman revealed her private opinion about her superior. "I think that Miss Smith focuses on the girls who have been formally accepted into the training school – the First Years, the Intermediates, and the Seniors. The probationers are dispensable. If they don't make the grade, another three dozen candidates will replace them in April."

She pleaded once again: "But most of us who are young have the energy and the urge to sign up for overseas service. Even Miss Smith's face lights up whenever someone talks about it."

The nurse recruiter stood up, walked to the window, and raised the blinds. Drops streaking down the pane showed that it was still raining. The sky was a mix of grays; exhaust columns spewing from factory smokestacks dispersed into the cloud banks that scudded eastward. March in Rochester— that month when mud-spattered snow banks and soot-stained buildings complemented the sky's dreary monochrome palette.

"Margaret, I'm sorry, but I've decided to eliminate hospital staffs from this recruitment drive. You're needed too much here. At this stage, we want nurses employed by private patients who don't need round-the-clock nursing. Or nurses who retired from the profession when they married. And as the Army drafts more and more doctors, their office nurses will help fill the Red Cross's demands. The hospitals need all the trained nurses they can get if the America enters the war. Without instructors like you, they won't be able to prepare the incoming students."

Margaret stood. It was time for her to use her most telling argument. "But didn't you do just what I want to do, Miss Palmer? When you began the crusade to raise trained nursing to a profession, didn't you resign as General Hospital's Superintendent? You wanted the time to write petitions and lobby in Albany. Look at all you've been able to accomplish by branching out into the world. That's all I want."

Sighing, the gray-haired woman turned toward her petitioner. "That's just my point, Margaret. When I left the hospital, I knew that Mary Keith was more than capable of filling my shoes. And she has proved that in the past fifteen years. But at this time there's no one with your skills who could replace you."

She approached the younger woman and put her hands on nurse Scarry's shoulders. "The fact that you've been given an important hospital post at such a young age indicates that someday you'll be a qualified hospital administrator. You have a bright future ahead of you. But right now, I cannot consent to your leaving the General. I'd be disloyal to the hospital and to my friend Mary Keith."

Without a word Miss Margaret Scarry R. N. put on her coat and hat and walked to the office door where she retrieved her still wet umbrella. Her sight was as blurred as the office window was.

"If, on the other hand," she heard the Red Cross Nurses Recruiter's voice say through the closing office door, "America joins the Allied nations in the war, the draft will bring together young men from all over the country. They'll be crowded into tents, sharing the germs they bring with them from their hometowns. They'll need dedicated nurses like you. And I believe our boys will soon be fighting on French soil. They'll be wounded and maimed, needing the skills that only trained American nurses can give them. In that case, I'll reconsider your situation."

"Thank you, Miss Palmer," the younger woman said, her voice lighter now, hope filled.

That evening, six graduate nurses lingered over coffee until all of the pupils had left the cafeteria in the basement of the Nurses Home. Around a circular table toward the back of the large room sat three head nurses: Katherine Gray, Mary Olds, and Charlotte Sherman. Social Services Director Mary Laird, Superintendent Keith's assistant Emma Jones, and Margaret Scarry, Instructor of Probationers, were also at the table.

Sounds of the kitchen staff at work gradually faded, and only the clink of silver spoons against china coffee cups and the hushed conversations of the nurses remained. Hurried footsteps approached the entryway, and the women looked up expectantly.

Quickly removing her coat and her gloves, the training school's Principal, Eunice Smith, joined the group. "The meeting was exciting," she panted. "Dr. Swan is already organizing a Base Hospital to be ready when war is finally declared. And he needs nurses."

Members of the group eagerly leaned forward as the newcomer pulled another chair up to the table. "They're not sure whether the unit will serve stateside or overseas. It'll take time, though." She ticked off three items on her fingers: "They have to collect enough beds, pillows, and blankets for five hundred patients. And recruit enough physicians and technicians. And raise a lot of money to buy equipment and ambulances and such." She inhaled deeply to catch her breath.

"Who's in charge of getting the nurses?" Nurse Jones asked.

"Sophia Palmer. She's already in charge of finding Red Cross nurses for national service."

"But…," began Margaret Scarry, the youngest member of the group.

"How do we sign up?" broke in Mary Laird. "Who do we contact?"

"But…," Miss Scarry tried again.

"They'll be enrolling nurses and physicians at the State Armory next Thursday evening."

Margaret raised her hand this time. "But…."

"How many nurses will they take?" asked Miss Jones. "We can't all go, can we?"

"They didn't say, but I suspect nurses from the Homeopathic, the Hahnemann, and the State Hospital will want to sign up. And there are sure to be nurses in private practice dying to get in on the action." The speaker's nose wrinkled with distaste. "Tending to a rich patient who really isn't sick must be the most boring job in the world, even if it does pay the best wages."

The group agreed. They turned to each other naming nursing friends from the other hospitals who had confided in them about volunteering for Red Cross service. If they didn't sign up right away, the competition for a place in the local unit would be fiercely competitive.

"But…." Margaret was surprised when the murmurs stopped suddenly. Everyone looked her way.

Principal Smith finally acknowledged the young instructor. "Yes, Margaret? What is your question?"

"It's not a question." The young instructor paused briefly, surprised that her opinion did matter. "A week ago I met with Miss Palmer to volunteer for the national recruiting drive. But she told me that she isn't accepting hospital staff nurses. She said if she did, there wouldn't be enough registered nurses left to instruct and supervise new training school candidates."

Disappointed mumbling circled the table.

"She has a point, I think. But I don't believe Miss Palmer can hold back this steamroller, as respected as she is. The men in charge are passionately patriotic, as you can imagine. They're positive our boys can straighten the whole European mess out, and they're eager to keep our troops healthy and able to do just that."

"She did say, though, that if the country goes to war, she will have to reconsider her decision," admitted the youngest nursing staff member.

"But what will the hospital do? If we all volunteer, where will Miss Keith find enough nurses to staff the General and carry on the school?" asked Assistant Superintendent Jones.

After a moment's thought, Miss Smith replied, "I'm positive that Miss Palmer will be able to meet Rochester's quota of nurses for the national drive. But the Base Hospital would really benefit from a group of women who have worked together in the same community and who know the area where the servicemen come from. Jessica Heal over at the Homeopathic told me privately that a few of their staff want to enter the service. Rochester nurses caring for Rochester boys will lend a touch of home, you might say."

"That's all well and good for the Base Hospital and for us, but what about Mary?" reiterated the Superintendent's right-hand woman.

"Look around the table, Emma. Except in your case and Mary Laird's and mine, each of us has a counterpart who can manage her department until a new supervisor can be found and acclimated to the job." She gestured toward Margaret Scarry. "I'm sure Margaret's education partner could manage both teaching the Probationers and orienting a new instructor. And my assistant, Alice Gilman, knows just about as much as I do about directing the school."

A crash of pots and pans in the kitchen startled everyone. When they relaxed, she continued.

"Besides, it'll take some time to assemble the Base Hospital's staff and to collect all of the equipment. We probably won't be leaving for quite awhile. Miss Keith should have plenty of time to find replacements. After the Seniors graduate on April 16th I'll be able to recommend the most promising ones for the General's staff. Mary will have the whole summer to troll for graduates from other schools too. They'll be young, but Margaret here has demonstrated that even nurses without much administrative experience can step into important roles in the hospital."

The nurses nodded in agreement, and a spark of pride shone in Margaret's eyes.

"Then let's vote. All in favor of volunteering?" Seven hands raised immediately. "Anyone opposed?" There was no response.

"So," instructed Miss Smith, "those of us who are scheduled for duty next Thursday evening should trade off the time with a replacement. And since we've all agreed, the rest of us can take the trolley to the Armory as a group."

As a single organism, the white uniformed group stood, replaced their chairs neatly under the table, carried their coffee cups to the serving window, and filed out.

The school's Principal waylaid Miss Keith's assistant just before leaving the room. "Emma, will you tell Mary what we're planning? I admit to being a coward; I just can't bear to tell a friend I'm leaving her."

A reluctant pause preceded the response. "I will, Eunice."

"But be gentle, will you? The past couple of years have been difficult for Mary."

"I'll be as gentle as I can."

"...for Alice Denny." The faint words distracted Alice from the anatomy textbook.

"A visitor for Alice Denny." The message, relayed by a pupil on the second floor landing, was fully audible this time.

Using her note pad to save her place, Alice closed the book, walked into the hallway, and yelled down the stairs, "If it's my mother, please ask her to come up." Returning to her room, she quickly put Norma's pajamas, thrown in a heap onto her bed, in the roommate's half of the chiferobe and straightened the blankets. Canadian teenagers were about as tidy as American teenagers were, it seemed.

Alice finished buttoning up her "civilian" dress as she heard footsteps ascending the stairs. They were labored, a pause between each one, and Alice regretted expecting her mother to climb the two flights.

Sarah Denny was panting when she appeared in the doorway. Alice led her to her own bed and sat her down. "Here, Mama, rest. You look paler than you did last Sunday. Can I get you a glass of water?" Her mother shook her head no.

Sarah looked at least a decade older than her 56 years. The death of her husband William three years before and her own health problems were clearly wearing her down. She was very thin. The effort to get up to the third floor should have brought a flush to her face. But her skin was nearly white, and there were gray circles under her eyes.

Nevertheless, she was stylishly dressed, as always. Ready for an outing with her younger daughter, one of the few pleasures she still had the stamina to engage in and could afford. An early spring freeze had burst one of the water pipes at 916 South Avenue, and the widow had had to vacate the homestead while workmen repaired spaces behind the walls where the water had seeped through. Renting a room at Kent Hall was economical, but room and board at $1.00 per day stretched her dwindling monthly income nearly to its breaking point.

"Where shall we go?" she asked when she finally caught her breath.

"Want to see the movie that's opening at the Regent?" Alice suggested, combing her hair in front of the smaller mirror. Sitting in the theater would be preferable to the exhausting round of shopping and visiting with friends in Sarah's social circle that they used to enjoy. "It's *The White Raven* starring Ethel Barrymore."

"That sounds about right. Then we can join my house mates at Kent Hall for dinner and spend a quiet evening together. If you have any mending to do, why don't you bring it with you?"

"Okay, I'm about ready," Alice said, helping her mother to her feet. "Let's go." Grabbing her purse and sewing bag, Alice led the way down the staircase, concerned that her mother might lose her balance and tumble down them.

Sundays were always easy days to travel in downtown Rochester. The Main to West Avenue trolley was nearly empty when they boarded it, and for once, the car didn't lose power along the way. At the Four Corners stop they transferred to the East Avenue bus for the short ride to the Regent.

As they left the theater, the Denny women agreed: Miss Barrymore's performance was first rate, but the plot was too improbable, too melodramatic. Alice engaged a cab waiting at the curb. In the past, they would have enjoyed the stroll from the Regent to Kent Hall, window shopping along the way. But today Sarah's condition discouraged that kind of exercise.

During the short ride to South Washington Street, Sarah related the history of her new residence for her daughter. In the 1880s, the YWCA had opened Kent Hall to single immigrant women looking for employment as domestics and other unskilled work. It was one of several similar boarding houses scattered among downtown side streets. When the flood of immigration lessened ten years later, boarding house clientele changed. The Hall was now the residence of Rochester's fast-growing population – widows and single women in the work force. Repairs to her house had forced Sarah to temporarily join their ranks.

Dinner at Kent Hall was a sprightly affair. The pot roast, potatoes and gravy, and boiled carrots were tasty, and the conversation at their table of six was stimulating. The women began by discussing their day: comparing sermons at their various houses of worship and describing afternoon outings. Then they progressed to news of the day: guessing when the country would officially enter the European war, debating whether women would be given the vote in New York State, and wholeheartedly agreeing that the nation would benefit if the production and sale of alcoholic beverages were outlawed.

After ice cream and coffee, her mother and Alice excused themselves and retired to Sarah's apartment.

"I have a roommate," the older woman explained as they entered the third floor sitting room furnished with matching wicker rocking chairs and a small table. "All of us on this floor have to share one bathroom," she continued, leading her daughter through a door to the tiny bedroom. "But the ladies here are very accommodating, so there's rarely a conflict. Miss

Miller, my roommate, lost her husband too, so we have much in common." She gestured toward the interior where twin beds separated by a table with lamp were crowded by two small dressers. "I like to pretend I'm in nursing school, like you. And that this is my room in the nurses' residence."

Returning to the sitting room, Alice settled into the chair closest to the dormer window. The pink floral print of the drapes blended nicely with the chair cushions. But it clashed with the cinnamon and beige geometric patterns in the wall paper. She drew out a pair of the stockings she had brought to mend. "You're in luck being compatible with your roommate, Mama. Sharing a room, especially with a teenager from a foreign country, has been one of my biggest challenges."

"I can imagine. Are your meals at the hospital as good as the one we had this evening?"

"Better, I think. They treat us well. They want us healthy and strong. If we get ill, the head nurses will have to change the soiled bed linens, empty the bedpans, and mop up the vomit themselves. Actually, I've gained four pounds."

"It doesn't look badly on you, dear. I hadn't noticed." Sarah took up the camisole she'd been hemming from the shelf under the table top.

"I think the weight is turning into muscles. We're always running to class or to an assignment in another building or to seven a.m. inspection." Alice inserted a wooden egg into a stocking, cut off a length of black darning cotton, and threaded her needle.

"If you don't have much in common with your roommate, are there others you can relate to?"

"They're nearly all younger than I am. Some of them have boyfriends. Others came from distant towns and want to explore Rochester. That's why I've been spending most of my half days off with you. I'd really rather be at home than leading city tours."

Sarah stopped hemming and looked at her younger daughter. "I'm so sorry our lives have been disrupted, Alice."

Dropping her almost mended stocking onto the table between them, Alice went to her mother and knelt in front of her. "Oh, Mama. It's lonely not having you around every day to talk with. I'm home sick, even though I see you twice a week. And I worry about you so. Your health, I mean. You need me there to collect the rents and to tell the maintenance men what to do and to manage your social calendar so you don't overtire yourself." She laid her head on her mother's lap and encircled Sarah's tiny waist with her arms. "I want to withdraw from the school, at least until you regain your strength."

Sarah smoothed her daughter's hair and lifted her chin to look directly into her moist eyes. "Alice, I think I understand how you feel. But no, you cannot withdraw."

"Why?" the daughter demanded, standing abruptly.

"Because you have to have a way of supporting yourself, now and after I am gone."

"What do you mean?" Alice was pacing now.

Sarah decided that a direct confrontation with the realities of their lives was better than softening the blow. "Remember the securities your father invested in before he died?"

"Yes."

"Well, at that time the company was growing and very profitable. But the European war has drastically reduced its export business. And there was a bad fire at the plant early in February. A couple of weeks later, the firm declared bankruptcy. Today the stock is worth only a fraction of what your father invested in it."

Alice stopped walking. "What about the cottage rents? Don't they bring in enough?"

"No. The maintenance on our house and the upkeep of the cottages barely covers my living expenses. Eventually, I'm afraid, they'll have to be sold."

Alice knelt and hugged her mother again. "Mama, I'm so miserable. What can I do?"

Sarah stroked her daughter's brown waves. "You'll do quite well, sweetheart. I have confidence in you. You're bright, so I know you'll pass your examinations. And I'm sure you'll eventually learn to like nursing."

She lifted her daughter's chin and looked deeply into her eyes. "There's a bit more bad news, I'm afraid, Alice. I need to keep an eye on this situation first hand. As a major stock holder in the company, I'll have to be in Buffalo while the court settles the creditors' accounts. For several weeks I'll be staying with your brother Will and his family."

"But Bess is so far away in Hornell! And Buffalo's even farther." The daughter paused. "It's not fair! Can't I go to Buffalo with you, to be <u>your</u> nurse?"

"I'm afraid not." The mother lifted her daughter's shoulders gently. "There's always the telephone. I'll call you every week to let you know how things are coming along and to see how you're doing. You can keep writing letters to Bess, and I know she'll write back. And I'll scold your brother. Will needs to telephone you more often."

"You'd better give him the nurses' residence number. He's never used it."

It was dark when Alice finally boarded the trolley that took her back to the hospital. As worried as she was about her mother's situation, self pity kept intruding on her thoughts. *I hate the dormitory and my roommate! I despise those officious instructors! I don't want to spend the rest of my life nursing strangers! Why can't things to go back to the way they were before Daddy died?*

....You'll be tired reading of my life here but really there's nothing else for me to write of for I don't know what is going on outside. It seems as though I'm in another world. Probation is over 7 weeks from yesterday and then - wonder if we'll be accepted.

My love & best wishes, Alice

Chapter 3

Dear Bess,
....Our theory medicine & practical
classes are over but we still have A[natomy]
& P[hysiology].... Nothing has been said to
us about our uniforms & caps as
yet....Wonder if all our class will stay....

Mary Keith had been poring over the balance sheets for an hour when she heard the familiar sounds of her assistant, Emma Jones, hanging up her raincoat and umbrella in the outer office. The hospital Superintendent was both relieved and disappointed. Her disappointment came from the fact that she still hadn't been able to finish the task she had risen so early to complete. Her relief arose from knowing that Emma's interruption would stop this exercise in self punishment, at least for awhile.

"Well, we're finally in it." Emma appeared in the doorway carrying a cup of steaming coffee in one hand and a folded *Democrat and Chronicle* in the other. A few rain drops still glistened in her brown curls.

"Who's in what? Emma, I truly wish you'd use nouns," Mary complained.

Setting the saucer down on her superior's desk, the assistant retorted, "And I truly wish you'd let me work on those figures. Remember, I'm the number person; you're the word person. Then maybe you wouldn't be so testy this morning."

"Sorry I'm in a bad mood, Emma. But I wouldn't give this chore to anyone I cared about. It's impossible! The city doesn't pay nearly enough for the patients they send us. The part-pay patients are more of a drain. And I can never raise the private patient rate enough to cancel out the deficit. Maude Johnston over at Homeopathic says she's in the same boat, and it's listing dangerously. She and I can't let our ships sink."

Miss Jones unfolded the newspaper and placed it on the desk with the banner headline oriented toward her superior:

PRESIDENT SIGNS WAR RESOLUTION AT 1:13.

"To get back to my opening comment: the country's not neutral anymore. The United States is officially in the European war."

"Doesn't Congress have to vote on it? It seems to me that politicians debate for years and still can't agree. Look at prohibition…and women's suffrage." Miss Keith picked up the newspaper and scanned the other articles on the first page.

"They already have. Besides, the president is the Army's Commander in Chief. And most of the politicians have been itching to get into the fight any way. Don't you ever read the front page?"

"Since women don't have a voice in the matter, what's the sense? I read the local news first and then go to the business page." Mary sighed. "Our opinions don't matter. And since we don't have a voice, most of us don't know how the government works."

"President Wilson has plenty of allies, both Democrats and Republicans. And except for Montana, they're all men."

"Thanks for filling me in, Emma." The Superintendent gathered the balance sheets in a neat pile and moved it to a shelf behind her. "The news makes my work on these figures absolutely futile." Then she began to pace. "Sit down, Emma. What we have to do today is try to figure out how the war will affect the hospital. Do you think the Army will siphon off most of our staff?"

"They'll ask for volunteers and call out the National Guard first, like they did in the last war. Then, if this one keeps up, they'll have to institute a draft." She looked down at the desk top, avoiding eye contact. "But there's something else you need to know."

"What?"

"A group of volunteers is already forming into a medical unit in Rochester."

"So?"

"It's called Base Hospital 19."

Miss Keith faced her assistant. "I've read about that. And…?"

"Some of the General's staff have joined it."

Mary Keith stopped pacing. "Who?"

Emma raised her eyes and then spit the answer out all at once, like bad-tasting medicine. "Well, there's Eunice, and Mary Laird, and Margaret Scarry, and three head nurses…and me."

Miss Keith slumped into her chair.

Now it was Emma's turn to pace. "Mary, you must know that we've been thinking about this. All of us have committed ourselves to caring for the sick and the injured. Surely, there's a need for us here in the hospital. But we see a greater need. None of us was sure that the Base Hospital would ever be activated, or I would have told you earlier. We were hoping the country would remain neutral. Then I wouldn't have had to tell you."

"I suspected something like this was going to happen, Emma. A few weeks ago Eunice hinted that a few of our head nurses were tempted to volunteer as Red Cross nurses. Frankly, I envy you young ones. Compared with wrestling with finances and placating the hospital's Board of Directors and the Board of Lady Managers, the prospect of doing some actual nursing is very tempting."

Raising her head and straightening her shoulders, the Superintendent resumed her usual confident posture. "Let them know I don't blame them, will you? I'll find some way of filling your places, but it'll be hard. You're all so competent." A glint of humor returned to her gray eyes as she shifted the balance sheets back to her desk top. "There must be someone else on the staff who can help me with these numbers."

"Thanks for understanding, Mary. Why don't I get you another cup of coffee? That one must be cold by now."

"Thank you, Emma. And thank the others for holding on to their idealism and maintaining their sense of duty."

Miss Keith waited a few moments after her assistant left. Then she closed her office door. Returning to her desk, she pushed the button on the intercommunicating telephone set. "Please get me the Red Cross office, Gladys."

Lifting the speaker to her ear, she waited for the receptionist's voice. "Hello, this is Mary Keith at General Hospital. May I speak with Miss Palmer if she's not too busy?"

When she heard Sophia Palmer's voice, she launched right in: "Sophie, the Army will need all of the medical personnel they can get. What will the hospitals do for nurses and house staff when that happens?"

"What do you think, Alice?" Norma asked as she and her roommate walked across the campus toward inspection and breakfast. It was spring, and the sun had been up for at least an hour. "Miss Reid has always given me passing marks. But Miss Scarry never liked me. I think Canadians disgust her. Will I be here next month? Or will I have to go back across the border tomorrow?"

Alice tried to be positive, although she was tired of tutoring her roommate nearly every day. "You do so well with the patients, Norma. I can't imagine that the instructors haven't noticed that. Your pulse, temp, and respiration numbers are always accurate and recorded consistently. And the patients clamor for you when it's time for their evening backrubs."

She inhaled a deep breath of the spring air and then continued candidly, "I don't know how you can stand some of them. They're so weak and so needy, so messy. The women's ward is all right. And the children can be cute sometimes. But the men's ward is a place I just don't want to be."

The cafeteria was especially noisy when they entered after morning inspection. The Seniors had been animated for weeks, sharing and comparing their future plans. For most, their careers would begin on the day after graduation, when they could finally don the white dress and wing-like cap with the coveted black velvet band. It was a tradition in Rochester's training schools; each school's nurse cap displayed a distinctive pattern formed by thin strips of black velvet ribbon, identifying its graduates. There were so many choices open to young women with their skills —private nursing, school nursing, industrial nursing, and now Red Cross nursing with the Army— the list of new possibilities grew every year.

The Probationers were adding their enthusiasm to the buzz. This morning the grades they'd earned in their examinations would be announced. The ones who had been teetering on the edge of academic disaster, despite extra tutoring, huddled together, anxious and quiet. But those who had excelled could barely conceal their excitement. If their grades were good enough, their three-month probation period would end this day. Tomorrow they would be "First Years," *bona fide* pupils in the General Hospital's Training School for Nurses.

Canadian Norma Whitely was a part of the former group. She hadn't been able to master all of the bandaging schemes, and she still went totally blank on a couple of them. The class on solutions hadn't been too bad. She was able to memorize most of the chemical terms. But anatomy and physiology had overwhelmed her. There was so much to learn. Too much.

Alice Denny belonged to the latter group, although she hadn't joined any clique. She still resented having to study for a career, any career. Until last January, her future had appeared to her as an unbroken path of charitable work, religious worship, social intercourse, and shopping. Her opinion about settling for marriage and babies mirrored her attitude toward becoming a nurse. Any intercourse beyond the social kind was most definitely not part of her imagined life.

The Probationers, directed to assemble in the large classroom they had first met in, broke into friendship groups. Norma Whitely joined her Canadian country women, Ina Bramley, Bernice DeNiord, and Mary Sheppard. Alice Denny sat alone.

The room was just as spartan as it had been at the orientation meeting. In direct contrast with the reception rooms in the floor above, with their tall windows and huge potted ferns and cushioned wicker chairs, the school's subterranean cafeteria and the classrooms didn't try to disguise sickness and pain. Here horizontal window slits peeking just above ground level admitted almost no light, their mud-spattered panes obscuring any view of the early spring campus outside. This morning the student chairs were crowded into two-thirds of the large room.

Standing in the third section were three movable garment racks on which hung dozens of ankle-length, powder-blue dresses. Behind the racks, a long table held stacks of white bib aprons and columns of starched, stand-up white collars, ready to be buttoned to the necklines of the uniforms. On the floor underneath were boxes of the regulation high-button shoes, each box with a size number printed on its side.

"Welcome, Class of 1920 of General Hospital's School of Nursing," shouted Principal Smith, trying to reduce the excited chatter. As the voices trailed off, she continued. "Congratulations! You have all passed your examinations, some of you with exceptional results. We are not going to announce individual grades at this time. This afternoon, we'll hold interviews with each of you. At that time you will learn your rotation schedules and which of the wards you'll be assigned to first. That is when your interviewer will tell you about the grades you've earned."

A murmur rose as the women looked around the room to discover which members of the class were no longer with them.

"We're going to keep this morning simple. First, you should select your work uniforms. They're arranged by sizes on these racks. Take three uniforms and four aprons and collars each. Later, your allowances will be reduced to purchase a brand new uniform for special occasions, like open houses. Then find a pair of shoes that fit. Be sure to walk around in the shoes to be certain they're comfortable. From now on, you will be walking and standing a major portion of your days."

The newly admitted pupils began to move out of their seats. "Wait! Wait!"

They sat back down.

"The interview schedules are posted on the wall. Check them before you leave so that you know which head nurse you'll be interviewing with and when you'll meet with her. Once that's over, you may have the rest of the day off. But remember, punctuality is essential both for the interview and for reporting to your first assignment tomorrow."

Alice held back while her classmates surged toward the garment racks. Then, as the crowd thinned, she took a place next to the "Size 10" uniforms. They were not new, but they were clean. Recycled from previous classes, some of them were badly worn around the cuffs. They wouldn't last through her first year. And, of course, they made everyone look the same. She cringed at the thought of someone mistaking her for Norma, her roommate.

Another woman accidentally nudged her as she inspected the "Size 12" collection. "Excuse me," she apologized.

"That's all right," Alice replied. "I thought it would be less crowded by now, but tens and twelves seem to be very popular."

"Hi, remember me? Florence Austin." She pressed the size twelve against her athletic body, sizing it up. "But everyone calls me by my last name.

Alice kept moving hangers. "Oh, yes. That end of exams party I went to last week was in your room on the second floor, wasn't it?"

"Yes."

"You know, it was the first time I've been social with anyone besides my roommate. It was fun."

"You can thank the frogs for that."

Alice held a uniform up against her front, checking the length of the hem. "How will I look in this?"

"Just like everyone else in our class." Florence selected a dress. "This one looks good."

"You mean the frogs that didn't come?"

"They didn't come, so we didn't have to write up dissection reports that night. Thus a free evening."

"But we did have to dissect them when they came the day after."

Austin checked the frayed edges of the neckline of another dress. "This looks like it can be repaired." She surveyed the room. "The other girls are somewhere around here. Would you like to meet them again?"

"Oh, yes. Especially that funny one… Ernestine, was it?"

"Wait a minute. She's over there trying on shoes."

Austin returned a moment later leading a short, chubby woman, probably a size 14, whose left arm was weighed down with uniforms, aprons, and collars. Putting the shoes she held in her right hand on the floor, she extended it. "H-H-Hi again, Alice."

"I'm glad to meet you again, Ernestine."

"Th-th-the pleasure's mine. But 'Ernestine' is too darn long. If you want to be friends, just call me 'Bong.'"

Austin rolled her eyes. "She does that all the time. She wants to be called by her last name, so we use that. Be careful, though, the rhyming can be contagious."

"And from now on, you'll need to know," Bong nodded toward her friend, "If she didn't prefer 'Austin,' we'd call her 'Flo.'"

Alice giggled. It was the first time she had smiled since the day her mother had left for Buffalo.

"Be careful; she'll give you a nickname too, one that rhymes easily," commented Austin.

"That's all right. I don't mind."

"Well, everything I need, I've got right here. It's time for me to disappear." Ernestine picked up the shoes and moved toward the interview schedules.

"Why don't you stop by my room at eight o'clock this evening, Alice? I'll reintroduce you to the other girls in the second-floor group. Oh, and bring whatever goodies you've got squirreled away. It's a pot-luck party. "

Having selected their uniforms the two women moved toward the collar and apron table. Then they proceeded to the boxes of shoes and to the interview schedules posted on the wall.

Norma wasn't in their room when Alice got back, but she had left a note on the bed. The Canadian friends had gone to a movie downtown to celebrate having advanced one degree on their career thermometers.

Her interview had gone well, Alice thought as she removed her shirtwaist and tried one of the uniforms on for size. Other than a suggestion that she should spend more time with her classmates during their time off, her test results were excellent, and she'd executed the demonstrations capably. Miss Reid had no doubt that at the end of her training, Alice would be a credit to her profession and to her training school.

She carefully slipped the neck chain tethering her eye glasses over her topknot and examined her reflection from every angle in the long mirror. Her probationary three months had seemed to drag, but now it felt like only yesterday when she had first entered this room. She finished off the outfit by tying the black velvet ribbon that held her treasured time piece around her neck and tucked the instrument into the uniform's tiny breast pocket. Then, careful to straighten her skirt so it wouldn't get too wrinkled, she lay down on the bed and closed her eyes, intending to rest them for only a few moments.

When she awoke, Alice looked at the time. It was already 7:30, too late for supper in the cafeteria. That was all right, though. Florence had invited her to a party on the floor below. She thought there would be enough there to satisfy her, even if the snacks weren't as nourishing as the cafeteria served. She could make up for it with a more healthful meal tomorrow.

She searched the top shelf on her side of the chifferobe. Nothing but dust up there. She found a cloth on the cabinet's floor, and standing on a chair, wiped the shelf off. Then she looked in the bottom drawer of the dresser. Aha! A box of saltines. It had been opened, but it was still half full and hadn't been discovered by rodents. Apparently the atmosphere on the third floor was too thin for mice. Cracker box in hand, she descended to the second floor.

Like the rooms on her floor, a name card identified the occupiers of each room. She read the labels until she came to "Miss Austin – Miss Sheppard." She knocked tentatively, and the door opened promptly.

"What's the password?"

"I…I don't know, but I brought a contribution to the party." She handed the cracker box to her hostess. "Here. Should I call you "Flo," like Bong said?"

"No, just call me Austin. All my friends do. She just used 'Flo' because it rhymed with whatever else she was saying. Sometimes it's annoying, but most of the time she's just too funny." Austin slid the crackers onto a plate and lined it up next to a platter of cake slices on the study tables under the windowsill. "Unless someone brings a liquid with flavor, we'll have to rely on water to wash these down, I'm afraid."

"Water will do for me. Where's your roommate?"

"Same place your roommate is, I suspect. Those Canadian girls tend to stick together."

"Who else is coming?"

"Well, there's Bong and her roommate Hilda Mehlenbacker from this floor. And Emily Donnellan and Susan Kelsey. They live downstairs. Susan's the youngest of our group, only 19. She's kind of bossy. But we like Emily. Susan's attached herself to Emie like a puppy, always tagging after her."

There was a knock at the door, and Austin opened it.

"The party can start. It's certainly clear! Bong and Hilda are finally here!" Two red-haired women sidled through the door, single file, hefting a wooden case of green ginger ale bottles between them. The shorter one was in the lead.

"It is a party now, Bong. Where'd you get those?"

Bong rolled her eyes. "It was hard on the trolley, and it took us hours. But it was on sale downtown at Duffy-Powers."

The newcomers heaved the case onto the party tables and everyone took a bottle.

"It's Cliquot Club, no less. How can you afford that?"

"Well," Hilda chimed in, "my dad sent me a check at Easter, and since this is a kind of graduation day for us, I thought we should have a sparkling beverage to celebrate with. We can have Welch's any old day."

Austin slapped Bong's hand playfully as it reached for a piece of cake. "Not until Susan and Emily get here, Bong. Then we'll toast to our success."

Scolded, Bong flopped onto one of the beds. "But I'm hungry now, and I can't wait. You know those two; they're always late."

Austin mimicked her chubby friend, "Just be patient, it's not quite eight. Anyway, you could stand to lose some weight." They all laughed.

"What's so funny?" asked Susan Kelsey as she and her roommate Emily appeared at the open door. "Come on, share the joke."

"Austin's just teasing Bong again," answered Hilda. "The usual. Come on in and have a ginger ale on me." She handed each of the newcomers a bottle. They had prepared a platter with a pyramid of dainty sandwiches and now added it to the party table.

"Good thing I slept through supper," Alice said.

Austin remembered, "Oh… yes. Everyone, this is Alice Denny from upstairs. I asked her to join us." The group all welcomed the newcomer.

"Let's see," Bong thought aloud. "Alice rhymes with palace? chalice? malice? That won't do. There's some other name we'll have to call you."

"How about just 'Al,'" suggested Susan.

"No. Another sound at the end…." her face brightened. "I've got it now. How about 'Ben?'"

"I like it!" Alice responded. "I've always thought the name 'Alice' was way too formal."

"So it's all agreed: this moment's when," Bong raised her green bottle, "I hereby christen Alice, 'Ben.'" The other young women raised their ginger ale bottles joining the salute.

"And here's a toast to our future successes," shouted Bong, lifting the bottle a second time. "May we all survive the 'white skirts' and messes!"

They clinked their bottles and took long swallows of the sparkling liquid.

"So, what's our agenda?" asked Hilda, passing around the sandwich platter.

"Let's compare rotations."

"Then we can see if any of us are teamed together."

Four of the group had been assigned to the same two duty areas: Alice and Susan would spend the first leg of their training in the women's ward, and Emily and Hilda had drawn the children's ward. Bong was on men's, and Austin would start in maternity.

"I was thinking. The Seniors will be moving out of the nurses home as soon as they graduate in a couple of weeks. Do you suppose they'll move us all over there now that the new Probationers will be coming in?" asked Emily.

"They can't do that!" yelled Susan adamantly. "It would split us up." She looked fondly at her roommate. "What would I do if they put us in with all the Intermediates and the new Seniors? I'd hardly get to see you all."

"It wouldn't be all that bad, Susan," her roommate replied. "Sometimes it's good to get used to moving to new places and meeting new friends. Keeps us on our toes."

"But she's got a point, Emie. We've drawn close in these past three months. We know each other pretty well now and help keep each other out of trouble. It'd be a shame if we had to separate," Austin argued.

"Consider my problem, please, this time. There'd be new names that would not rhyme."

"That's a good reason, Bong, even if it's a minor one. I'm sure you can talk without rhyming."

"If you want me a mute, if you'd rather I mutter ...," she held out both hands, palms up, and shrugged, "if I can't rhyme, I j-j-just stutter."

Austin passed the cake plate around. "Okay, for Bong's sake, and for the rest of us, let's ask for a meeting with Miss Smith and request not to be relocated into the nurses' home. Agreed?" They all nodded.

"You know, we won't have the same half days off anymore. I think it depends on when the heads of our departments want their time off. How will we get together?" Alice asked, more comfortable now that she'd been initiated into the group.

"There's always Sunday afternoons."

"I can't be there if my Mama's in town, though. She needs my help."

"We always had Sunday afternoons off when we were Probationers. As head nurses' assistants we'll have to work when they're on duty. And I've heard we'll have to cover for them if they're late, including Sunday afternoons."

The partiers began depositing their empty bottles into the wooden case partitions.

"In the next month, let's figure out some time, like a meal time, when we can all get together."

"Sounds good to me."

"And everyone has to have a story, something exciting, to share. The highlight of their month. Okay?" Susan commanded as she and Emily took their sandwich platter, now empty except for a few crumbs, toward the door.

"That should be fun." Alice returned the crackers to the box she'd brought them in. No one had touched them.

"Thanks, Austin," called Hilda as she and Bong lugged the ginger ale case out the door.

"We'll save the rest of the soda till we party again, no matter where or exactly when," added Bong.

Alice helped Austin replace the furniture and, thanking her hostess, left the room. As she ascended to the third floor, she determined to bring something more substantial when the group held an impromptu party again. She liked her new friends, even if she wasn't any more interested in becoming a nurse than she had been last January.

...One hears so many things here. I heard that the price of caps was to be 25 [cents] *and that the uniform sleeves were to be different style. Isn't that fine when one just has* [bought] *a new uniform?*

My love & best wishes, Alice

Chapter 4

Dear Bess,
Susan ... is as important & bustling as
ever. I went for a shampoo yesterday on
my time [off] & today donned a new
cap that M[ama] made me. It isn't a
larkspur, I'm thankful to say....

"Eeww! What is that? It won't move!" The hair brush Susan Kelsey was using clattered to the floor, and alarmed, she jerked backward, upsetting the chair behind her.

Across the ward, Alice was helping Mrs. Lupinski to get back into her bed, Alice finished fluffing the pillow and pulled the fresh sheet over the elderly woman.

"What now?"

Susan had been parting another patient's jet black hair from behind, preparing to weave it into the long braid that the full-figured woman always wore. "I drew the part, and there was something dark against her scalp. I thought it was a freckle. Then I saw the other ones, lots of them. Those are not freckles!"

The woman let forth a torrent of Italian, wild gestures punctuating her words. The dozen other patients in the ward were alerted by the commotion. One by one, seven women who were able sit up in their beds,

38

did so. The five who were too weak, raised their heads and looked toward the commotion, curious.

"Here, let me help." An older patient, gray haired and somewhat plump, moved from the next bed to her frightened ward mate's side, opposite Susan.

The young pupil nurse glanced at her and frowned. "Get back into bed!" she ordered, unwilling to let someone else take charge. She picked up the hairbrush. "Now, now. Just sit back and relax, all right?" she pleaded and pressed the agitated woman's shoulders toward the pillow.

The volunteer patient sat on a chair between the beds. "You frightened her. She's in a strange place with people who don't speak her language. I understand Italian," she explained. "*Calmati, cara mia,*" she soothed the distraught patient.

But Susan persisted. "You stay out of this! I'll handle it."

Alice saw her classmate shiver. "You'd better let her help, Susan," she advised.

"I need to look into her eyes and touch her," the motherly volunteer said, and she took hold of one flailing wrist and gently stroked the hand. Gradually the voice became less strident, and she relaxed. But she kept a suspicious eye on Susan.

As the two First Year pupils retreated from the bed, still cautiously observing the Italian pair, Miss Jutsum, the Senior pupil in charge of the Women's Ward, stepped out of the prep room at the end of the long ward. "Miss Kelsey. Miss Denny. May I speak with you a moment, please?"

Susan shrugged in innocence as the younger women walked toward their supervisor.

The other patients, having enjoyed the interruption in their morning routine, lay down again, most of them privately wishing that another distraction would brighten this otherwise uneventful day. They were so very tired of having nothing to do but wait.

"Just what was all the commotion about?" Miss Jutsum asked as she closed the prep room door behind her.

Hoping that admitting her involuntary reaction would gain the Senior's sympathy, Susan spoke up first. "I was brushing the hysterectomy's hair, and I noticed a couple of dark spots on her scalp. At first I thought they were a strange kind of dandruff, but they wouldn't budge. Then I thought maybe they were freckles, but there were scores of them, maybe hundreds." Her tone betrayed a conviction that <u>she</u> had been offended, not the patient.

Trying to minimize Susan's petulance, Alice interceded. "When I heard the gall bladder patient in the next bed speaking Italian, I suggested to Susan that we probably ought to let her calm the agitated woman down. Her surgery isn't scheduled until tomorrow, so she wasn't in any danger."

"Well, ladies, this will be a valuable learning experience for you," Miss Jutsum said. She turned toward Alice first. "In the first place, the patient in bed three isn't a 'gall bladder'; she's Mrs. Privitera." Then, turning to Susan she added, "And the patient in bed four isn't a 'hysterectomy'; her name is Mrs. DeCecco."

Both of the First Year pupils blushed and cast their eyes down at the linoleum floor.

Miss Jutsum turned toward Susan. "In the second place, what you saw, Miss Kelsey, was pediculosis. It's more common in the Children's Pavilion, but we sometimes find entire families afflicted with it. Mrs. DeCecco's husband's head is probably crawling with lice. And her children, if she has any, are probably infested, too." She jotted a note on a form on the table. "We'll need to send her home with instructions in Italian about how to get rid of them."

Susan shivered again. "It's disgusting. I feel all creepy and itchy."

"The third thing you should understand from this is that most of the patients are caring people. Yes, they do complain about their pains, but they forget them when they can help someone else in distress. In a way, caring about others is a step toward healing themselves." Again she addressed Susan: "If you're that squeamish about nits, Miss Kelsey, you'd better get used to them."

She paused and continued in a more sympathetic voice. "I must admit, though, that's just how I felt when I was a novice and first saw the ugly vermin." She walked toward the instrument cabinet along the far wall. "Now, for your final lesson: how to get rid of them. You'll need to do this together so that both of you won't feel so helpless when this happens to you again."

She opened a drawer underneath the counter top, revealing silver instruments arranged in neat compartments.

"Go over to the pharmacist in the Administration Building, ask for a large bottle of Tincture of Larkspur, and bring it back here to the prep room. Pour some into a basin, and soak a clean rag from that pile in the corner in the solution. Keep this door closed, though, because full strength the stuff smells awful, and the patients at this end of the ward will complain. Once you've wrung it out, wrap Mrs. DeCecco's head in the rag, turban style."

She withdrew a comb with tiny notches between its teeth. "Then every morning for the next several days, you'll need to unwrap the Larkspur cap and use this special comb to remove the eggs. Be sure to sterilize the comb after every use. Reapply a fresh cap daily until the comb shows absolutely no sign of eggs or nits."

Then Miss Jutsum opened the door and the three reentered the ward.

The patients, many of them still grinning at the excitement the novice had caused, watched as, with heads bent, Susan and Alice walked the long center aisle between the bed rows toward the ward's entrance doors.

"I don't think we should share this story with the rest of our group, do you? Too embarrassing," said Alice.

"Well, the Anatomy and Physiology text book didn't say anything about pediculosis, did it? And Miss Scarry didn't mention it either," Susan whined. "But maybe we should share what happened with the others so that they don't react the way I did. It's kind of a funny story when you think of it — that woman yelling words we couldn't understand and waving her arms so violently. She could have knocked me over."

"You may think it was funny, but Miss Jutsum was definitely not amused."

Whirling away at its highest and noisiest speed, Principal Smith's desk fan flipped the corners of the reports she was working on. If she didn't anchor the top page of each pile with her forearms, the papers threatened to become airborne and scatter her work all around the room. All of the pages, that is, that her sweat hadn't glued to her skin.

According to this morning's *Democrat and Chronicle*, the thermometer had reached 92 degrees yesterday. The newspaper was predicting more of the same today, to usher in August. Factories had released their workers the previous afternoon, and they were considering letting the second shift find relief at Lake Ontario beaches again today. To handle the added traffic to the Lake, the street rail company was scheduling extra car runs.

And today, she knew, more outdoor laborers, overcome by the heat, would add to the hospital's census. Four patients had been admitted yesterday, with the Hahnemann and the Homeopathic accepting even larger numbers. One elderly street cleaner had collapsed on St. Paul Street and died of heat prostration at the Homeopathic. This heat could be deadly.

Miss Smith wished that Superintendent Keith could shut down early too, but you can't close a hospital and release the nurses, no matter how hot it gets. Even with ceiling fans going all the time, you can't make patients comfortable. The noisy machines were just circulating more of the same heavy, sticky air. *If you believed in Purgatory, this is what it must be like. And the pupils will be dragging.*

She wasn't looking forward to meeting with the contingent of them, the first item on her schedule this morning. Nursing Instructor Reid had reported a disturbance on the First Years' floor of the nurses' residence last night. She had felt that the pupils had been disrespectful toward her, and she wanted them disciplined.

Although they happened rarely, these situations were most distasteful to the school's Principal. A tentative knock on her door signaled their arrival.

"Come in," she said. Six young women entered. *Looking a bit sheepish*, she thought. Sweat had dyed the powder blue of their uniforms a darker shade around their glistening necks. Their stand-up collars had collapsed into soggy cowls. In the lead was the shortest of the group, damp ringlets hanging limply from her regulation cap, which always reminded the administrator of an upside-down cupcake.

"Good morning, Miss Smith," their spokesperson said, her eyes averted, avoiding contact with the administrator. "You asked us to report to you this morning?"

"That's correct, Miss …?"

"Emily Donnellan. And this is Florence Austin, Susan Kelsey, Ernestine Bong, Hilda Mehlenbacher, and Alice Denny."

"I know your names, Emily. We've been referring to the few of you who stick together like glue as 'those First Year Pupils.' I just didn't know which of you was which." The administrator picked up an official looking paper from her desk and glanced at it. "Your names are all on this report that Miss Reid submitted to my office this morning. It's about last evening's disturbance. In fairness, I want to hear the story from your perspectives."

"Well, Miss Smith, it was the bat that started it all."

"A bat?"

"Yes, Miss Smith," Susan volunteered. "I had left my window open to see if a breath of air might find its way into the room. It was so hot I couldn't sleep. And a bat flew in."

"I see," the Principal replied, quelling an urge to smile.

"I'm frightened of bats, Miss Smith. My older brother loved books like *Frankenstein*, *Phantom of the Opera*, and *Dracula*. Our parents left him in charge when they went out for an evening, and he would tell me the stories in the dark. Dracula was the scariest of them for me, and I've been terrified of bats ever since. So I screamed and ran out when a bat came in and began squeaking and running into the walls trying to find a way out."

"We all ran to her rescue, Miss Smith," explained Austin. We got Susan into the hallway and closed the door. "She's younger than most of us, and we're a little protective of her."

Emily continued the story. "Well, Susan's screams woke up the whole floor. Miss Reid came down from the third floor to see what the noise was about."

"Like she always does in our classes, she took full charge," added Hilda.

"She yelled, 'Don't move!' and then grabbed a broom, opened the door, and went into the room," put in Bong.

"After she closed the door behind her, we heard loud crashing and furniture being shoved around. She was yelling at the bat, too." Alice stifled a snicker.

"There'd be a bang, a crash, a lurch, and then some words you won't hear in church."

"Anyway," Emily continued, "when she came out, the room was a shambles, and so was Miss Reid. But the bat had gone and she'd slammed the window shut. She ordered us to go to bed and left the floor."

Miss Smith had turned her back to the group, hoping that they would think she was pondering the situation. The pupils waited silently, and then noticing the involuntary movements of her shoulders, they grinned at each other. The Principal found the situation as funny as they had.

Finally regaining her composure, Miss Smith decided to change the subject without exploring the incident any further.

"Aren't you that group of girls who petitioned me to be allowed to stay at the house on Reynolds Street? I'm sorry I couldn't accommodate your request, but we've found that First Year pupils benefit by living with the Intermediates and Seniors. You can learn almost as much from them in your off-duty hours as you learn in the wards."

"We understood your reason, Miss Smith. But now we have a different request." Emily ran a forefinger around her limp collar. "It's our uniform collars. They just won't stand up in this heat." Then she held out a catalogue opened to a dog-eared page. "We've found a collar that looks just as neat, but it won't wilt when it gets hot like ours do."

The Principal took the catalogue and examined the collar styles pictured in it.

"It's the Peter Pan collar at the bottom right."

"It does look prim, and I believe you're right, Miss Donnellan."

Members of the delegation looked at each other, at first surprised at how easy their task had been, and then delighted that their crusade had succeeded. They wouldn't have to argue about the merits of the change in tradition, a problem they had anticipated during breakfast.

"And, in view of the weather we've been having, I'm going to give all pupils permission to dispense with the corset requirement, but only as long as this heat wave lasts."

Grins widened into smiles.

"But everyone must agree. Corsets give your spine extra support. When you are not protected by one, you should not lift a patient or even try to help an overweight one to move. You <u>must</u> get an orderly or a porter to do any kind of heavy lifting."

"That would be a wonderful relief, Miss Smith," said Susan, struggling against an impulse to click her heels together, and yell "Yippie!"

Thanking the Principal with as much decorum as they could muster, the delegation filed out of the office.

As soon as the door closed, the Principal Smith gave herself a mental pat on the back. *There, I've done at least one good deed today. But I'll wager they won't announce the news to the other pupils until they've gone back to their rooms to remove the corsets. That's what I'd have done in my student days.*

Then she got busy again, gathering and sorting the reports that, aided by the slight breeze that had come through the closing door, the desk fan had propelled all around the room.

A thunderstorm last week had cooled things off, so the pupil nurses no longer had the freedom of going corsetless. But the new Peter Pan collar was indeed a relief from the clerical neck brace that disintegrated whenever they worked up a sweat.

One of the new crop of Probationers had taken the last bed pan to the utility room and Alice could hear her sluicing the receptacle out in the hopper's wash sink. As far as she could see, everything in the ward was in good order. Susan was stationed at the door to the corridor, ready to admit the evening-hour visitors. The wall clock clicked precisely 8:00; the sentinel swung the door open and welcomed the visitors.

A dozen people streamed in and dispersed among the long rows of hospital beds. Jutting perpendicularly from the walls, they looked like so many teeth with big spaces between them. One by one the visitors drew chairs up next to their ailing loved ones. The two pupil nurses went about collecting the few bouquets that the newcomers had brought. They would take the flowers to the prep room, arrange them in vases, and return them to the bedside tables.

A young man entered the ward late. Dressed in a khaki Army uniform, he carried a small bouquet of forget-me-nots and baby's breath sprigs. "Excuse me, miss," he said, removing his cap and glancing from bed to bed. "I'm looking for my mother. Mrs. Privitera? She's one of Dr. Edwards's patients."

"She's in the fifth bed on the left," Alice directed. "Here, let me take your lovely flowers and put them in some water." Struck by the appearance of his neat uniform, she looked closely at the young man's face. The blue of his eyes matched the color of the forget-me-nots in the bouquet he handed her – exactly. She had seen that color somewhere. But where? When?

In the work room, Alice searched through the containers on the shelves under the counter. The vases there were bulbous, suitable for show-off peonies, not for delicate baby's breath. The shelves above the sink were just as disappointing. A dozen roses would feel comfortable standing in those vases. Forget-me-nots would look ridiculous, like little topknots, peeking out of their long necks. Then she saw the tiny, goblet-like glassware on a table behind the door. They were just the right size.

Where did I meet him before? she puzzled , turning on the cold water spigot and filling one of the miniature vases. *It must have been recently.* She was sure it hadn't been a formal meeting. She didn't know his name or anything about him.

The young man was kissing his mother's forehead when Alice reentered the ward. "Sorry to be in such a rush, Ma, but I've got to catch tonight's train to get back to camp. I should be back in a couple of weeks," he said.

"*Via con dio, Alphonso.*" The middle-aged patient's voice was still weak, muted by the after effects of anesthesia. He patted her hand and kissed her forehead again.

Alice handed him the vase with its tiny blue flowers.

"Thank you, miss---? Wait a minute. Haven't we met?" He placed the arrangement on the bedside table.

"Alice Denny. But most of my friends just call me Ben. And yes, I believe we've met. Recently, but I can't remember when or where."

"You weren't in that uniform then, something more dressy."

"You weren't in uniform either, something more formal. . . . Now I remember; it was your bright blue tie."

"What was my tie?" They walked toward the entry doors.

"Your tie matched your eyes, like those forget-me-knots you brought your mother tonight do. But you had a topcoat on."

"And you wore a fancy feathered hat….It was the trolley….your suitcase….early morning….last January."

"That's it! I knew we'd crossed paths, but not formally."

"A lot's changed since then, obviously," he replied.

"It most certainly has," she agreed. "Did you volunteer, or did Uncle Sam snag you?"

"Uncle Sam drew my number. And you? Following a life-long dream?" They paused at the doorway.

"No. It's a necessity. I came here under pressure, but I'm beginning to be able to tolerate the regimen." Alice's eyes shifted down the room toward Mrs. Privitera. "How's she doing?"

"She wants to get out of here. But she's still got a couple of days to recover from the operation, Dr. Edwards told me."

"That's the trouble with some patients with gall stones. They tend to come back. As pleasant as we try to make it, a hospital ward is too sterile, almost too regimented to endure. A student nurse's life is like being a patient, except that we can go anywhere we like --- as long as it's on this campus."

"Sounds like being in the Army. Except that they gave me a couple of furlough days to visit Ma for her operation. You have a regimen; I have a regiment."

"Will they send your regiment overseas?"

"Them, yes, but not me. My eyesight's not good enough to aim a gun. So when I finish basic training, I'll be assigned to stateside duty. I hope my posting'll be nearby."

"Well, we'll take good care of your mother while she's here." Alice looked down the row of beds again. "It's so good of you to visit her. Some of the patients are here for weeks, and no one comes to see them."

He glanced at the wall clock. "Got to go. Say, don't you ever get a chance to escape?"

"We have a couple of half days a week. But I spend a lot of that time working on class assignments."

He paused, reluctant to leave. "If I get another furlough, will you still be here?"

"Until a year from next April."

"Can I telephone you?" He stepped into the hallway.

"Yes. What's your name?" she called holding the swinging door open and watching him stride down the corridor.

"Alphonso, but my friends call me 'Al,'" he yelled back. "Hey, you can call me 'Al' and I can call you 'Al.' It's a smaller world than we thought!" Then he disappeared around a corner.

A bell rang, signaling the end of the evening's visiting hour. As soon as the visitors had cleared the room, two Senior nurses came in to help settle the patients. One of them brought out the tray of medications she had prepared and handed it to Alice for distribution.

"That's so cute, Alice – or rather Ben," Susan said as she finished tucking Mrs. Privitera in. She picked up the little vase of flowers and held it up toward the ceiling light.

"I looked all over the prep room to find just the right container for them," Alice explained. She had just given meds to the last patient and was returning the tray to the prep room.

"Such a novel idea."

"What?"

"Using a urine sample cup as a vase for such delicate flowers."

You'd probably be amused to see me
working in the wards especially when I
put flowers in a urine specimen glass
and marched it into one of the women.
I found the glass with several others in
the work room and thought what nice
vases.... One of the girls nearly went into
hysterics laughing when she saw my
vase.

As ever,
"Ben"

Chapter 5

No one on the floor has gotten off duty before 7:30 all week. We just seem to work in a circle every minute & never reach an end. Poor Emily is distracted too but we do manage to get in a few good laughs over it all. . . ..

Alice and Emily Donnellan boarded the east-bound trolley at Main and State. As usual on a Sunday afternoon, there were plenty of seats, so they had their pick. The motorman engaged the electric wire above the car, and they were on the way to the double feature at the Colonial Theater. Pledging not even to mention their classes, their instructors, or their classmates, they had decided to make the most of this sunny, brisk autumn day.

The week had been especially hectic with examinations in all of their classes along with their duties in the wards. While they had gotten used to the routines – bed baths and linen changes, keeping records of which medications to give to individual patients and when to give them – each young woman had been challenged by problems that weren't covered in textbooks.

When the matinee was over, they window shopped all the way from the theater to the Four Corners. On impulse they stopped for "a late lunch or early supper" at the Canton Restaurant, just up the street from the movie emporium. Learning how to manipulate chopsticks without dumping a load of rice in her lap prompted Alice's embarrassment and Emily's giggles. "Look. It's easy," the younger woman bragged, and skillfully shoveled in another mouthful.

Tea topped off the meal perfectly. Emily's fortune – "A pleasant surprise is in store for you," and the one in Alice's cookie – "A thrilling time is in your immediate future" inspired fantasies about traveling to exotic places and meeting famous personalities.

Reluctantly they boarded the west-bound streetcar to return to the nurses' home. As the trolley "rumbled," "dinged," and "zapped" its way past the Powers Building and the BR and P Railway station, the young women talked about the afternoon's feature, *Hell's Hinges*, a western starring William S. Hart. Charlie Chaplin had been uproarious as usual in *The Adventurer* shorter movie, but it was the longer film that had enthralled them.

"Had you ever thought you'd rather be a man?" Emily asked Alice after they had reviewed the *Hinges* plot.

"What? Why would I?"

"They have all the fun. The women in films just sit around waiting for the men to come back. Brace was so heroic, wasn't he? Shooting Silk and his cronies after they'd burned down the church like that. He was so moral, so courageous."

"Courageous, yes. But moral? That was just taking revenge, not being moral, don't you think?"

"I suppose so. "

The trolley took on passengers at Canal Street and then continued its prescribed route.

"But wouldn't you like to have more of a say in your life? First you're your father's daughter. Then you're your husband's wife. Finally, you end up as your children's mother. Until we women get to vote, we're like this street car, rolling on rails we can't get off, powered by a source outside of our control."

Alice drew back and frowned at Emily. "I kind of enjoyed being my father's daughter. I don't like it now that he's gone, when Mama's sick and I have to take over the responsibility of the house and learn how to be a nurse so I'll be able to support myself. Besides, I doubt I'll ever have to act as 'my husband's wife' or my 'children's mother.' That isn't in my fortune cookie."

Emily's expression brightened a bit. "Why do you say that?"

"The war's taking all of the single young men away. When it ends, the ones who come back'll be in wheel chairs or on crutches. I'll be twenty-eight when I finish training, definitely not a young, marriageable woman. I probably won't be attractive to any man, either the lamed or the maimed."

Emily laughed. "Bong's rhymes are contagious, and you've been infected. But think; if women had been able to vote in 1916, we could've helped to elect more candidates that wanted the country to stay neutral."

The Reynolds Street stop was coming up on the left, and Alice reached for the buzzer to be let off.

Emily stopped her. "Let's not get off yet. Let's keep the afternoon going. We can ask for a transfer and pick up a returning car at the end of the line."

"I'm in no hurry to get back."

"Did you ever think about becoming a suffragist?"

Alice wrinkled her nose. "No. Never been interested in politics. That's men's work."

Emily pointed at the Madison Street sign on the right as the trolley rolled on. "Susan B. Anthony lived right down that street," she said. "I haven't told anyone, but I've been a suffragist since last February. That's when I started going to the Suffrage School. I went to every meeting I could get a late pass for."

She fairly bounced in her seat as she described how she became convinced that women must have the right to vote. She talked about the Suffrage Shop on East Main Street. They sold Wade corsets. "They're the best! And they have these darling Chinese embroideries made by a student at Mechanics Institute. He's earning his way through school. Chen's short like me, but he's cute. And he has jet black hair just like I do."

She put her hand to her mouth. "Don't tell anyone, but Chen and I had a date. I don't think Miss Smith would approve."

"So that's how you learned to use chopsticks. No, Miss Smith would definitely disapprove."

To change the subject, Emily described the celebration at Suffragist Headquarters when the State Senate agreed to take up the issue again this year. She knew that some men who favored a second referendum really hoped it would finally die like it had two years before, but that couldn't be helped. After all, only men were allowed into the polls, and she knew that most of the men in Western New York were determined to squash a state suffrage amendment. She was optimistic, though.

The trolley reached Bull's Head, and the two women glanced at St. Mary's Hospital as they rode past. Here the streetcar veered to the right, shifting from West Main Street to West Avenue.

"How do you know what the men think?" asked Alice.

"Ads in all of the papers have been urging readers to defeat the amendment. They list the men who believe women shouldn't 'dirty their hands' by getting into politics. The anti-suffragists are including us suffragists on their list of subversives, like German spies and Socialists and unionists. Someone's even linking suffragists with abortionists."

Emily suddenly sat straighter, alert as they approached the Ames Street stop. "I wonder what goes on in that place." She pointed to a house on the opposite side of the street.

Shadows had lengthened as dusk approached. With the changing leaves still clinging to the tree branches and the lush surrounding landscape, the structure was in deep shadow, but Alice could make out the acute angle of a center gable flanked by two smaller gables. Gothic arches framed the windows on the street side, and vertical staves gave the wooden façade a texture of wide-whale corduroy.

"Looks like a scary place for trick-or-treaters. What's so interesting about it?"

"Mr. and Mrs. Danforth live there. Edwina, the wife, has been a leader in the county Suffragists for years. I met her last May. And Henry, the husband, is a Republican conservative. He used to be a member of the House of Representatives in Washington. Many of his supporters believe that women belong in the home, not parading in front of the White House and going to jail for it. "

"Their dinnertime conversations must be a bit tense, then."

"If they have dinnertime conversations. Mrs. Danforth told me that she hardly ever sees him, she's so involved with suffrage and other causes."

Alice looked at the buildings on the Ames Street side. Factories lined the avenue, dark and empty on a Sunday afternoon. The trolley line was like a border between the rich and the working class. She had crossed that boundary in the past few months, she knew. But Emily's crusade made the side she was now on a little more intriguing. Maybe having to earn a living wouldn't be so boring, after all.

"Theirs is the kind of life I was hoping to have before my father got sick and died. Then my mother had to go to the sanitarium in Buffalo. That meant I had to enter nursing school last winter."

"There's a vote on women's suffrage in New York State early next month. The men will decide whether they'll share decision making with us women or not. If the referendum passes, I'll be able to vote in next year's election, when I turn 21."

"If women had the vote, I wouldn't feel as helpless as I do now, I think. Is there some way we could encourage this? We're pretty isolated at the school. And our work load keeps us from joining outside activities, other than a weekly movie like today."

"I think I have a plan. I'll tell you about it on the way back to the hospital."

Florence Austin switched on the table light. The ceiling fixture would have attracted the attention of all the other First Year pupils on this floor; attendance at this monthly gathering was by invitation only. She drew six chairs from nearby study tables to the large table at the center of the room. Two-by-two the other attendees began to shuffle into the library. Clad from neck to floor in flannel nightgowns and pastel bathrobes, with their hair set free from the confining bobby pins and uniform caps, they appeared more distinctive now.

Bong and Hilda arrived first, carrying a pitcher of milk and a tray of glasses. "Never fear, the red heads are here." With the lanky Hilda following directly behind her much shorter roommate, the two resembled a carrot-colored exclamation point, Hilda's long straight cut dotted by Bong's closely curled hair do. Bong placed the pitcher in the middle of the table. Hilda arranged the glasses at six places. They gathered their bathrobes around them and chose adjoining seats. Hearing the sound of hushed voices, they glanced toward the darkened doorway.

Susan and Emily emerged from the corridor next. Emily carried a box of graham crackers and a platter. She opened the cracker box and arranged its contents in a neat, overlapping mound that filled the plate, and then placed it in the table's center. Susan followed her, distributing a napkin at each of the six places, her lips silently mouthing the number of each place, "One, two, three…." Then she sat next to the chair Emily had chosen.

Alice, as usual, came in alone. She carried a two-pound box of Lowney chocolates, removed its lid and unfolded the gold foil inner wrap, exposing its contents. She placed the box next to the graham crackers.

Bong reached for one of the dark brown delicacies. "M-m-m-m. What a treat! Wonder what else we'll have to eat." She bit into its chewy nougat center and looked expectantly toward the hallway.

"Where's Norma?" Austin asked Alice.

"In bed. She had night duty a couple of days ago, and she hasn't caught up on her sleep yet."

Susan frowned and removed the napkin and glass from the extra place. "Five," her lips pantomimed. Alice removed the extra chair, and took one of the remaining two seats.

"Where'd you come across these, Alice – er, Ben?" Hilda wondered, reaching for a chocolate.

"Mrs. Privitera gave them to me the day she was discharged from the women's ward. She was such a pleasant patient."

Susan raised an eyebrow. "I've heard that name before. Didn't her son come for a visit? Wasn't he in uniform?"

Frowning, Alice abruptly changed the subject. "I've been gaining so much weight lately, that I decided to limit myself to one a week. There were enough to share at our meeting. If I don't watch it, I won't fit into my uniform before long."

The students chatted about the problem they were all having, some noting that Thanksgiving, Christmas, and New Years were approaching and others warning that they had all better start watch what they ate. Nevertheless, milk glasses were draining, and the remaining chocolates were disappearing one by one.

"Okay, let's get started." Austin's alto voice was all business. "First on the agenda is reports of unusual experiences we've had so far this month, followed by New Business." She poured the last of the milk into her glass.

This meeting's reports weren't as humorous as last month's had been, less about the mistakes the first-year pupils had made and fewer complaints about the officious head nurses and the Seniors who, the First Years felt, lorded over them. Hospital work seemed to have settled into a calm, if boring, routine. There had been no real crises, like that string of women who had attempted suicide during the heat wave last summer. And now that colder temperatures prevailed, there were fewer motorcycle accident cases in the men's ward. The weather, the young women agreed, had a lot to do with the kinds of patients that filled the General's wards.

"But colder weather hasn't stopped automobile accidents," Hilda argued. "The men's ward is crowded with pedestrians hit jaywalking in the busiest streets. Collisions at intersections are increasing. The drivers don't want to give way to any other vehicle, even the streetcars." She paused, remembering. "And then there are the railroad crossings. I was on duty in the women's ward a couple of weeks ago when that hideous accident happened at the Lyell Avenue crossing."

Different members of the group contributed what they remembered about the affair, which had been reported by the newspapers in detail. A BR & P train had crashed into a motorcar car full of family members. There were so many in the demolished auto that one ambulance took the grandparents and an infant to St. Mary's. The mother, her teenage daughter and a young niece came to the General. The younger girls hadn't been injured badly, but the mother had a skull fracture.

"How could you miss seeing a locomotive in full daylight?" asked Susan.

"It was an open car, and it was windy and rainy. The passengers had pulled the curtains down to keep from getting wet." Hilda replied."The grandparents both have broken pelvises, and the four-month-old infant's skull was fractured, like his mom's."

"Was fractured?" asked Austin.

"I still wake up at night hearing that poor woman's wails when the head nurse told her the baby had died."

The group was silent for a moment. Then they all agreed: someone ought to make train engineers blow their whistles when they approached a grade crossing.

"That's the point," said Emily. "Who? Who's that 'someone?'"

"Couldn't we?" Susan suggested.

"We're only students, and women at that. Who would listen to us?"

Emily turned to Austin. "Can we get on to New Business? I have something important to bring up."

"Certainly, if no one else has a report." Austin surveyed the group. "All right, go ahead Emily."

"Wait here just a minute, please." She nodded to Alice, and they both went behind one of the tall bookcases. They returned to the table carrying two cartons.

"On the way home from the theater last Sunday, Alice – er, Ben and I were talking about how limited women are. But then I remembered that there's an election coming up."

"That hasn't anything to do with us," Susan interjected. "That's men's work. We're here to serve, to heal. No one wants to hear our opinion about cars and railroads or candidates running in an election."

"That's what I said," Alice replied. "But then we thought about it more. And what Emily told me made sense."

Energized, Emily continued. "Rochester's Suffragist Society is intent on convincing men that we women should be able to vote. A proposal to that effect will be on the ballot in a couple of weeks. All of the Society's members are nagging their husbands, sons, male employers and neighbors to say yes. If the men want their women to stop nagging, they'll agree, just to shut them up. After all, women in a dozen western states already have a political voice; some of them have been voting for nearly a half century. There's even a woman in the House of Representatives in Washington. "

The speaker's enthusiasm was compelling. Everyone except Susan had drawn closer to the table, enticed by the conviction in her voice.

"What's wrong with New York?" Alice added. "We're called the 'Empire State.' Why can't we call ourselves the 'Democratic State' or the 'Equality State?'"

Thumping sounds coming through the ceiling alerted the young women that their voices were carrying beyond the library's walls. They "shush"ed each other.

"Here's the plan," Emily went on. She opened her carton and drew out packets of blue brochures. "If we place a handout on every flat surface in the hospital, someone may be curious enough to pick it up and read it. If it's a man, he might be persuaded to vote yes."

"And even better: if it's a woman," Alice went on, "she'll take the hand out home and nag her husband, or her brother, or her son to give her the same rights he has." She opened her carton and brought out a fistful of miniature purple, gold, and white banners attached to small sticks.

Unfurling one of the tiny flags, she read the words printed on it, "'We demand an amendment to the New York State Constitution Enfranchising Women.' If we put a banner on every meal tray we deliver, in every vase of flowers we arrange, in every centerpiece on the cafeteria tables, even in every bathroom, someone will see it. If they take it with them as a souvenir, all the better."

The speakers' enthusiasm was contagious. Bong raised one of the flags and waved it. "Let's all complain. Women can't be happy, won't be content, until men approve the suffrage amendment!"

Again, the thumps came from above, this time dislodging dust motes from the ceiling fixture, which drifted downward. Everyone covered her milk glass, protecting its contents.

"I'm not doing that," Susan said adamantly, and she picked up her glass and plate. Tossing her wiry locks, she whined as she entered the dark corridor, "Besides, even if you all get to vote next year, I won't be twenty-one yet. It doesn't matter to me."

Speaking in subdued voices, the remaining students each took a packet of brochures and a handful of banners, gathered her dishes, and left to go off to bed. The mound of graham crackers had disintegrated into a few crumbs, the Lowney box was empty, and only a white film coated the pitcher.

"How can you stand her?" Austin asked as she gathered the remaining utensils. "She's so self centered."

"Susan's young. Besides, when I'm on night duty, there's always a warm hot water bottle in my bed when I get back to my room the next morning. She's is my good gremlin. She'll mature, I am sure."

"You're sounding like Bong again."

Alice placed the last chair where it belonged, the lamp clicked out, and the two friends left the library.

Superintendent Keith slapped the morning paper down on her desk, front page up, her eyes still glued to a headline a third of the way down on the front page:

15,000 COAL MINERS QUIT IN ILLINOIS

She pushed the receptionist's button on the inter office communicator. "Grace, please call Mr. Danforth's office." As she waited for the connection, she remembered last winter's fuel crisis. She hoped that this year would not be a repeat. Of all of the things that had been unpredictable in her life recently, a coal shortage was number two, right there under America's declaration of war.

A male voice came on the line, neutral, but business like in tone.

"I'm fine, Mr. Danforth, but I just read about the coal miner's strike in this morning's paper. I'm assuming that the hospital and essential industries will be exempt from fuel rationing this will cause. Do you know if our exemption will cover the nurses' residence and the four houses where the probationers, the interns, and the maintenance staff live?"

She paused as the baritone voice responded.

"Well, will you please look into it? Those people are as important as the patients are, in my estimation. I can't run the hospital without them. If they quit because we can't keep their dormitories warm, I won't be able to replace them, not with the draft taking all of the able-bodied young men and the Red Cross siphoning off our nurses."

Again, she waited while the voice came through the earpiece. The conversational tone had turned into a lecture, and as the speaker's volume increased, she had to tip the earpiece away from her ear.

As she listened, the hospital administrator's complexion colored until her face was almost crimson. "No, I didn't know that, sir....Yes, sir.... I'll have the staff look into it immediately, Mr. Danforth."

The voice was shouting now, and she moved the earpiece farther away.

"I assure you that I will attend to this situation personally, Mr. Danforth.... Good bye, Mr. Danforth." She replaced the earpiece on its hook and, sitting down, she laid her head on her crossed arms.

Her graying head rose abruptly at the buzz of the desk-top loud speaker. Her complexion had returned to normal. She pressed the button on the machine. "Yes, Grace?"

"A telephone call from Miss Palmer, Mary," the office assistant's tinny voice responded.

"Thank you, Grace. Please connect me."

The hospital Superintendent sighed, lifted the telephone stand again and unhooked the earpiece. "Yes, Sophia? What can I do for you today?"

This disembodied voice was a soprano. Its tone was urgent.

"More nurses? No, Sophia, I don't have any more nurses to spare. As it is, I'm assigning women who haven't finished their training yet to supervisory duties. I have to hire brand new graduates to fill head nurses' places when they leave for army service.My assistant has already gone; Emma left for France a month ago, and a half dozen of the senior staff have volunteered for the Base Hospital 19 unit. The paper keeps threatening that their departure is imminent."

The telephone voice moderated a bit.

In contrast, Mary's responses grew impatient, and the color began to rise in her neck again. "No, Sophia....I don't care what the government has ordered; I can't spare anyone....I know the Red Cross is doing a wonderful job, and I'm happy they're doing it, but I have a hospital to run and I need every nurse and pupil we have to keep it running."

The voice coming through the earpiece turned sympathetic, soothing.

"Nursing aides? What kind of training have they had?....Well, maybe, if they don't get in the way of our pupil nurses....I'll ask the Seniors, but first I have to plug a hole in another dike....Good bye, Sophia. I sincerely wish you good luck."

Mary replaced the earpiece in its cradle and resumed the head-down-on-crossed-arms posture.

The desktop speaker buzzed again. This time the tinny voice-in-the-box announced, "Miss Whitely to see you, Miss Keith."

Mary sighed. "The First Year pupil or the housekeeper?"

"The housekeeper."

"Send her in, then."

"I will. Then I'll get you some coffee. I think you need another cup this morning."

"You've got that right, Grace."

When she entered Mary's office, Edith Whitely in her white uniform reminded Mary of a fluffy cloud floating against the sky blue of her office door. The middle-aged woman's fine, tight curls had turned from chestnut to pure white, and she had put on weight since the Superintendent had arrived at the General in 1901. Then the housekeeper's major characteristics had been efficiency and an inordinate pride in the institution that had trained her. Her nurses cap, with its distinctive black velvet band, was still her proudest possession.

She remained efficient, not only because she was a superb organizer, but now because the pupils loved and trusted her. The girls, especially those who had come to the big city from small towns, adopted her as their surrogate mother. They wouldn't disappoint her for the world.

A packet of blue brochures peeked out from her apron pocket, and her right hand held a clutch of furled pennants attached to small sticks.

What appeared to be a folded, satiny version of the little pennants, white, gold, and purple, was folded across that forearm.

"Good morning, Miss Keith," the newcomer said, her eyes cast downward, almost in reverence to the leader of this wonderful institution.

"Come in and have a seat, Edith." Mary drew two chairs together, seeking to dissolve the disparity in their positions. "I think you have in your hand the items that I want to ask you about."

"These?" The older woman sat and proffered the pennants and brochures to her superior. "The maintenance staff have been finding them all over the hospital for the past two weeks, even in the men's lavatories." She unfolded the larger, satiny cloth, revealing its legend: "WE DEMAND AN AMENDMENT…."

"When Mr. Howard took down the American flag at dusk yesterday, he found this had been run up along with it."

"Those are what Mr. Danforth is so angry about. We'll have to find and remove all of them. And we need to identify who has been distributing them."

"I think I know, Miss Keith. During daytime, the brochures and little flags always begin appearing in the same wards and classrooms where a few of the First Years have classes or are on duty. And again around 7:30 in the evening when they've finished their routines. I believe Miss Donnellan and Miss Denny are the leaders, although there are a few others. I thought of talking about it to Miss Smith, since she's in charge of the school. But they aren't breaking any rules that I know of."

"You're right, Edith. None of the school's written rules forbid this. I'll take care of it. Just leave the materials on my desk."

"Please be kind to them, Miss Keith. They're just girls. They don't mean anything by it." Edith Whitely, RN placed the items on the Superintendent's desk and floated out of the office.

As she left, receptionist Tailie entered and handed her superior a cup of coffee.

"Thank you, Grace. I certainly need this. Would you please ask First Year pupils Emily Donnellan and Alice Denny to see me as soon as they get out of their morning classes?"

"Yes, Mary. Why don't you sit down and relax a bit. It's been a busy morning."

"And it promises to get busier," her superior responded, blowing across the cup and taking a sip.

"Come in," Superintendent Keith invited, responding to the timid knock on the office door.

Emily Donnellan entered first, with Alice trailing behind her. "Good morning, Miss Keith, they said in unison. The first of the pair to see the satiny pennant on the Superintendent's desk, Emily frowned. Then Alice noticed the items, and her left eyebrow rose.

"Sit down, girls." The team obeyed. The Superintendent remained standing. "I've had a telephone call this morning from an important person, Mr. Henry Danforth, the President of the Board of Directors of the General Hospital."

In addition to being surprised, the revelation of Mr. Danforth's connection with the hospital struck Emily funny. A title with so many words – she counted them —ten to be exact— must belong to a man of great privilege and esteem. Her left lip quivered, the involuntary beginning of an impulsive grin. If she looked at Alice, she was sure she'd burst out laughing. But when she did glance toward her accomplice, the latter was studying the toe of her high-top shoes.

"Henry Danforth," Miss Keith went on, pacing around the room now and seeming to ignore the pupils, "has been the most dedicated Board President that this institution has ever had.He has served the hospital, not as a figure head, but as a hands-on leader, since before I got here, and that was a long time ago."

She reversed her path and looked at the ceiling, as if a script was printed there. "As a respected lawyer, he has many powerful and prestigious clients in Rochester. Some of them are very generous contributors to this hospital which, as you know, serves everyone regardless of race, creed, gender…," she paused, "…or political leanings."

The Superintendent stopped pacing and picked up the large pennant, but her voice remained calm. This was turning into a long lecture, Emily decided. She wished Miss Keith would hurry up and get it over with.

"Some of Mr. Danforth's clients believe that women should be able to vote in elections. Others do not believe women's opinions should affect what they regard as men's prerogatives. A few want to wait until all of the states agree and a federal amendment enfranchises women. Quite frankly, I'm not sure which side Mr. Danforth favors. That's his business, and he keeps it to himself. His wife, on the other hand, is quite outspoken on the issue, but only in public.She has served on the hospital's Board of Lady Managers for as long as her husband has been President of the Board, but she has never involved this institution with her suffrage activities."

Alice jerked to attention. *Both of the Danforths were on the General Hospital's governing boards? Who would have guessed?* Emily shrank in her chair.

Miss Keith's tone was assertive now. "These pennants and brochures associate this hospital in patients' and visitors' minds with a controversial political campaign. They could damage this institution's reputation in doing so. They must be removed from wherever you've put them at once!"

Both young women stood and quickly gathered the suffragist materials, anxious to escape before their superior exploded in anger.

But Miss Keith modulated her voice a bit. "I do not expect to see a single suffragist item or to receive a telephone call from an angry board president about them again. You are dismissed."

The girls nearly tumbled over each other in their hurry to retrieve the offending relics before lunchtime.

The following week, Alice and Emily were assigned to night duty in neighboring wards in West Hall. Pushing carts with coffee urns for the head night nurses' break, they paused in the hallway.

"We won!" Emily shouted. She jumped up and clicked her heels together.

"Sh-h-h," cautioned Alice. "Not by much according to this morning's paper. We're only ahead by about 4,000 votes in early returns."

"You realize, though, that downstate ballots haven't all been counted. That's where the big support is."

"Still, there's only two unreported districts in the county. And the 'no's are ahead by more than three thousand votes."

"Don't be so pessimistic, Ben. You know we won. And one or more men might have voted for suffrage because he saw a brochure or a pennant in the hospital."

A night nurse poked her head into the hallway. "Come on, you First Years. Get that coffee in here."

"At least Miss Keith didn't expel us."

"I bet she's been hoping women would get the vote as much as we have," said Emily, and she danced a jig down the hall behind her cart.

Well I guess I've raved enough, more than usual perhaps, so I'll close. Emily just came in and said she caught a mouse by the tail in the desk drawer. They surely run rampage around here.

Love to all,

Ben

Chapter 6

The nurses had a sleigh ride last night.... Went out the Chili road, back to the house.... I fell out the sleigh. My head on the ground and feet up in back of the sleigh. Of course I laid in the road after I loosened my feet and then had to run to get in the sleigh. The girls said I was some sight but it added to the fun.

Snow came early this year, in mid October, but then it disappeared for a month. By Sunday, December 9th, there were nine and a half inches on the ground. It was a perfect opportunity for the hospital's Board of Lady Managers to arrange a treat for the pupil nurses —a sleigh ride on their half-day off. Since noon Billy Mahoney, the ambulance driver, had been chauffeuring small groups around town before the street shovellers had had a chance to expose the grimier pavement and while the white blanket still masked the sharp angles and edges of the buildings. The upperclassmen had gotten priority. It was dusk when "those First Year pupils" finally had their turn.

Alice and Norma hurried out the door and down the steps of the Nurses' Home. Large flakes were falling, but they could still distinguish the path that their friends had taken around the corner to Reynolds Street. The new snow glistened, and it was so cold that it crunched under Norma's flat-heeled boots. Alice had to pump her legs faster to keep up with her roommate's long strides. She should have chosen sensible foot ware rather than given in to vanity.

"Come on!" "Let's get going!" the girls yelled from the sleigh's bed. Norma, used to hoisting herself into farm wagons, hiked up her long skirt and mounted the slippery ladder rungs easily. Emily made room for her on her hay bale and handed her a horse blanket. Norma sniffed the blanket, smiled contentedly, and spread it across her lap.

"Sit here, Ben!" Susan invited. She shifted to make room on her bale. Alice got to the second step when the horse abruptly moved forward, and she fell backward into a snow bank. A hot rush of embarrassment counteracted her icy landing.

"Whoa!" yelled Billy Mahoney, reining up Dobbin a couple of yards away. Some of the girls giggled at the slapstick comedy scene. It was like watching a Charlie Chaplin movie.

Alice struggled to her feet, shook some of the snow off, and ran to catch up. Susan stretched out her arms, nearly lifted her friend bodily onto the sleigh bed, and brushed the rest of the snow off with her mittened hands.

Her sense of decorum recovered now, Alice could join in the chatter. She sniffed the horse blanket that Susan had snuggled around her legs and wrinkled her nose. "It's perfume to me," said her roommate grinning from the opposite side of the sleigh bed. The sled moved again, its runners gliding smoothly over the firmly packed roadway.

"First, a tour of the hospital campus," announced Billy, and they turned eastward onto Troupe Street. Alice eyed a hulk of a building across the street from the hospital grounds. It was a four-story box that an architect had tried to disguise by pasting on an assortment of porches and gables to its walls. Every window was lit, indicating that all of the rooms were in use, from the first floor to what was probably an attic.

"What is that place?" asked Austin. "Whenever I've walked by it, it's given me the creeps. No one ever seems to go in or out, yet the windows are all lit up at night."

"It's called the House of Hope," Hilda answered. "It's where unwed mothers stay in the weeks before they give birth. They're admitted to the hospital for the delivery and a week later they return to the house for their lying in."

"Why don't they ever come outside?"

"The house matrons are teaching them domestic skills so that they can support themselves when they leave. Besides, the neighbors scorn them."

"What happens to the babies?" Susan wondered.

"Most of the new mothers agree to put them up for adoption. It's rare for a single mother to find work in Rochester, let alone an employer who'll allow her to keep her baby at her side."

"How do you know so much about the place?" Austin asked.

Billy had steered Dobbin back into West Main Street now, heading westward. Since this was his last run for the day, he decided to treat his passengers to a much longer ride.

"When you've lived in Rochester all your life, you hear about some places, even though no one seems to want to talk about them in public," came the answer. "Am I right, Ben?" Alice nodded her head in agreement. She had heard voices whispering about the House of Hope in the Christian Endeavor meetings she used to attend with her mother.

Sensing a new crusade, Emily broke in. "Where did you hear about it?"

Hilda looked around at the friends, considering how much she needed to share with them. "I knew someone who was a resident there," she finally admitted.

"Go on," Emily encouraged.

"The girl's father had emigrated here from Germany. He is a good man, and a religious one. But he sees everyone's actions in black and white; in his world there are no shades of gray. A person's choices are either good or evil. You should hear him on the subject of the Kaiser's war."

"So how is he connected with a resident at the House of Hope?"

"Well, when his daughter was young, she and a boy classmate had a close friendship. It blossomed into love when they became teenagers. They planned on getting married last summer, but his number was drawn in the first Army draft."

The riders huddled together, leaning elbows on knees, closing the gaps between them. The vehicle approached a street lamp. For a brief minute it became a spotlight, illuminating Hilda's white knit hat with a fringe of red hair peeking out from underneath. And then her face faded into the shadows again.

"But my —the girl— had become pregnant. Since she and her beau weren't married yet, he couldn't get a deferment."

"Then what?"

"The father was furious! He would not have an evil woman living under his roof. He disowned the girl and forbad anyone else in the family from contacting her. He packed up all of her belongings and committed her to the House of Hope."

"Couldn't her mother have done something?" Susan asked.

"Of course, not," replied Emily, turning away and staring into the snow-studded darkness. "She's a woman. She has no legal standing."

The group was silent for a few moments, listening to the rhythmic bells jingle around Dobbin's neck as he trotted and the *sh-sh-sh* of the sleigh's runners. Susan broke their reverie. "Can't we do something for them? Maybe help them keep their babies?"

"There's nothing we can do, except when they're admitted to the General's maternity ward. They're the saddest patients in the hospital," Emily answered.

"I'm on maternity duty next week," Susan declared. "That's what I'll do. When I bring the babies to the mothers at feeding time, I'll look for the saddest one. Then I'll be especially nice to her until she and her baby are discharged."

"We all could do that," agreed Emily. The sleigh riders nodded in silent agreement.

A few seconds later, a happy rendition of "Jingle Bells" lasted until they got to the intersection of Chili Road and West Avenue. "Which way?" yelled Billy.

"Chili Road!" they demanded in unison.

Then Austin got serious. "Listen, girls. The Board of Lady Managers is hosting an annual Christmas party for the pupils in the training school. But the ladies have decided there should be entertainment along with the cranberry punch and cookies and group carol singing. So they're running a contest. Volunteers from each class will compete in a Christmas sing. Miss Keith and Miss Gilman will be the judges."

"Aw, we'll never win. It's only our first year. The Seniors and Intermediates have been working together for three years," whined Susan.

"You may be right, Susan. But Bong has a great idea. Tell them, Bong."

Bong began her explanation in the key of C major. "It's a simple melody and we're all familiar with the words."

"What's wrong with Bong? Why isn't she rhyming?" Alice whispered to Hilda on her left.

"When we're alone in our room, she doesn't rhyme. She'll either stutter, which doesn't embarrass her if she's just with me, or she'll sing. If she sings, she doesn't stutter."

Bong's singing voice was pleasing, even though the tune wasn't familiar. Her lyrics told them that she was composing a new Christmas piece based on the Gospel of St. Luke. If the First Years team practiced faithfully for the next two weeks, they'd have a chance of winning because their selection would be original. But, she warned, her voice dropping to a lower register, Austin would have to agree to just mouth the words. Then she lapsed into speech: "I love you, Austin; you're such a dear. But for singing music, you've got no ear."

Austin nodded, almost enthusiastically. She knew that her speaking voice could command attention. But if she sang, she was sure to spoil Bong's creation.

"We've got a really good chance," Hilda agreed. "Bong has a beautiful singing voice, and she's had professional training on the piano."

An hour later, when the sleigh slid to a stop back at the nurses' residence, the girls piled out, excited to start learning their entry in the Christmas Sing, and anxious to warm their hands around steaming mugs of hot chocolate.

The Nurses' Home parlor sparkled on the evening of the competition. A canopy of red crepe paper streamers draped from the central ceiling light fixture to the top edge of all four walls. At the back of the room long tables, arranged end to end, wore gleaming white linen table cloths. A huge glass punch bowl filled with a cranberry red beverage was at the center of the tables, crystal cups surrounding it. Platters of decorated Christmas cookies, fudge, and candies hugged the centerpiece.

Behind the bank of tables stood members of the Ladies Board of Managers of the General Hospital, all attired in their finest holiday outfits and each wearing a broad-brimmed, be-feathered hat. Tonight these upper-class women, who were accustomed to being served by others, became servants themselves. Their benevolent smiles welcomed the classes as they filed in. The room buzzed with polite conversation.

The Seniors and Intermediate pupils were already sitting in the rows of chairs aligned for the audience when the First Year pupils entered the parlor. The upperclassmen also wore a variety of gaily colored Christmas outfits, although the off-the-rack type rather than the tailor-made kind. Within each class, the competing septets or octets, wearing green or red skirts with white blouses of a similar cut, sat together.

The team representing the First Year class wore floor length black skirts topped by simple white blouses. As their director, Bong's shoulders were draped in a black shawl, attached by a brooch at her neck. As they took their seats, Norma whispered into Alice's ear, "Guess I'll have to put on my good manners tonight and make polite conversation with the ladies. How do you hold a glass punch cup? Like the china tea cups they give us at the Wednesday teas, with our pinkie fingers extended? And will I have to curtsey?"

"No, Norma. Just use your index finger and thumb like you normally do. Curtseying may be a Canadian custom, but Americans don't do that."

Mrs. Dr. Fitch, President of the Lady Managers, welcomed the guests of honor – Superintendent Keith and Principal Gilman – and the pupils. She introduced Mrs. Hoyt who would accompany the contesting teams on the piano if they so wished. The order of appearance would be Senior pupil's team first, then the Intermediate team, with the First Year's team performing last.

As the Senior septet assembled at the front of the room, Bong opened the bag she had brought with her. She took a piece of segmented lemon out and passed the bag to Hilda, who took another wedge and passed the bag on down the line. That morning, Bong had forbidden anyone in the group from drinking milk or eating a milk product, like cheese or ice cream. The offending foods coated the vocal chords, she insisted. Sucking on lemon wedges would keep the singers' voices clear, the notes precise. Even Austin took a segment from the bag, just in case she'd have to make an acceptance speech at the end of the competition.

The Seniors' skirts were various shades of green. They had chosen "O Holy Night" as their selection, perhaps hoping to extend their vocal ranges to their limits with success. The higher notes were barely audible, but some of the singers struggled mightily to reach them, their eyes rising toward the ceiling, their chins straining upwards. Mrs. Hoyt played *fortissimo*, with vigor. She may have had a special love for this carol, or perhaps she hoped to drown out the somewhat screechy rendering. The audience applauded politely the instant the carol was over.

The Intermediates wore an assortment of red plaid, striped, be-flowered, and plaid skirts. "God Rest Ye, Merry Gentlemen" was their choice. They had a much better command of the carol's range, but the fragile soprano voices could hardly do justice to this hearty traditional carol. There were a couple of false starts while the accompanist tried to match her instrument's keys to the range that the girls had practiced in. And she played *pianissimo*, afraid that her next note or her tempo might clash with the team's. The applause at the end was stronger this time, more appreciative.

First-Year septet rose, dropped their spent lemon rinds in the open bag on Bong's chair, and walked to the front of the audience. Each held a black folder with the music and lyrics, something they were afraid might reduce their rating. But they needed the notations desperately since this was not a traditional carol, learned by heart from childhood. Bong faced her team and shook her head "no" toward the pianist, indicating that this selection would be performed *a cappella*. With her wiry red hair and pudgy torso, she looked for all the world like a Raggedy Ann doll in mourning.

When she had made direct eye contact with every singer, she raised her arms. They started on the beat:

> At that time there went forth a decree from Caesar Augustus
> That all should be enrolled.
> And Joseph went from Galilee to Judea
> To the town of David
> Which is called Bethlehem….

The melody could not have been simpler. In fact, it was Gregorian chant, blending six voices into precise, crystal-clear notes, unadorned by harmony or a distinctive rhythm. An ancient story sung in an ancient style.

The tempo changed a bit when the singers came to:

> …and she brought forth a newborn son,
> and wrapped him in swaddling clothes,
> and laid him in a manger.

Hushed, breathy "Ah"s descended from high C to middle C, but this time with soprano/alto harmony.

Bong slowly turned to face the audience and sang the first verse of "Silent Night" in a sweet soprano. She beckoned to the audience to join her and the team in the second verse. Finally, she turned to her group once more, commanding their undivided attention with her smiling eyes. The haunting, chant-like melody returned, this time with harmony.

The selection ended with the joyous announcement of the angels:

Peace on Earth; Good will toward men.

The conductor relaxed her arms and bowed her head. The choristers closed their folders and lowered their heads too. There was silence.

The sound of one person clapping followed by a second and then more, filled the parlor and the hallway beyond, until everyone, the Lady Managers, the Seniors, and the Intermediates, were applauding enthusiastically. When the team returned to their seats, their fellow classmates whispered their appreciation to the group, the ones closest to the singers and their leader patting them on the back.

Mrs. Dr. Fitch wedged the handkerchief she had been using to blot her teary eyes into a sleeve and handed paper and pencils to the judges. Then Miss Keith and Miss Smith huddled for just a moment before returning their decision to the chief Lady Manager, who announced the unanimous results: The First-Year team had won. The applause was again generous, with only two indecorous hoots eliciting frowns from disapproving matrons.

Mrs. Dr. Fitch invited all of the attendees to join her and her fellow Lady Managers at the punch bowl. Mrs. Hoyt began a Christmas carol-a-thon with "Oh, Come All Ye Faithful," and the guests sang and sipped and nibbled and smiled for the next hour and a half.

At the evening's end Mrs. Dr. Fitch handed the first prize, a huge, cherry-studded fruitcake, to Bong, who was able to thank her hostess with only a little stammer: "I kn-new we'd w-won. Just because, when we finished, there was no applause."

Miss Keith and Miss Smith helped the Lady Managers clear away the party paraphernalia and straighten the room. Eunice walked with the Superintendent to the Nurses' Home door to bid her good evening. "What a pleasant evening it was, wasn't it, Mary?"

The Superintendent eased each finger into her leather gloves and replied, "You know, Eunie, if we had more evenings like this one, I wouldn't be the exhausted administrator I've become in the last couple of years. Let's hope the Lady Managers will come up with more entertaining activities for the girls in the coming year." She hugged her friend and, bending against the cold, she made her way back to her suite in the Administration Building.

When Bong and the rest of her team returned to Austin's room to enjoy their victory and their prize, the First Year song leader observed, "F-fruitcake's immortal – if we don't finish it all, it'll still taste good well into next fall."

Alice turned to Hilda who was sitting next to her. "You know, Hilda, if we had more activities like this one, when we can all be together at the same time, turning into a nurse wouldn't be such a chore for me."

"Just keep at it a while longer, Ben. I know you'll come to love it like the rest of us."

It was cold! Her automobile merely growled when she'd first turned the key. This Saturday Mary Keith, Superintendent of General Hospital, wanted to growl back. She didn't like using her only day off for hospital business. She'd much rather have stayed in her warm apartment in the Administration Building reading a good book and visiting patients informally.

It was cold - <u>again</u>! Like it had been for the past week. Her nose hairs froze up with every inhalation, and she blinked as each exhalation condensed on her glasses. She could stand a day or two of sub-zero weather, but this cold was relentless. The thermometer in the ambulance garage where she kept her auto registered a minus 6 this morning; it had registered zero yesterday. There'd been a warm up at the beginning of the week, the high all the way to 27 degrees on Monday, but like her spirits, it had plunged again. February was probably going to be just like January had been, bleak and icy cold.

But this is important, she thought as she shifted the floor rod into first gear. She had made an appointment to meet a dear friend, Maude Johnston, her counterpart at the Homeopathic Hospital.

Hospital superintendents were rare in Rochester, a city with only four major health care institutions, and female hospital administrators were becoming even rarer. Maude and Mary were the second generation of strong female managers. Their predecessors, Eva Allerton and Sophia Palmer, had paved the way, fighting to establish a new career choice for women and the scattering of men who could ignore the gender-exclusive title, "nurse." Hospital trained, registered nurses now enjoyed a unique status. For the past thirty years or so, the profession had gained the respect that, in previous years, had been given to male Board directors, female overseers, and learned physicians. But now elsewhere female hospital administration was slowly being infiltrated by men.

Main street had been cleared by the army of snow shovellers as had Monroe Avenue. But when Mary turned east on Alexander Street, the roadway was slippery, with ruts that shoved her chugging machine around like a canoe in choppy water. She parked and, bending to protect her body from the sharp edge of icy air, she made her way up the sidewalk to the Superintendent's cottage.

Back in 1901 when the Homeopathic's Women Supervisors had the frame building erected, Mary had felt a twang of envy. But now its isolation from the main hospital buildings bothered her. She needed to be at the heart of her institution, in her suite in the Administration Building. True, she was awakened occasionally at night when the ambulance brought in emergency patients or noisy drunk and disorderlies, but those disturbances were the institution's pulse, and she wanted to monitor it in person.

Maude's sitting room was much like the one in her own suite, the walls lined with professional books and the fading Persian carpet weighted down by overstuffed furniture with large, flowery patterns. Flames licked around the edges of logs in the fireplace, warming the room. Colorful prints of far-away places revealed Miss Johnston's lifetime dream of traveling to exotic places. To Mary's delight, the hostess had a large urn of hot coffee and mugs with which she could warm her numb fingers.

"It's good to see you again, Mary," Maude Johnston greeted her professional counterpart, hanging her visitor's coat on a hall tree in the foyer. She was younger than Mary, but slender like her. Her raven hair, unrestrained now on her day off, brushed the shoulders of a frilly white blouse. She poured a steaming mug of coffee, handed it to Mary, and sat across from her guest at the small dinner table in the center of the room.

Spooning sugar into her own cup, Maude guessed, "I'm afraid, though, that this isn't just a friendly visit. I suspect the predicament we're in will need two heads to solve."

"You're right, Maude. By the way, that was a generous offer you made to share Homeopathic's laboratory facilities with the General when the army took our lab technicians. It's nice to know that you and I are in this situation together, not competing," she frowned, "–like the Homeopathic and the Allopathic physicians arguing over which medical theory is better– but as collaborators."

"So, what brings you here on our day off?"

Mary leaned forward. "This morning's *D & C* said that all of the hospitals are running at full capacity except for the General. Is that really true for the Homeopathic?"

"Unless we set up cots in the hallways, we haven't a bed to spare. Aren't you full, too?"

"I downplayed the General's overcrowded condition to the reporter that interviewed me. I didn't want the public to suspect how many of our pupils are sick. Did you count everyone?"

"Yes. I reported both patients and staff." The younger woman sighed. "We're painfully understaffed."

Her fingers now warm, Mary sipped her coffee. "I didn't want to admit how much of our nursing services are being affected by this coal famine."

"Last fall it was the coal miner's strike. Now it's the weather, Mary. The trains can't get from the mines to the cities that desperately need it. People are shivering in their homes, sharing their germs with each other." She slumped in resignation and then straightened. "At least Washington has exempted hospitals from the temperature regulations, and we can keep our patients warm."

But I think the 65-degree limit may eventually force us into turning away patients anyway. The hospitals are fine, but our Nurses' Home isn't. In December we had nine staff members sick. They take up hospital beds. Then last month nineteen of our staff couldn't report for work, and many of them are still on the sick list. Our healthy nurses are working overtime, and their disease resistance is suffering. The patients keep exposing them to cold and influenza germs. If this keeps up, there won't be enough healthy nurses and staff to care for new patients."

"What else can we do, Mary?" Maude counted on her fingers. "Dr. Lewis at the Hahnemann, you at General, and I all petitioned our Board of Directors' presidents to lobby in Washington for heat in the nurses' homes. I'm not sure about Sister Clementine at St. Mary's; she serves a higher power than a mere board president. But I'm fairly sure she's approached Bishop Kearney."

Mary stood up and paced around the table. Stopping abruptly, she said, "Suppose we asked Sophia Palmer for help. She's the director of Red Cross nurse recruitment, so her reputation for supporting the war effort is unquestioned. If she were to approach Mayor Edgerton and the City Council, they'd listen to her, I think. In fact, it would be unpatriotic for them to ignore her."

Maude joined Mary on her side of the table. "Let's do that, Mary. Monday morning, let's make an appointment with Sophia." Smiling, they hugged each other.

"We have a plan," the older woman agreed. "Once we settle on a date and a time, I'll pick you up…if my ornery car starts. We could all go to lunch and reminisce about the old, simpler times."

"But they were exciting times, weren't they, Mary? Eva and Sophia arguing with the physicians, who were sure they should regulate the new profession and then lobbying with the politicians in Albany for self governance."

"In order to continue doing what we pledged to do, though, our hospitals need to keep their nursing pupils and staffs healthy."

For the next hour the two Superintendents, pioneers in their own way, reminisced about their activities in the very exclusive career they had helped create.

The temperature was a shock to Alice as she entered the tunnel that connected the nurses' home with the Administration Building. Her busy duty that night had made her forget about the weather. New patients, sometimes whole families, were constantly being admitted, all of them with high temperatures, flaming sore throats, violent chill spasms.

As she trudged along, she said a weary "hi" to pairs and trios of pupils who passed her on their way to their morning tasks. They walked briskly, not in anticipation of another day of serving others, but so that they could reach the warmer hospital buildings as quickly as possible.

It was nearly as cold in the Isabella nurses' home when she exited the tunnel and went to her room. As always Norma had left her bed unmade, decorated with discarded pajamas.

Exasperated and exhausted, Alice decided to keep wearing yesterday's undergarments. At least they were still warm. Lifting her chemise, she unlaced the corset and tossed it toward the bottom of the bed. She slid her flannel nightgown over her head, scuffed her feet into slippers, and burrowed under the blankets. Forget brushing anything – hair, teeth.

There it was! The blessed hot water bottle that Susan always put in her bed before leaving for day duty. It had appeared every morning that Alice was on night duty. The squishy rubber bag had spread its warmth to the sheets, rising to just above her ankles. Comforted, Alice fell asleep quickly.

The knocking on the door wasn't part of her dream. It was real. "Yes?" she complained.

"A phone call for you, Alice," was the apologetic answer.

"I'll be there in a minute."

Her face instantly knew how cold the room was. Nevertheless, still clad in layers and warmed by deep sleep, she slowly extracted herself from a mound of blankets. Norma must have come off duty and, rather than making her own bed, she had used her blankets to cover her sleeping roommate. *Exasperating, yes. But considerate, too.*

Alice shuffled down the hall to the little alcove in the corner of the parlor. They called it a telephone booth, but it had no privacy. The black ear piece lay on the table next to the post it was tethered to. She picked the instruments up.

"Yes?"

"Alice," came a familiar male voice, distorted a bit by long distance. Her brother Will in Buffalo.

"Yes, Will. It's me. Why are you calling? I had night duty, and you got me up out of a sound sleep." She yawned.

"Alice." The voice hesitated; the tone was somber. "Mama died in her sleep last night."

Alert now, Alice merely placed the receiver gently back on its hook. Oblivious to the cold she hurried to her room where she could weep alone.

Oh, how I wish I could see you all. I like the girls here and they're kind to me, but it's not like your own and I do miss home and mama so much. Seems as tho' I must phone her sometime, and I almost catch my self making for the phone booth when the awful thought that she isn't there comes to me.

Chapter 7

Dear Bess:- …. Had my [cap's] *stripes* [as a First Year pupil] *a year* [ago] *last Mon.,… and how proud I was to get them. The next goal will be the white uniform and black velvet* [band] *and then I wonder what…. I dread to take the "weary road" again without M*[ama]*'s loving support & comfort…. Seems as tho' everyone I love is going somewhere.*

It was quiet, unnaturally so, Alice concluded, scanning the parallel lines of sleeping patients. Night duty on men's ward normally meant a chorus of snores, snorts, and grunts as the sleepers turned over in their beds, punctuated by the occasional shouted epithet provoked by a vivid dream.

It was ironic. Here it was, the shortest night-duty assignment she had yet experienced, and there was nothing to do. She yawned and settled into a wicker chair. Miss Lee, the Assistant Night Supervisor, was bent over patient reports in the work room at the end of the ward. Alice had already taken her break, wheeling the night duty nurses' coffee urn from ward to ward on this floor and returning the cart to the kitchen in the basement. There must be something she could do to relieve the boredom and stay awake.

Just past midnight, she decided to reset her timepiece. The government was instituting the daylight-savings plan for the first time today, in the hope that adding a night-time hour in the spring and taking it back in the fall would somehow ease the winter's coal famine. It didn't make sense to many people, including Alice, but she knew she had to conform. She'd do anything that would shorten this twelve-hour tedium.

As her fingers began to loosen the black velvet ribbon that suspended her timepiece from around her neck, the thing she yearned for —sound— happened. A male voice echoed faintly down the hallway that connected the wards on this floor. "Too-ra, loo-ra, loo-ra" an unsteady tenor drifted through the swinging doors, the volume increasing as its source approached. "Too-ra, loo-ra, la-a-ay" it continued, going flat as the doors swooshed opened.

Alice stood, rushed to an empty cot, and turned the blanket and sheet down. It was hard to determine whether the crooner, his front half covered by a long sheet draped toga style, was being supported by his smaller companions or whether he was holding them up.

The inebriated patient's right arm was hugging the thin shoulders of Charles Muldoon, the hospital's elevator operator. At 50 years old, the balding, white-haired man was too ancient for the Army to be interested in drafting him. Under the tenor's left armpit, George Edmonds, one of the General's young ambulance drivers, was limping along on a club foot. *A hospital in war time is a strange place,* Alice mused. *There are so few men here, and they're either sick or decrepit or physically impaired. The few healthy ones – interns and resident doctors – appear for a few short weeks, and then the Army always whisks them away.*

"Over here," she directed the struggling human crutches. "Sh-h-h-h!" she admonished the soloist as he paused, apparently to get up steam for the finale of his aria.

"Been here before, Miss. Jist tryin' ta soothe the sufferers," he slurred, and he finished his rendition -- "That's an I-rish" – a huge breath – "lull-a-a-a-by!" – in a very unsteady note.

A somnolent patient in a neighboring cot swore, turned over, and burrowed his head under the pillow. Another opened one, semi-sedated eye lid, and then clamped it down tightly. A man on the other side of the center aisle sat upright and yelled, "Welcome back, Mick. Wondered when we'd see ya!"

"Best celebrate while ya can, Mick. Them prohibition folks 're tryin' to dry us all out!" a second man added.

Several other patients stirred, wiped sleep from their eyes, and then sat erect, eager for a little unexpected entertainment. What would the fragile young nurse do to subdue this behemoth?

"He messed his pants, Miss, but we took 'em off in the ambulance. Didn't have time to clean the rest of him up, though. It's a short ride from Front Street. Celebrating St. Paddy's Day, he was, when he fell."

"That's all right. George. I'll take over from here." *St. Paddy's Day?* she wondered. *That was two weeks ago.*

The elevator man and the ambulance driver exited quickly, relieved to be returning to matters that they knew they could control.

Removing the toga and exposing a hulking, hairy chest, Alice winced, and she gagged when the odor reached her. Hastily, she drew the bed sheet up to the man's waist. The angry red scrapes on his knees were surface wounds, and they could wait. Then she began unbuttoning the vomit-stained work jacket, exposing a graying undershirt, still moist from expelled stomach contents and drying sweat. The quickest way to examine the body was to cut the shoulder straps and abdomen of the undershirt, which she did with the blunt-nosed scissors in her apron pocket.

The shoulders were as hairy as the rest of him, more like fur than individual strands. Even the knuckles sprouted with wiry, reddish stuff. The left hand was matted with blood that had trickled down from bicep to forearm, its source another bloody wound on the left shoulder. But this hair wasn't like the fine, gold highlighted manes that Hilda and Bond had. The body hair was a darker red, almost russet, a shade deeper than the wiry mass that covered the giant's head, cheeks and chin. She supposed, the facial hair, exposed to the elements, had been bleached by the sun. Or perhaps the man had bathed those areas more often. The stench suggested that might also have been the case.

"If you iver go across the sea to Ire-land...," the soloist began again, and he struggled to rise.

"Shush!"she commanded, loudly now since everyone in the ward was awake and watching.

"Aw, the only thing that'll get him quiet is a knock on the head," insisted the patient in the next cot.

"Yeah!"

"Put his pillow over his face 'n' smother him."

"Naw, let 'im sing till he passes out!"

"We can join in! We know the words."

"Th'n, maybe at the closin' of yer da-ay,..." the tenor continued, and sat upright.

Night Supervisor Lee, alerted by the disturbance and unsure whether her protégé could handle the situation, was hurrying up the aisle between the bed rows. She held a large amber bottle and a clean cotton rag.

"...you c'n sit an' watch the moon – " The singer's voice stopped abruptly, the pupils of his eyes rose toward the ceiling and rolled back into their sockets. The immense torso fell back, the bulging biceps flailed wildly.

"Try to hold him down," ordered Miss Lee, uncorking the bottle and pouring a clear liquid into the rag. The aroma made one's eyes water, but it was preferable to the reek emanating from the body.

Alice secured one wrist, but when she grabbed for the second, the first escaped. Her hands weren't large enough or strong enough to immobilize both huge arms at the same time. A beefy elbow drove into the side of her chest; luckily her corset protected her ribs. One fist flew up, heavily grazing her right temple. Miss Lee thrust the moistened rag under the patient's nose, and after a couple of jerks, the body went limp.

"Chloroform," the night supervisor said. "Does the trick every time. But it won't last. Stay here, Alice, while I get something that'll keep him out longer."

"Aw, why stop the fun?" asked one disappointed patient. Grumbling their disappointment, the ward mates lay down again, pulled their blankets over themselves, and worked at getting back to sleep.

Miss Lee returned with a syringe and a vial.

"What's that?"

"Veronal. It'll knock him out 'til he's slept it off." She inserted the needle into the vial and withdrew a measure of the medicine. "Mick's been here before; he's kind of a tradition. Starts celebrating St. Patty's day and carries on until he's too drunk to stand up. Sometimes it takes days before he falls down." The night supervisor inserted the loaded needle into the man's bicep and plunged the sedative into his blood stream.

Stepping back, she examined the wounds. "Contusions as usual. Nothing serious unless he's broken something. We'll have X-ray take some pictures tomorrow to make sure." She tucked the sheet and blanket around the unconscious, red-forested mountain. "He'll be in no mood to serenade in the morning. He'll have a huge hangover, but at least he'll be quieter. And if he remembers anything about tonight, he might feel a little guilty."

Then she looked closely at Alice. "By the looks of things, you won't feel good tomorrow either, Alice. You'd better put some ice on that eye of yours. And if you have any energy after you get some sleep, you could stop by here to see how he's doing. You might bring back his memory of tonight. Guilt can be good sometimes. With the luck of the Irish, he might not be with us at this time next year. But I doubt it."

The remaining hours of her shift went on without incident. Alice put some ice from the refrigerator in a rubber sack and held it against her right cheek, which was red and swelling. The adrenaline rush kept her from nodding off from sheer exhaustion, or boredom.

When the Probationers came on duty at dawn, Alice still didn't feel tired enough to go back to the nurses' residence to sleep, so she helped the newbies with their chores: taking temps, recording pulses, and emptying bedpans. They were respectful enough of their seniors not to ask why her cheek and eyelid had taken on a purplish hue, but she knew they were speculating about it.

Emptying one filled bed pan into the hopper in the supply room, she recalled that she hadn't yet reset her pocket clock ahead one hour. So, while waiting for the spigot to flush out the receptacle in the secondary sink, she reached behind her neck to finish untying its black velvet tether. As she released the ribbon, it slipped smoothly through her fingers. She grabbed for the timepiece, but missing, she watched the clock's face disappear down the dark drain of the hopper.

Her training had been effective. Thrusting her hand into the pipe to search its contents for the treasured instrument would mean contact with millions of invisible microbes. No amount of scrubbing and disinfectant would rid them of the contamination.

For a moment, a wave of guilt washed over her.

Aunt Anna had had a healthy sense of humor, she remembered. In that instant her mind transformed the treasured heirloom into a mere hand-me-down *"Tempus' certainly does 'fugit,'"* she thought, knowing that Aunt Anna would have laughed at the irony of the situation. *But after a night like this*, she wondered, *how could Anna ever have devoted the rest of her life to being a nurse?*

"Who should we assign to march in the Liberty Loan Parade on Saturday, Mary?" Eunice Smith asked after draining her coffee cup. The head nurses had finished their meal, and the wait staff were noisily clearing the tables in the dining hall.

"Another cup of coffee, Miss Smith?" inquired the waitress hovering near the administrators' table.

"No, I don't think so, Catherine." The Principal handed her saucer and empty cup to the young woman.

"You, Miss Keith?"

"No, Catherine. I've had enough, thank you," and the hospital Superintendent leaned back while the waitress removed the china. "You've read about it in the newspaper, Eunice. How big will this thing be?

"They anticipate even more marchers than the Preparedness Parade back in '16. They've decided that nurses who have volunteered for the Base Hospital 19 unit should march with their regular hospital contingents. That way the spectators won't notice how limited hospital staffs are now. I think we should send as many nurses as the hospital can afford to release."

Miss Keith sighed. "Any word on when the unit leaves?"

The clatter of dish clearing had moved from the dining hall to the kitchen, allowing the women more privacy. Eunice pantomimed quotation marks in the air. "'Any day now.' But, your guess is as good as mine."

"Quite frankly, I don't think that group is ever going to be deployed. It's been —what?— over a year since Dr. Swan began recruiting you folks?"

The Principal thought for a moment. "Nearly a year and a half. And it's <u>Major</u> Swan now. Received his commission sometime at the end of last year, right after he began organizing six months ago, four months before we actually entered the war."

"It seems like all they do is hold benefit dances and perform military drills for the public." Superintendent Keith walked her index and middle finger toward the center of the table. "And every Sunday contingents of them march to the churches in full uniform."

"They were delayed because Washington sent orders to double the unit's size a couple of months ago. That meant enlisting men from outside the city, raising money for more armored vehicles, and equipping the bigger unit. It all takes time."

"<u>And</u> siphoning more nurses from the hospitals." Mary straightened up, warming to her subject. "What about that fund drive to buy them overcoats? You'd think Washington would provide overcoats, for goodness sakes. Privately, Eunice, I believe they keep the men marching around town just to recharge our patriotic spirit. And to raise more money for the war. This will the third Liberty Loan they want us to subscribe to. A quota of fifteen and a half million? On top of the ones we met in the first two drives."

Eunice frowned. "That's a pretty cynical way of looking at it, Mary."

"I've been too long in Rochester and seen too many unexpected–" she pantomimed quotation marks in the air "'coincidences' not to be suspicious. Anyway, let's get back to your question. Who should represent the hospital in the parade?"

The Principal sat back in her chair, relieved at the change of subject. "I think we ought to send a few of our graduate nursing staff, but most of the contingent should be the pupils. Saturday afternoons are usually pretty calm here, and the regular staff should be able to handle the routine without students' help." And it'll be a treat for the younger ones.

The chief hospital administrator frowned. "By evening, though, some of the marchers and the spectators will be high on more spirits than just patriotic ones. They'll have to be back to cover the surge in admissions."

"A good idea, Mary. And the blue uniforms among white ones the other hospitals will show that we're giving nearly as much to the war effort as the draft is. Shows that we're training new nurses to keep up the growing demand. At the very least, marching in the parade will give the girls some exercise and a healthy whiff of air that doesn't smell like ether and alcohol.

The Preparedness Parade of 1916 had been only for show, a demonstration of how loyal Rochesterians were if the federal government decided to enter the European war. When news of the patriotic fervor reached the Kaiser, maybe he'd give up invading his neighbors, fearing that the U.S. would join the Allied countries against him. But, of course, that hadn't happened.

The planners of this parade had scheduled the extravaganza for a weekend afternoon to encourage factories to give their workforces the time off to march. Any group that was connected to the war effort, no matter how large or small, had been invited to participate. Whether there would be many people left to watch the pageantry was a valid question: More than 40,000 workers had agreed to join the marchers.

Military units, both new enlistees and veterans from the Civil and Spanish-American Wars, would head the parade. Following them would be the wives, mothers, and sisters of soldiers currently serving in the Army and Navy. There would be a huge increase in women marchers, the number swelled by hundreds of female factory workers, those from Symington wearing pants, the uniform adopted by all munitions workers.

Led by a color guard, a group of lady equestrians, and a distaff marching band, Red Cross nurses and nursing representatives from the city's four general hospital staffs would come next. Following them would be members of Rochester's women's clubs who had been knitting soldiers' caps and mittens, raising cigarette money for the boys overseas, collecting wholesome books and uplifting magazines for army canteens, serving coffee to men being transported through the city, and writing homey letters to the servicemen abroad. The Women's Motor Corps, dressed in their new khaki uniforms and driving their volunteered automobiles, would bring up the end of the women's section.

The nurse's staging area on Culver Road was a scene of organized confusion at 2:30 when the General Hospital's pupils arrived. The women flag bearers, flying banners of the embattled allied countries, were arguing about which flag –Great Britain's, France's, or Belgium's– should take the place of honor to the right of the American flag. Hospitals' nursing contingents were mixing and milling around in disorganized groups. Women's marching band members were busy tuning their instruments.

The lady equestrians were valiantly trying to control their steeds. The matrons had agreed to wear blue riding habits, since they all had at least one of that color in their closets. The shade or tint didn't matter; a midnight blue mingled with a peacock blue, a royal blue, and an aqua. Style didn't matter either; solids mingled with stripes. Two items unified their attire, however –a red and white striped sash draped diagonally from each horsewoman's left shoulder across her body, its ends meeting in a navy blue nosegay on her right hip. And peeking through the feathers on each broad-brimmed hat was a miniature American flag attached to a short dowel.

Since it was a lovely spring day, the division's grand marshal, Mrs. Van Hoosen, had chosen a pastel blue outfit. Astride a high-spirited, white Arabian that kept turning her now toward the assembly, now away from them, she shouted through a megaphone. "Ladies! . . . Ladies!. . . Please listen. . . . This is important!" Her lieutenants began "Shush"ing everyone.

Finally, Mrs. Van Hoosen's mount settled down, and the marchers began to pay attention to her amplified voice. "You need to march in lines of sixteen!" she bellowed. The marchers began to comply. "That's it! . . . That's good! . . . Now, with your hands on your hips, spread out so that there is about an arm's length between you and the person on your left and the one on your right!"

The marchers organized themselves into neat lines, spaced more or less equally across the pavement. They looked obediently toward their leader. "Now, listen carefully! When you turn onto East Avenue and again when you turn onto East Main Street, the persons on the left ends of the lines need to march in place for several seconds! Those in the middle may continue at the pace they have been going, but the women on the right side of the line will need to quick step in order to catch up!"

The standard bearers, having finally agreed about the flag order, lined up with the mounted matrons behind them. The band struck up its first marching tune, each instrument joining in almost simultaneously. The General Hospital's nursing pupils in their powder blue uniforms followed the musicians; the First Years led the contingent, Intermediates followed, and Seniors brought up the rear. Behind them came the white-clad units of the nursing staffs from the Homeopathic, the Hahnemann, and St. Mary's hospitals.

Aware of Bong's talent for music, the classes from General Hospital's training school had chosen her as their *majordomo*, and they had practiced under her orders –"Left! Right! Left! Right! Marching forward with all our might!"– for more than a week. But they hadn't tried turning a corner yet, so the group's Culver onto East Avenue pivot was a little ragged. By the time the Division reached the Main Street East intersection, though, they had gotten the knack of the maneuver. Their steps and their patriotic spirits were high, fueled by the enthusiastic cheering of the flag-waving spectators along the route.

Just as they passed the Clinton Avenue intersection, however, a loud explosion coming from behind them startled the participants. The neat lines faltered, the rows behind threatening to walk on the heels of the ones in front.

"What was that?" Susan was especially startled. As usual, she had elbowed her way to Alice's right side.

"I don't know."

"It came from behind us," yelled Austin from down the line. "Probably the Motor Corps from the Armory. The *Times Union* said they're supposed to have a tank."

"Nobody said anything about shooting off a canon," observed Hilda on Alice's left. "They should've warned us. Hope they don't keep doing that."

But they did. The canon roared again when they got to the St. Paul intersection, and again at Front Street, and once again where East Main turned into West Main at the Four Corners. Each boom was a shock to the marchers who were busy concentrating on avoiding the droppings from the New York mounted police unit, which headed the parade. After every resounding "BOOM!" the lady equestrians' mounts would bolt, ready to charge ahead or to retreat in panic. Those animals added to odorous mounds already dotting the parade route. And the curb-side observers roared their delight at each cannon roar.

By the time the contingent approached the Court House reviewing stand, the training school pupils were drooping and soaked with sweat. But they perked up and quickened their pace, which they were able to maintain for one more block.

At the corner of North Washington Street, just in view of the fall-out point at Elizabeth Street, a figure in an Army uniform invaded Alice's line from the sidewalk and began marching in step between Susan and herself.

"What are you doing?" she demanded. "Go away!"

Susan tried unsuccessfully to push him back to the curb. "Get out of here!"

Then Alice saw the blue eyes. "Alphonso!"

"It's the only way I could think of to talk to you, Alice. Been here a couple of days, but have to go back right away. Got a furlough coming up in a few weeks, though. Think you can get Lilac Sunday off?"

"I don't know. I'll see."

"Great! I'll call the nurses' residence when I get back in town. Bye." The young man performed a perfect "about face" and, marching backwards, saluted the students in the lines behind. Then he ran back to the sidewalk.

"You're not going to meet with him, are you?" asked Susan. "He's so bold!"

81

"I don't know. I'll see," Alice repeated. She could feel the blush rise in her cheeks, but she wasn't sure if the vigor of the march or the surprise of seeing Alphonso was causing it.

"He's cute!" Hilda yelled. "Go ahead. Go out with him."

"He's got spunk!" Emily agreed. "Breaks rules that aren't important."

"With those blue eyes, you shouldn't reject him. I like him already, though I haven't even met him," observed Bong.

Mercifully, the parade's end was just across the street from the nurses' residence, and the spent pupils dragged themselves home. As they trudged across the street they agreed: Serving as a nurse on the war front couldn't be much more demanding than the march down Main Street in Rochester, New York.

Principal Smith was pacing at Miss Keith's suite entrance when she returned from church services. *Something's important*, Mary thought, extracting her key from her purse. *What could it be? Another sick pupil? A disagreement between a head nurse and a visiting physician? Disappointing scores achieved by last year's graduates on their State Boards?*

"What can I do for you on this lovely May morning, Eunice?" she asked, removing her spring coat and her hat and laying them on a chair.

The Principal poured out the news all at once. No sense in dragging it out – prolonging the agony. "The six of us who signed up for the Base Hospital 19 unit have to report to the armory late this afternoon, all packed and ready to go. We'll need a ride if you can spare an ambulance. The unit leaves at 10:00 this evening, destination unknown." She moved closer to her superior ready to sooth a tirade or to offer a comforting shoulder to cry on.

But Mary didn't react as expected. She smiled and embraced her friend. "I envy you and the others so much, Eunie. If I were younger, I'd be packing right along with you today."

"You're not disappointed, Mary? I thought it would be a blow. Our assignment's going to complicate things for you, maybe even compromise the hospital's welfare."

Mary led her guest into the kitchenette and began making tea, talking as she worked. "You forget. I've known for over a year that you were going to leave and I'd have trouble replacing all of you. I've been planning ahead. Alice Gilman is a very capable assistant, as you've noted in your monthly reports. She's earned the respect of both the students and the instructors. She just needs a little more backbone so the physicians won't shove her out of the driver's seat and take over the school. She should do fine."

Their long association had made Eunice familiar with the kitchenette. She withdrew cups and saucers from a wall cabinet, extracted spoons from the silverware drawer, and set two places.

"Alice and I have been revising the curriculum. The class work will be on the same schedule, but the clinical experiences will have to accelerate. We'll let the Intermediates observe operations earlier, and the Seniors will assist at surgeries at the beginning of their last year rather than at the end. Intermediates will visit milk stations, factories, the settlement centers, schools, and physicians' offices so that they can decide what kinds of nursing they'll want to do when they graduate." She turned the gas on under the kettle.

Eunice found napkins in the drawer under the table top. "You've got it pretty well planned out, Mary. Shows why you've been such an outstanding superintendent all these years."

The kettle whistled. Mary brought it to the table and filled the cups. Tea bags and a sugar bowl were already there. Neither woman used cream. They steeped their tea bags.

"Maybe too long, Eunie. It's been years since I've done any actual nursing. Too busy keeping the Directors, the Lady Managers, the Twigs, the donors, and the rest of the hospital staff satisfied. It's women like you who have helped me last this long."

"But it hasn't been all work, Mary. You have to agree. Remember the day that....?"

The question prompted an hour-long chain of reminiscences, interrupted with hearty laughs. When the second serving of tea had been imbibed and the table service cleared, Eunice said good-by with a lump in her throat. And Mary, her eyes tearing, hugged her teammate and wished her and the others –United States Army Red Cross nurses now– God speed in their grand adventure. "Stay well, my friend."

At noon the Principal ran up the stairs of the columned porch of the nurses' residence. She had only a few hours to get ready. A young man in uniform removed his cap, stepped aside, and held the door for her. For an instant she noticed his electric blue eyes and then the black velvet strip of cloth circling the top of his left sleeve. Thanking him mechanically, she hurried to her suite, mentally separating what she needed to pack in her suitcase from what she'd have to leave behind.

Alphonso waited patiently while the probationer on receptionist duty relayed news of his arrival to Miss Denny. He smiled when Alice appeared almost immediately; she must have anticipated their outing with at least a little enthusiasm. From her old wardrobe, so out of fashion now, she'd chosen a filmy white dress sprinkled with dainty pink rosebuds for the excursion. A broad-brimmed hat with bold yellow dahlias completed the outfit.

Alphonso offered her his arm, and they descended the porch steps and strolled to the trolley stop. The passengers on the streetcar were chatty, in a festive mood. The women wore their Sunday finest, and their escorts sported jackets in light shades, collared shirts with bow ties, pinstriped trousers, and spats. Most of the men carried straw skimmers. It was too warm to wear them.

"I miss that," Alphonso said, surveying his male counterparts in their natty jackets.

"What?" his companion asked.

"The chance to choose what you want to wear every day. Uniforms are good; you don't need to decide what to wear. And, if you don't notice ornaments, like stripes and epaulettes and medallions, they erase social class differences. But choice is all mixed up with freedom, and even though freedom is what we soldiers are fighting for, we've given our personal choices away to the U. S. Government."

Alice recalled the day she had exchanged her fashionable wardrobe for her nursing outfit. She glanced at the earnest young man; Alphonso was certainly a much deeper thinker than their previous short conversations had indicated. She asked him about the black velvet band around his sleeve.

"My little cousin Albert died a week ago. He was only four — diphtheria. It's an Italian custom. The arm band shows that our family is in mourning. All of the Priviteras and Desiderios will wear them for a month as a sign of respect for my Aunt Mary and Uncle Nicholas."

The couple was silent for awhile as the trolley rumbled down West Main Street. Then they began to debate whether to transfer at the South Clinton stop or wait until Goodman Street. Alphonso wanted some exercise. Alice held out for Goodman. She lifted one foot revealing a high-heeled shoe. "Besides, I won't make it through the whole park with these on."

"You win!" he said, his palms raised in surrender. "Can't have you hobbled. Besides, we can see most of the popular attractions that way."

During the second spur of their ride, they compared impressions of their childhoods in Rochester. The Dennys had been in the city for a long time. The Priviteras had emigrated a generation before from Italy. Her family had been protected, Protestant, and privileged. He'd grown up in an ethnic neighborhood. A nominal Catholic, he'd decided that if a non Catholic ever became dependent on him, he'd embrace their religion. He had just gained enough experience in men's clothing retail to become a department manager when Uncle Sam had tapped his shoulder.

Their Highland Park tour began with a circuit around the Pansy Bed and continued past the Rhododendron Valley. The uphill path turned their amble into a hike, and Alice was panting when they arrived at the Children's Pavilion at the top. Alphonso bought ice cream cones and a nosegay for Alice – forget-me-nots, of course. Dossenbach's Parks Band played popular tunes, the ones everyone knew the words to. "There Are Smiles That Make You Happy" and "I'm Always Chasing Rainbows" lasted through the couple's circuit of the reservoir.

Up here, the aroma rising from hundreds of multi-hued lilac bushes, the cycloramic view of the spring-clad hills in the distance, and the sweet melodies were intoxicating. The euphoric effect began to crumble barriers of shyness. Alice asked Alphonso what being in the Army was like.

His life as a soldier was far different from most draftees, he told her. After basic training at Camp Dix, he'd been reassigned to Fort Syracuse because poor eyesight prevented him from joining the fighting forces. Otherwise he was in good physical condition. That camp was near enough to Rochester to take short trips home. He was very worried about his mother's health. The gall stones kept reappearing.

In camp he lived in a huge tent with at least a dozen other recruits whose training he was responsible for. His trainees all had physical issues that kept them from directly engaging the enemy overseas. Most of them would be assigned guard duty at critical points along the east coast: looking for enemy submarines along the Atlantic, guarding canal locks and railroad bridges from saboteurs, patrolling munitions depots. He taught them how to use surveillance and detection devices.

"You live in tents? All crowded together? With newcomers arriving all the time bringing all kinds of infections? What happens when someone gets sick?"

"Well, there's a Base Hospital at Fort Ontario near Oswego. It treats patients from all the training camps in Central New York. In Syracuse, we put the sick men on stretchers in a reserved rail car, and ambulances transfer them from the city's train station to the army hospital at the Fort."

The Parks Band began a new tune as they sauntered downhill toward the Lamberton Conservatory. Comfortable with each other now, they sang along: "Hail! Hail! The Gang's All Here."

"When's nurses' training finished?"

"I'm scheduled to graduate in 1920. That is, if I don't get too sick before then. No time out for illness; we have to pay back the days we can't work in the wards."

"Excited at the thought of living on your own?"

"Not really. Nursing's been in my family, and it seemed like the best path for a single woman.

"I'm not like most of my classmates. They're dedicated; nursing's in their blood. But their burning desire isn't contagious for me. I have a hard time sympathizing with people who won't take care of themselves. No offense to you, but especially men. They seem intent on drinking way too much alcohol, careening around on those awful motorcycles, racing their automobiles against locomotives. And they haven't a care about anyone they could hurt while they're doing their dare-devil stunts."

She stopped herself and looked at his alarmed expression. "Sorry. I didn't mean to preach."

His frown relaxed. "I know what's wrong. Everything you see looks diseased. Living at the hospital, you haven't a chance of noticing the beauty in the rest of the world."

Alice was embarrassed. She wanted to change the subject. "Let's go a little farther, across Mt. Hope Avenue and into the cemetery. I'll show you Papa's and Mama's graves. Then we can take the Mt. Hope car back downtown."

She found the tombstone easily. It had only been four years since her father had died. The marker was dark gray, polished granite with an incised rectangle. The legend—
William J. Denny
May 19, 1855
Sept. 16, 1914
— stood out in relief. Next to the stone was a mound of fresh dirt.

"I forgot that today would have been Daddy's birthday," she said, a quaver in her voice.

Alphonso reached for her hand and held it. "When did your mom die?"

"Last February," she replied. The quaver had become a tremor. "I haven't talked to anyone except my sister and brother about it since then — and Miss Keith. I had to tell her so that I could be at the memorial service and the interment a month ago. The ground needed to thaw before we could bury Mama." She concentrated on her shoes. "I'm a private kind of person."

Alphonso lifted her chin with his free hand, compelling her to look directly into his eyes. "Thank you. I feel privileged."

"For what?"

"For allowing me into your confidence."

She lifted the little forget-me-not bouquet. "May I leave these here?" she asked. "Their color matches your eyes. It'll be kind of like introducing you to my parents."

He nodded, and she carefully placed the flowers on the fresh soil.

After brief contemplation or meditation or prayer, or maybe just a private working through the awkwardness of first-time intimacy, the couple turned and left the cemetery. Strains of "After You've Gone" drifting with lilac fragrance from the Pavilion followed them as they strode toward the northbound trolley stop.

The 19th is set for "lilac Day" and I presume there'll be a concert and great crowds. We are going to Highland Pk. for, as usual, it must be beautiful.....The base hospital [left] Sun and I do hate to see some of them go.

Love to you all,
Ben

Chapter 8

Miss Keith is on her vacation but in spite of her & Miss G[ilman]'s absence the R. G. H. seems to be running smoothly & everyone is apparently far more happy & contented than when G[ilman] is here [alone] *but no doubt she'll make us all suffer on her return.*

The corner of Jefferson and Bronson Avenues was a busy one. A hardware store, a saloon, a market, and a drugstore anchored the intersection. When he had volunteered to solicit for donations to Rochester's Community Chest drive, saloon keeper William Siggelow had been assigned the north Jefferson Avenue area to canvass.

Siggelow's pocket watch showed 10:00 when he glanced at it. If he made the hardware store at 170 Jefferson his last stop for the morning, he reasoned, he'd be back to his saloon in time to help his wife make sandwiches for the lunch crowd.

He parked his Model T in front of the house next door. He had geared his sales approach particularly toward small shop owners like Max Braunstein. Sure he would need only a few minutes to make his pitch, he engaged the brake, shifted to neutral, and left the motor running.

The bell above the door jingled as he opened it. The proprietor was doing paperwork at a scarred counter that was dominated by an ornate cash register. Behind him was a wall of drawers that undoubtedly held the smaller tools of his trade: screws and nails, nuts and bolts and such, neatly arranged according to size. Leaning against the wall to his left were shovels, hoes and rakes, saws and other long and bulky tools. The hand tools covered the tops of several tables on his right.

"Nice shop you've got here, Mr. Braunstein."

The shop owner kept his attention on the order form he was filling in. "Thanks. Let me know how I can help you."

"I'm not here to buy anything."

Braunstein looked up, annoyed at being distracted.

"I'm here to <u>sell</u> you something."

Irritated, the proprietor punched the "No Sale" button on the cash register, and it dinged. "Here, let me save you some time. I'll give you a couple of bucks."

"No, you can put those away, sir. I'm William Siggelow." He gave the man a firm handshake. The little bell on the door jingled again, and another man entered.

"Hi, Max," the newcomer said, and he turned toward a table holding an assortment of wrenches.

"Hi, Lou," was the automatic response. To Siggelow he said, "So what are you selling?"

"I'm here to save <u>you</u> some time."

The proprietor frowned.

"I notice that you were annoyed when you found out I wasn't here to buy something. What I am here for is to eliminate people like me from interrupting your work, wasting your valuable time."

The sales pitch had attracted the newcomer's attention, and he moved closer to the two men at the counter.

"I know that people come in here every two weeks or so asking for a donation to a worthy cause, like a hospital or an orphanage or cigarettes for our boys overseas. I also know that their visits sometimes irritate you. Otherwise you wouldn't have automatically reached for the cash register there and tried to brush me off with a couple of dollars."

Siggelow's listeners were now giving him their full attention. "Suppose there was only one person who solicited you for a donation every year, rather than dozens of them. One substantial donation that would benefit all of the charities that now eat up your available cash and their solicitors who take up your valuable time."

Noticing that his friend was equally intrigued, Braunstein introduced the stranger to his Lou Haitz, the owner of the bar across the street. They shook hands warmly.

"They're so annoying," Haitz said. "Especially the ladies who come all dressed up with their noses in the air, like my place doesn't smell good. Most of 'em are temperance fanatics, and they hate my place. But if I kick 'em out, I'm called heartless or unpatriotic."

"They don't like the smell of my place either," Siggelow agreed. "They're bad for my business. I'm a barman, too. Just call me Will."

"Okay, Will," said Haitz. "What's this 'product' you're sellin'?"

"It's the Community Chest. You can get rid of those do-gooders who're interrupting you all the time by just giving a single donation once a year to one solicitor like me. And you can pledge it. You don't have to take dollars out of your cash drawer right away. You could pay the pledge off a little bit at a time.

"But it should be a substantial amount," he continued. "If every breadwinner in Rochester gave once a year, all the worthy charities would get a cut, enough to support their programs for the next year. And you could feel justified in turning any other beggars away without giving them anything. Just tell them to go down to the Community Chest office and beg there."

"Sounds good to me," said the hardware man. "Give me a pledge card. I'll sign up." The neighborhood saloon keeper held his hand out as well.

The two filled in the forms and handed them back to Siggelow. "Thank you, gentlemen," he said.

The saloon keepers bonded immediately. They compared their sales and their clientele. Business was good now, but the temperance clan had infiltrated the state and national politicians. Requiring state liquor licenses hadn't been too bad, but then commandeering grains used in making alcoholic beverages for the soldiers, taxing beverages by the barrel and then doubling that tax, and finally prohibiting sales of alcohol to military men had brought the industry nearly to a halt. The barmen's former resentment was escalating into contempt for powerful authorities: "They're going to close us up, take away our livelihoods," they agreed.

Siggelow checked his pocket watch. "I'd love to stay and continue our conversation, gentlemen, but it's getting late. Got to get back to my own place and help the wife with the lunch crowd. I know you won't regret your donations, and I'm sure the hospitals and orphanages and all of the rest of the worthy causes'll appreciate your generosity."

The solicitor congratulated himself as he left the store, examining two filled-in pledge cards and tucking them into his breast pocket. *Glad I didn't turn the automobile off*, he thought glancing at the watch again. *It's almost lunchtime. Minnie'll nag at me all afternoon. She doesn't think I should spend time on any good cause besides herself.*

The blue rubber ball had rolled to the edge of the front porch at number 172 Jefferson Avenue, the white frame house next to the hardware store, and, bouncing on each step, it gained momentum. Reaching the curb, it rolled under Siggelow's auto and stayed there. Two year old Mildred Wright looked back toward the front door of the house. *Mommy isn't there. I'm a big girl now, two almost going on three. I can get my ball by myself,* she thought.

The hand railing was too high for her to hold on to, so she turned around, knelt down and, descended each step backwards. At the bottom she stood up and toddled across the sidewalk to the curb where she bent down and peeked under the vehicle. But the ball was too far away for her short arms to reach.

The toddler looked at the porch steps. It hadn't been difficult to come down them, but climbing back up to the porch without a hand railing for balance would be too hard. She decided to sit on the Ford's passenger side running board and wait for Mommy. After a few minutes, the bored youngster shifted so that she could put her feet on the running board and lean against the front fender. In a few moments, the gentle vibration of the machine and the purr of the idling engine lulled her to into a nap.

At 11:30 William Siggelow slid into his Model T's driver's seat, engaged the clutch, released the brake, and pressed the gas pedal.

A high-pitched scream shot adrenalin throughout his body. In a single, fluid motion, he squeezed the brake handle, turned off the ignition, and burst out of his door.

What he saw behind the vehicle nearly sickened him. The bleeding, wailing child lay on her stomach at the curb, her little arms pawing at the pavement in agony. Carefully Siggelow picked the tiny body up and shouted "Help!" to Haitz who was just leaving the hardware store.

"I'll get my car!"Haitz yelled and ran across Jefferson toward his saloon. Siggelow was cooing to the toddler and gently cradling the frightened child in his left arm when Haitz's car pulled up behind his own. Haitz leaned over and opened the passenger door from inside; Siggelow slid into the seat and closed the door with his free hand.

"General's the closest hospital," Haitz said. "I'll drop you there and come back to check the neighborhood to find out where she lives. Her mother'll be frantic when she can't find her."

The weather was sunny and mild when Mary Keith had boarded the west-bound New York Central Express in Boston. By the time the engine pulled into Syracuse, though, the sky had begun to cloud over. Now, as she descended Pullman car steps and took her suitcase from the porter at Rochester's train station, the sky was slate gray. The locomotive's engine belched a puff of soot into the air, a homecoming that put an abrupt period to her restful summer vacation.

Entering the cavernous building, she met Alice Gilman, now the Acting Principal of General's Training School. "You're going to wish you hadn't come back, Mary," Miss Gilman warned as she took the suitcase from her superior.

"Why? What's happened?"

They were weaving a path through the crowd of travelers that rushed through the station, all intent on catching the late afternoon train to Buffalo. A glimpse through one of the huge Romanesque windows lining the main concourse revealed that the cloud cover had thickened even more.

"Remember that toddler that was so severely injured when a car ran over her? It happened just before you left for vacation. "

Exasperated, Mary sighed, "Unfortunately, Alice, children being hit while running into the street is all too common in good weather. But I think I recall that one. At first they didn't know where the little girl lived. Did she survive? It was pretty bad, as I remember."

"Her injuries were serious, and she wasn't expected to live at first. She's still with us, and the doctors are beginning to be a little optimistic. But she'll be scarred for life and maybe have some paralysis."

By this time, they had reached Alice's coupe in the station parking lot. She stowed Mary's valise in the rumble seat, and the women got into the auto. The Acting Principal started the vehicle and put it in gear.

"What makes this case so unusual?" her passenger asked.

"The parents claim that the hospital mistreated their daughter. Mr. Wright, the father, has been complaining to his co-workers, telling them to boycott the Community Chest drive because it'll benefit the General along with the other hospitals."

Alice turned right onto Main Street and skillfully maneuvered through the late afternoon traffic.

"Where does he work? He can't do much damage if it's only in a factory or a department store."

"He's on an assembly line in a shoe factory, but he's an officer in the Shoe Workers Union. The Chamber of Commerce is worried that he'll convince the entire union to refuse to join in the drive. The General's Board of Directors believes it's all a misunderstanding. They've passed the problem on to the Board of Lady Managers to straighten out. We've all been waiting until you got back to schedule a hearing. So that's on your agenda for next week."

Mary took a pad and pencil out of her purse. "Okay, tell me who we need to alert. We won't have to ask everyone who was involved to the meeting, just have them standing by. Who's the physician in charge of the case?"

"The toddler's in pediatric orthopedics. Dr. Prince is the physician of record."

"He'll need to be at the meeting in person, so he should head the list."

The traffic was much thinner by the time they approached the Plymouth Avenue intersection. Thunder was rumbling in the west. They parked Alice's little runabout in one of the ambulance bays and made it into the Administration Building just after a flash lit up the campus, thunder cracked, and the skies let go.

Here I go again, Mary thought as she unlocked her apartment door. *Thank goodness they didn't call me back from vacation early. I feel like I can tackle this one now that I've had a change of scene.*

The fact-finding meeting convened in the General's Board Room a week later. A long mahogany table dominated the furnishings. Above it a ceiling fan disturbed the sultry air, but not enough to cool the room. In the table's center was a large carafe, and a water tumbler had been set at each of seven places designated by captains' chairs. Mrs. Dr. Ralph Fitch, President of the Board of Lady Managers, stylishly dressed in an emerald green suit and wearing a simple brown hat, a pheasant feather arching backwards from its headband, sat at one end. Three people were seated to her right.

Charles Wright, dressed informally in white shirt, brown trousers, and vest, was closest to the Lady President. The day was typical for mid June, hot and humid, and he had loosened his tie and opened his shirt collar revealing a stork-like neck and prominent Adams Apple. He was cleaning his fingernails with a pocket knife.

Mabel Wright sat next to her husband. Wearing a pink cotton shirtwaist dotted with tiny blue flowers, she looked older than her thirty-two years. Straight, dark brown hair, striated with premature gray strands, framed her fleshy cheeks.

To her right, portly William Siggelow, sporting a blue suit, vest, and striped bow tie, glanced continually at his pocket watch. His wife hadn't let him forget the last time he'd been absent from their saloon because of the Wright affair. He was afraid that he wouldn't be making the Friday afternoon rush again this afternoon.

To Mrs. Dr. Fitch's left were hospital administrators, Mary Keith and Alice Gilman, and orthopedic surgeon, Dr. Harry Prince. Misses Keith and Gilman wore their signature uniforms, long white seersucker business skirts and matching tailored jackets. Young Dr. Prince's street clothing was hidden by a white lab coat. A very high forehead and a large pair of shell-framed eye glasses were his most distinguishing features.

Mrs. Dr. Fitch stood and called the hearing to order. "I believe the most productive procedure to follow in this inquiry will be to allow the dissatisfied side to explain their perceptions of what happened on May 21st. Then Miss Keith, Miss Gilman, and Dr. Prince will detail the procedures that were followed after little Mildred Wright was admitted to the General on that day. Remember, our sole purpose is to review exactly what happened. This is not to be an indictment of any individual involved." She nodded toward Mrs. Wright and then sat down. "Since you were the first parent to learn that your child had been brought here, will you please tell us what you observed Mrs. Wright?"

"Well, it took awhile before Mr. Haitz found me," the woman began, her voice quivering slightly. "He knocked on my front door at about fifteen after noon, and when I answered it, he asked if a toddler lived here." The mother took a wadded handkerchief out of her black purse. "'Yes. She's right here,' I said. But when I stepped out and looked on the porch, little Millie wasn't nowhere to be seen." She dabbed at a tear with the handkerchief.

"How long had it been since you let Mildred go outdoors that morning?" Mrs. Fitch asked calmly.

"It couldn't have been too long. . . .She's never left the porch before. . . .I told her not to. . . .She's not been walking very long. . . .I didn't think she could get down the steps. . . .I couldn't imagine where she would've gone. . . .That was when I got scared." Like her words, the mother's tears flowed steadily, one after another now.

"Mr. Haitz drove me here, and I ran into this building. . . .Mr. Siggelow was still holding little Millie in his arms at the admissions desk. . . .They were just checking her in. . . .They hadn't washed the cinders off her face 'n' hands. . . .Hadn't given her laud'num or nothing. She was whimpering so. They wanted to know who was going to pay." The woman's handkerchief could not keep up with her tears and running nose. Her voice had risen to a whine. She hiccupped a sob into the handkerchief. Then she gave up and buried her eyes in the soggy cloth. "Please. I can't go on."

Mrs. Dr. Fitch leaned forward and patted the woman's free hand. "I know this is painful for you, Mabel, but it's necessary, I think." She turned to the husband. "When did you find out about the accident, Mr. Wright?"

The man folded the pocket knife and stowed it in a vest pocket. "The whistle'd just blown for lunch time. I was going outside with the boys. In good weather, we eat outdoors on the factory lawn."

Recalling the day, he glanced at the ceiling as if its details were written there. "Sometimes we get in a little game of bocce. The Italians like that, you know. A game in the middle of the day. Most days they bet a little, but I don't. I just watch."

"Try to stay on the topic, Mr. Wright, please." Mrs. Dr. Fitch was used to being in charge of things.

"Oh, yeah. Sorry. A secretary comes out and interrupts the game. She says a telephone message said I should come to the hospital, Mildred's been hurt. So I got on the first trolley and come here. Must've been about 1:30 by then. Mabel was waitin' at the admissions desk, but they'd taken Millie to the accident room. Said it was real serious.

"But they wanted to know who was going to pay, like if I didn't agree to, they were going to send the child home with us without doing anything." The color began to rise in his long neck, and the Adam's Apple bobbed up and down. "So I said I'd pay, and then they took us in to see her. She was a mess. Hadn't cleaned her up, but they must've given her something to put her out by then. She was quiet. Intern said they wouldn't know what was wrong for awhile."

"Excuse me please, Mr. Wright," the head Lady Manager interrupted. She turned toward the weeping woman. "I hate to upset you, Mrs. Wright, but what time did you let Mildred go out on the porch that morning?"

Keeping her eyes averted, the mother mumbled her answer, "About 11:15. It was just going to be for a few minutes, but then the telephone rang. It was my sister, and we hadn't talked in a week. So I guess time got away from me."

"So, you left your two year old alone on an open porch for an hour?"

Mabel Wright finally glanced up at the questioner. "I didn't mean to. We had so much to catch up on. And Mildred 'd never gone off the porch before. She's an obedient child."

The flush had reached Wright's perspiring face. He stood up, reached for the carafe, and poured a tumbler full of water. After downing it, he wiped his lips with his shirt sleeve. "Are you accusing my wife of neglecting the welfare of our child?" he growled.

"Now, no need to get upset, Mr. Wright. As I said before, we're not here to accuse anyone of anything."

Leaning forward, his hands on the table, the father shouted. "What kind of place is this! I think it wants money before it'll help fragile little ones. Talk about neglect! How about this hospital, leavin' the poor child, all dirty and in pain like that."

Now he was pounding on the table; the empty tumblers danced on the wooden surface. He glared from Mary to Alice to Dr. Prince and back to the fact finder. "You neglected her! Let her yell and scream in pain and then didn't do nothin' 'til you knew you'd get my money!"

Dr. Prince rose and leaned toward the angry father; his voice was calm, but firm. "That's enough, sir. You didn't get here until two hours after Millie was admitted. You can't possibly know what went on before you arrived." Wright sat down, still fuming. Mabel touched his shirt sleeve, her face gleaming with pride for her husband's outburst in her defense.

Mrs. Dr. Fitch broke in quickly, betraying a growing anxiety. "And now, Mr. Siggelow, will you please tell us what you remember about that morning?"

The saloon keeper sat up straight, searched the fold in his abdomen for the watch's little pocket and stowed the timepiece in its place. "I didn't know I'd hit the child until I heard her scream. I was in a hurry to get back and help my wife with the lunch crowd. When I saw her lying there, I picked her up as gently as I could and shouted for help. Lou Haitz was just coming out of Braunstein's store, and he ran to get his car."

Siggelow ran his fingers through thin strands of gray hair. "He dropped me here and said he was going back to find the mother. I told the receptionist what happened, but I didn't know who the baby belonged to. They made me take the child to the accident room myself. It didn't seem right. I'm not a doctor. Hardly know how to carry a baby, much less a bleeding, squalling one. Then they said I had to wait in another room 'til the police came and they found the mother." He retrieved the carafe from Wright's place and poured himself a drink.

"I didn't get back to the saloon 'til about 4:00. Wife was furious. She was even madder when she saw the blood on the front seat of my vehicle. Hasn't let me forget it ever since." He glanced across the table at three frowning faces and then spread his arms apart in innocence. "The policeman that took down my story said I wasn't to blame."

He turned toward the Wrights. "But I was glad I was able to help bring the baby here. I could've just driven away, but I brought her here." He retrieved the pocket watch again and opened the case. "Got to go. Wife's not happy about my leaving her tending the bar alone this afternoon. No sir."

Pushing back the chair, he stood and addressed the facilitator. "Hope that's good enough, ma'am. I'm leavin' right now."

"Yes, that will do, Mr. Siggelow. Thank you for coming." Mrs. Dr. Fitch called to the man's back as he hurried out of the room.

Dr. Prince reached for the carafe across the table and filled the three glasses on his side. The hospital administrators then passed the pitcher to the Lady Manager, who emptied the remaining water into her own tumbler.

With a sigh, she resumed the meeting. "Dr. Prince, can you tell the Wrights what went on before they arrived at the hospital?"

The orthopedist straightened his glasses. "Of course, Mrs. Fitch. When I came on the scene, Mr. Siggelow was holding the child at the admissions desk. By this time, little Millie was exhausted, and her cries had become whimpers. I asked the man to continue holding the baby still while I checked to see if an arm or a leg was broken.

"The limbs were intact. But the little torso was at an odd angle with respect to the pelvis, and I suspected that there was a fracture, and perhaps some internal injuries. So I didn't ask for an orderly or a nurse to take the patient to the accident room. The less we moved her little body, the less additional damage might happen. However, I did consult at that time with a visiting physician and two men from the house staff." He nodded toward Mrs. Wright. "That was when you arrived, Mrs. Wright."

"Like what damage?" demanded the father, his face nearly beet red. Mrs. Wright's tears had lessened, and she was now listening intently. She touched her husband's sleeve, attempting to calm him, but he jerked his arm away from her hand.

"Well, the pelvis is adjacent to the spine and protects important digestive organs. Jarring her fragile spinal cord could have killed Mille or crippled her for life. And if any bones were shattered, one of them might puncture a vital organ, like her stomach or intestine, or worse, her bladder. Keeping her immobile could save her life." He nodded toward the mother. "You first saw her, Mrs. Wright, when she couldn't be moved without endangering her abdominal organs." She nodded in agreement.

"When the X-ray team was ready," the orthopedist went on, returning his attention to the husband, "we asked Mr. Siggelow to gently transport her to that room. At that point the nurses took over. They cleansed her surface wounds and gently dressed her in a clean hospital nightgown. Mr. Siggelow went into a conference room for an interview with the patrolman who had been called.

The orthopedist sipped from his glass. "The X-rays showed that our preliminary suspicions were correct. Millie had a broken pelvis. Subsequent tests, which required her to be alert – not sedated– showed that her bladder had been punctured. We sped her to the Surgical Pavilion, administered ether, and performed the delicate operation that we hoped would repair the wound."

Wright relaxed a little, his high color beginning to fade. Mabel moved forward, eager to hear more. The other women sat quietly, occasionally sipping water.

Alice Gilman continued the account. "When you came in, Mr. Wright, the staff didn't keep you away from your daughter. She was in surgery, and no one who might be septic is allowed in the operating room. Mildred was under treatment the instant Mr. Siggelow walked through the front door. But before we could officially enter her name in the register, we needed to know who she was, who her parents were, and where she lived. Without knowing who to ask for permission to continue treatment, we weren't able to proceed.

"That information and the source of payment are required, whether the patient is a charity case –when the city will reimburse us for her treatment– or a paying patient. Her critical condition further prevented us from allowing you to see her until she was out of surgery."

"I went away shortly after the accident, so I was unable to follow up on it as I usually do. But you must agree, Mr. Wright," Miss Keith summed up the situation, "that as a not-for-profit institution, the General Hospital must account for every penny it expends on the excellent care we give to everyone who comes here for treatment. I have thoroughly questioned all of the people on duty that day. As the Superintendent of this institution, I agree with every step the physicians and the staff took to save your little girl. To have done anything else would have made us guilty of mistreating Mildred and might have caused her death."

"And, I hope when you visit her today," Dr. Prince went on, "you'll be pleased. It was touch and go for a few days, but your little girl is a fighter. This morning she was well enough to take her to the children's playground porch where she can breathe fresh air. In a week or two, little Millie will be able to join the other children in the sandbox there. She may have to remain in the hospital until mid July, but she is alive and out of danger.

"We're —No, you're— very fortunate," he continued. "Young children's bones heal quickly. Before you know it, little Millie will be toddling around your house and getting into everything again. But keep a constant eye on her, will you? All kids, even obedient ones, push the limits of their freedom once they find they can control their little legs."

Charles Wright's head was bowed, his chin now resting on his chest, completely obscuring the long neck and Adam's Apple. Mabel Wright was crying again, quietly this time, with tears of hope and joy, and a little embarrassment. The parents nodded agreement as the physician cautioned them. They stood and humbly thanked him, Superintendent Keith, and Acting Principle Gilman, shaking each panelist's hand.

"When I go in to work tomorrow," Wright promised Mrs. Dr. Fitch, "I'll take back everything I told the boys about not donating to the Community Chest. The hospitals deserve every penny they get."

Mabel enveloped the hospital personnel in cushiony hugs and inserted one hand in the crook of her husband's elbow. "Let's go find our miracle, Will, shall we?" Turning toward Miss Keith, she asked "How do we get to the children's porch?"

For a change, Alice and Hilda were on duty in the children's ward as a team. Hilda loved the assignment. Her partner wasn't sure. As Alice had described it in the letter to her sister Bess the previous night:

Surely have had very sick patients in the Children's Pavilion these past 3 weeks and they required constant watching as so many had the desire to crawl out of bed in their delirium.

"Isn't this fun?" Hilda was speaking as much to Alice as she was to the four year old she'd been reading a picture book to. She closed the book and gently laid the child, whose eyes were at half mast, in the crib for a nap. The pupil nurse surveyed the ward. "I want dozens of them when I get married!"

"Lie down, Anthony!" Alice yelled at the three-year-old who was bouncing up and down on his crib mattress, babbling something in Italian. This time the tone of her voice worked. The child looked at her, his exuberance momentarily interrupted. Alice motioned downward with her free hand, and the boy's black curls disappeared beneath his blanket. She finished oiling her current charge's bottom, fastened a clean diaper around the baby's buttocks, and took her to her crib.

"You must be insane, Hilda," Alice replied. "One is a handful. Twelve would be impossible."

The ward had quieted somewhat; only the wheels of two cribs continued to squeak as their occupants rocked themselves into an afternoon nap.

"You're just tired, Alice. Three weeks is a long duty," her partner observed. "Down Anthony!" she hissed at the hider who had stood again with the blanket over his head and was making ghost-like noises. The specter giggled and flopped back down on his mattress.

Hilda looked in the crib that cradled a wide-awake two-year-old in a body cast. "I know, why don't you take Mildred out for some fresh air. She's been cooped up here for too long. She needs some stimulation." She lifted the toddler and gingerly carried her to the baby carriage corner. "Wheel her over to the porch playground. Even if she can't get into the sandbox with the older kids, she can at least watch them playing in it. I'll stay here and handle nap time . . . . and the ghost."

Obediently, and feeling some relief tinged with guilt, Alice tucked a light blanket around the forlorn child, strapped her into a caned stroller, and wheeled it into the hallway. The passenger's expression, usually resigned to her pain, became alert as the busy corridors along the route distracted her.

Alice greeted the first few people who passed by, and then Millie joined in. "Hi!" Nurses in their white dresses and pupils in their powder blue stooped to coo at the toddler. Interns and resident physicians lightly pinched her chubby cheeks and ran their fingers through her honey blond curls. Porters shook her mittened hands and patted her chubby arms. Mercifully, the friction burns from landing on the pavement were nearly invisible now. She was too cute to ignore.

Alice recalled the first time she had liked a patient this much. It was spring a year ago, when as Probationers, she and her classmates had observed their first operation. She'd been especially touched by the case of a fifteen-month-old boy who was prone to putting everything he found in his mouth.

Floor-to-ceiling windows and strong overhead lamps, their brilliance magnified by stark white walls, had made the room so bright that the pupil nurses squinted when they entered. Once their eyes had adjusted to the light, they could see the state-of-the-art operating equipment neatly assembled against the walls. Most noticeable was the odor of the carbolic acid that disinfected every surface. A large, magnifying mirror had been positioned above the operating platform and angled so that the pupils and other observers, seated in tiered chairs, might watch the surgical team as they worked.

Three white-gowned figures wearing face masks were busily arranging instruments and murmuring to each other. A gowned porter wheeled the patient into the room, and the team gently transferred the tiny body to the platform. Alice nudged Susan on her right. "How helpless! That baby's not moving, not even looking around. It must be really sick." She glanced at her classmate. Susan's complexion was translucent, like parchment.

"Here, Susan. Put your head between your knees." Austin, who was on Susan's other side, gently pressed the frizzy head downward. "The fumes," she said to Alice. "Too much for her. I'll bet she won't choose surgical nursing when she graduates."

One of the operating team turned toward the class and addressed them in a baritone voice: "Lying before you is Harold Sisson, a toddler. When he was a little over a year old, the baby found its legs, and ever since, it has been exploring the world. At about this age, its permanent teeth are struggling to work their way out of the gums, which makes them tingly. So Harold puts his fist —and everything else that fits there— into his mouth."

A few of the pupils giggled at the thought.

"A day ago, the boy discovered that if he climbed up on a chair, he'd be tall enough to see what was on top of his mother's dressing table. Naturally, everything he found there, that was small enough to fit, went into his mouth."

The pupils winced and looked at each other. But the audience was silent. One of the attendants had placed a small cone over the baby's nose and mouth and was dripping drops of a clear liquid on it. The other attendant pushed a wheeled tray with glistening silver instruments next to the surgical platform and then painted the patient's abdomen with an orange colored liquid.

"I am a surgeon. Dr. Henry Williams. We 're sedating the boy with ether and painting the incision site with carbolic acid, an antiseptic."

He gestured toward a large photographic negative suspended by a clip against the wall. "That X-ray shows that the toddler swallowed three things. Two of them are small buttons; they will pass easily through the digestive system and be eliminated in his feces. But the third item is very dangerous and must be manipulated carefully."

Susan lifted her head, her pallor was better, and she now looked alert and attentive.

"The child swallowed a tiny safety pin, and it is open. If it makes its way into the small intestine, the sharp point will probably penetrate that organ, causing sepsis and almost certain death."

Susan's head dropped to her knees again. Ether vapors had reached the observers. Austin gently rubbed her back and held her hand.

"This morning I'm going to try an experiment that, if it succeeds, will revolutionize how we handle patients like this. It's too dangerous to make an incision into the stomach wall, and besides, that tiny muscle is too small for my fingers to fit inside." Using his fingers, Dr. Williams demonstrated the size of the child's stomach.

"So I will cut into the abdomen wall and gently palpate the empty stomach until I locate the pin. If I can find it, I'll pinch it. Once closed, the pin should pass easily into the small intestine and be excreted. Then I will close the incision, and we'll all cross our fingers. If the baby doesn't die immediately from shock, it has a fifty-fifty chance of surviving the operation. But if I don't try, it has no chance at all."

Dr. Williams began operating, murmuring commands to one assisting nurse who handed him instruments. His hands worked quickly, poking and probing in the incision he had cut. "Gauze," he commanded every now and then, and an attendant blotted up some of the blood, which gave the observers glimpses of the interior organs reflected in the mirror above.

Then he sewed the incision closed, finishing with a flourish stitch and a "snip!" like an expert tailor. "There we are, nice and neat and tidy." He turned his attention to the student observers again.

"Now, if the operation hasn't been too much of a shock to the baby's system, it should be ready in a week or two to swallow another notions counter —or anything else that looks like it will taste good."

The surgeon's delivery, clinical and impersonal, had offended Alice. Here was a tiny human being, innocent and just beginning life, his only sin being curiosity. Dr. Williams' tone was one he might have used to explain a repair he was making on his automobile engine.

Alice made sure to visit baby Harold every day he was in the recovery room. For a couple of days his skin turned rosy, and his eyes and arms and legs began to explore his surroundings. But then the grayish pallor returned, and the baby's eyes stared at the ceiling vacantly. Three days after Dr. Williams' experiment, Harold Sisson was not in the recovery room when she went to see him. When, hoping he'd recovered enough to go home, she asked about him, the head nurse's mute response told her. That had been the first time she had steeled herself against the wave of sadness and sense of powerlessness that threatened to overwhelm her. Her mother's death a few months ago had been the second time.

Alice maneuvered the stroller through the door to the porch playground where a trio of school-aged girls were playing in a large sand box. They had moistened the grains enough to mold them into shapes and were using toy shovels and multi-shaped containers to construct the interior of an imaginary house.

"Let's pretend the windows are here," said one tyke. "We can put the bed right under it and a dresser next to the bed."

"I think the stove ought to be opposite the sink," said a second tow head.

"This'll be the fireplace, across the room from the couch," the third youngster added.

Little Mildred strained her shoulders forward, reaching out with her chubby hands, mittened to prevent her from scratching the itchy scabs on her knees and elbows. "I want." She looked up at Alice, her eyes pleading.

Alice went to the sandbox and picked up a handful of dry granules. Squatting down to the carriage's level, she removed one of the toddler's mittens and encouraged her to feel the gritty texture.

"Here, Millie."

The little girl smiled and wiggled with delight, opening and closing her dimpled fingers around the warm grains in Alice's palm.

"Before you know it, you'll be out here playing with other little girls, making your own imaginary houses and furniture."

She brushed the sand off the chubby fingers and replaced the baby's mitten. Then she stood, bent over, and kissed the toddler's blond curls, burying her nose in their softness and inhaling the sweet baby scent deeply. "No telling what microscopic mites are in that sand. We'll scrub your hands thoroughly when we get back to the ward." Pushing the stroller through the sliding door to the hospital, she thought, *Glad there aren't any mites in your hair. The idea of having cooties up my nose gives me the creeps.*

Then she wheeled the stroller and its little passenger back to the Children's Pavilion.

Chapter 9

It will be 18 months ago on your
birthday that I entered the R. G. H.
Looking forward to the time I finish
Seems almost an eternity for I'm
anxious to be out and "doing." The year
and a half I've been here doesn't seem
long in some ways and then again it
does. Well it's time to turn out lights so
here goes.

Lovingly, Ben

 The knock on her office door had a tentative sound to it, so Superintendent Keith suspected that this might be another crisis. They seemed to have been a daily occurrence since she'd returned from her vacation. She put aside the inventory sheets she was working on and leaned back in her chair. "Come in."

 Dr. Joseph Roby, wearing street clothes now, rather than the white lab coat she was used to seeing him in, ducked his head under the lintel. The hand-tailored, navy blue suit fit perfectly on his tall, trim frame; only a salt and pepper dusting and slightly receding hair line revealed that he was no longer the dashing young physician she'd first met, when was it? Seventeen years ago?

Recalling her first years in Rochester, she smiled. The handsome attending physician had been a young nurse's dream then, and one of the city's heroes. Nineteen-two was the year of Rochester's last smallpox epidemic, and Dr. Roby had fearlessly tended two elderly victims at the Home for the Friendless. Then, to ensure that their housemates would not be infected, he had insisted that suitable arrangements be made for the impoverished women at the temporary Hope Hospital, hastily established to isolate and treat the epidemic's victims.

Dr. Roby had become Mary's personal hero back then, when the General was called City Hospital. Another visiting physician had admitted a distraught dowager here, rather than taking her to his own private institution. Unknown to anyone at the hospital, his patient was suffering from severe depression. She was assigned to one of the private rooms on the third floor in the old building.

Mary still recalled the horror mixed with guilt on a Senior pupil's face when she described what happened during the coroner's inquest.

"Mrs. Pierson walked over to the window," the pupil had said, her voice just above a whisper and her attention focused inward. "It was one of those crisp autumn days, and I thought she just wanted to open it to smell the leaves the groundskeeper was burning on the sidewalk outside."

"But suddenly she sat on the window sill and lifted her legs through the opening. I yelled for help and ran over and grabbed onto her skirt. I held on as long as I could." The young woman's shoulders shivered as she fought tears. "But she was a large woman, much heavier than I was. Her skirt ripped away in my hand, and she fell before an orderly got to the room to help me."

At that time, the Superintendent had focused on her own responsibilities. Had it been negligence on the Hospital's part? Would the family sue the institution? Was the attending pupil at fault? This was only the second year of Mary's tenure. Would the event be a blot on her record? Would the Hospital Board dismiss her for allowing such a thing to happen?

Fortunately, a team of physicians, including Dr. Roby, concluded that Mrs. Pierson had been mentally unstable. Without knowing her condition, the Hospital – personified by the Superintendent – could not have prevented the episode. Their report tempered any criticism that would have fallen on the brand new administrator. From that day on, Mary had thought of the post-mortem team as her champions. And she fantasized Dr. Joseph Roby as her personal white knight.

But the young physician was beyond a professional woman's league. He had married Alice Montgomery, a descendant of the city's founder, Nathaniel Rochester. Mary had attended the wedding, but she understood that her invitation was a professional courtesy more than a token of real friendship. Her position as a hospital Superintendent sometimes afforded her an entry into the homes of Rochester's upper social circles. But her middle-class, Boston pedigree had little currency here.

When Dr. Roby was appointed Deputy Health Officer the following year, the acquaintance became remote, limited to committee meetings and business-centered telephone conversations. The two would greet each other politely when the physician made weekly visits to his private patients. Last spring, their association had almost totally eclipsed when Dr. Goler, Rochester's Health Officer, joined the Army and his deputy was named Acting Health Officer in his stead.

So when Joseph Roby appeared in person at her office door this morning, his actual presence was a little surprising. "Hi, Mary. Hope I'm not interrupting you from doing something important."

"No, Joseph. Just the chores that I always seem to be doing nowadays. Invoices – inventory – ordering. Numbers! Any distraction will be a relief."

The physician drew a chair up next to her desk and after sitting down straightened the creases in his trouser pant legs.

"How are Alice and the children?"

"They're doing just fine. Joe Junior's approaching those teenage years, you know. Helen's five now and the baby just turned three."

"I'm glad they're doing well. And you? I haven't seen you in person in awhile."

"Being in full charge of a big operation isn't as much fun as being part of the troops, I've discovered. You must know what it's like, I'm sure."

She sighed. "Well, other than mundane things like I've been doing this morning, at least there's nothing boring about running a hospital. It's a challenge a minute. But I do miss hands-on nursing."

The Acting Health Officer leaned toward the Superintendent. "Well, I may be about to make your life even less boring, Mary. I need to ask you for a favor . That's why I'm here in person."

"I suspected this wasn't just a social call, Joseph. What does the Health Bureau want the General to do now?"

"You know, of course, that the Tuberculosis Sanatorium is filled to overflowing."

"I've read about that, yes."

"Well, the Army's asking us to accept some of the recruits who've contracted TB in the training camps. They want us to treat them, cure them, and send them back into battle. We'll need some beds to put them in and some nurses to care for them. Would the General have any room? With all of the open porches on East and West Wings, your setup would be ideal."

"How many are you talking about?"

"Not more than twenty."

The Superintendent opened the file drawer at the bottom of her desk and removed a folder. "Well, we could probably make room in the Contagious Disease Annex," she said, sifting through pages of floor plans. "There's a handful of diphtherias in there now, and a couple of scarlet fevers, and only one measles."

She stood behind his left shoulder and pointed to an area of a floor plan she had selected. *Bay rum,* she thought, breathing in the aroma of his cologne.

"We could partition the TB beds from the rest of the patients –a temporary wall right here, see?" She took the folder back to her desk. "There's one thing, though."

"What's that?"

"We don't have enough porters to move them from the annex to the porches. The Army keeps taking all of our strong young men the instant we hire them, and the ones that remain are hardly up to the chore."

"The Army will take care of its own patients with its own physicians and orderlies."

"Then I think we can do it."

Roby nodded. "That's generous of you, Mary." He looked directly at her. "Is there anything I can do to help you?"

Puffy folds under the lower eye lids, she noticed.

"Just let the Board of Directors know what I agreed to today. I can't overstep my authority, Joseph. But I'm sure they'll be enthusiastic about the plan. They're all in favor of anything that supports the troops, you know, like everyone else."

She placed the Annex floor plan on top of the inventory sheets and re-filed the folder it had come from. "Now that I think of it, though, there's another problem," she said. She began to tap a pencil on the blotter.

He frowned. *Smile lines around his eyes turned into crows' feet,* she realized.

"What's that?"

She shrugged. "Nurses? We're depending so much on the pupils now. Struggling along with just a skeleton staff of graduate nurses. Where am I going to get experienced nurses who aren't afraid of contracting TB? They all know they're in the most vulnerable age group for it."

He leaned forward. "I'll ask the Tuberculosis Association to loan you one of their visiting nurses. She could walk some of your nurses through the anti-contamination guidelines."

"That might work. Our housekeeper, Edith Whitely, knows the girls best." She sighed. "The hospital's so short staffed; we've had to put pupils in charge of some of the wards. It gives them early practice for their future, we tell them. I'll ask her for the names of some of our more courageous girls." She jotted a memo on a note pad.

"That would be wonderful, Mary." The health officer unfolded his lanky body. "I'll let the president of your Board know you've agreed the minute I get back to the Health Bureau. Right after that, I'll request that a Visiting TB Nurse schedule some times to train your staff here."

Mary rose, came around the desk and shook the physician's hand. *Grasp's still strong, but nails are manicured and skin's soft, not calloused.*

Feeling mildly guilty, she returned her attention to the business at hand. "There's something else I've been wondering about."

"What's that?"

"During the past couple of months, my Training School Principal noticed tiny items tucked at the bottom of the first pages of the morning papers, like they were trying to hide it."

"About what?"

"An epidemic in Europe. Portuguese? —or was it Spanish?— influenza, they called it. The *Democrat* said it was devastating the German troops, even threatening the Kaiser and his family. A few weeks later it seemed to have spread to France and England. Should we be worried?"

Dr. Roby looked deeply into the Superintendent's eyes, his expression all sincerity. "That's just propaganda, Mary. It's designed to make us feel like even nature's against the invaders. Besides, there's that great big ocean between us and Europe. Unless the influenza microbes have learned to swim in salt water, they'll never reach our shores."

His irises are so dark, like the pools of black velvet that I remember.

"I do hope you're right." Guiding the physician gently, she ushered him into the anteroom. "I know you're busy, but please keep in touch, Dr. Roby."

"I will. Have a good day, Miss Keith."

On her way back to her desk, Mary asked the receptionist, "Will you please ask Edith Whitely —the aunt, not the pupil— to stop into my office, Emma? As soon as she can."

Like a fluffy cloud, the housekeeper floated in through Mary's open door. "You wanted to see me, Miss Keith?" she asked.

"Yes, Edith. We've been chosen to do a special project for the Army, and we need some pupils with gumption to accomplish it. You know them best."

"What's it about?" the older woman inquired.

"We're going to be admitting some new patients whose condition is highly contagious. We need a few pupils who aren't afraid of catching it. Who would you recommend?"

Miss Whitely began to pace, her white head bent downward in thought. "Well, there's Emily Donnellan. She's not afraid of anything. Remember her? She was the instigator of that suffragist campaign in

October." She stood still, eyes rising to meet the Superintendent's. "Hilda Mehlenbacher would give her own life to save someone else's. Both of them are totally committed to patients, but they're realistic at the same time. Most of the other pupils are pretty idealistic. What is the disease?"

"Tuberculosis. You know how vulnerable young people are to it. Taking care of TB patients without catching the disease demands special precautions. We'll need nurses who have good heads on their shoulders."

The older woman smiled. "Then I have a perfect candidate, Miss Keith –Norma, my niece. She worked at the sanatorium in Muskoka the summer and fall before she came here from Canada. That was why she wanted to be a nurse, she told me. She's had experience, and she can help to train the others."

"But isn't Norma the one who didn't quite fit in with the Americans? Wasn't she in that Canadian clique that always stayed together? Didn't want to associate with American girls because this country came into the war so late?"

"You're right. For her first few months she was standoffish. A tomboy, proud of her country ways. But most of our Canadian pupils graduated last April. Norma's decided that she can't isolate herself any more. She's made a few close friends in her time here, and she's finally resigned to being just like the everyone else. In fact, she asked me to sew her a nice dress so she'll fit in better at social affairs, like the Wednesday teas.

"Thank you, Edith. That's the best news I've had today. Will you please ask Norma to make an appointment to see me? I'll explain to her what we'll need for this project and ask her to recommend another pupil she thinks she can work well with. Then she and I can work out a training schedule for a tuberculosis ward team."

"I'll do that, Mary," replied the housekeeper, and she turned and drifted back through the office door.

"Always remember to support the baby's head," Hilda warned. "And carry her with confidence. She's fragile, but she won't break." The Intermediate pupil gently handed the tiny bundle to the Probationer in front of her.

"Yes, Miss Mehlenbacher," the younger woman replied."Should I bring the baby back here as soon as she's finished nursing?"

"No, wait awhile. Give her mother some time alone with her daughter. Time to bond."

"Yes, ma'am." Holding the bundle carefully, the younger woman walked through the door that connected the Nursery to the Maternity Ward.

"Not too much time, I hope," objected a portly woman who had silently entered from the main corridor. She wore a fashionably cut, lavender cotton shirtwaist and white gloves, and she carried an over-sized beige pocketbook.

Startled, Alice Denny looked up from the bassinet mattress she had just flipped over. "I'm sorry, Madam, but maternity visitors aren't permitted in the Nursery. The door for visitors of new mothers is just down the hall on your left." Then she continued covering the tiny bed with clean sheets.

Noticing that the matron did not move as directed, Hilda approached the woman. "Please, madam," she said firmly, "you are _not_ allowed in this room. You _must_ leave."

"I have every right to be in this room, young lady. There are two newborns that I am responsible for here in this hospital."

"Just what gives you that authority?" Hilda challenged.

"I am Mrs. Eva Vunk," came the answer, " the Superintendent of the Door of Hope. Two of our residents gave birth here last week. I came to visit them, but I'm also here to make sure that their babies are being cared for properly." The woman began to make a circuit of the bassinets that lined the walls of the spacious, well-lit room.

"Isn't that the place you were telling us about last winter, Hilda? The one that takes in unwed mothers-to-be?" Alice asked.

"You're exactly right, young woman," interrupted Mrs. Vunk. "Those are the unfortunates we care for." She moved a bassinet back and forth, testing the stability of its legs.

"Why shouldn't the mothers bond with their infants?" demanded Hilda. "It's only natural. Babies don't thrive without their mother's love."

"Oh, they'll love them all right." The visitor moved a bassinet away from the wall, inspecting the floor beneath it. "Floor's dusty under here. Your housekeeping needs to be much better." She turned toward Alice and Hilda. "If their mothers bond strongly with their babies, it will be harder for them to give the children up. They need to keep the future in mind, both the mothers' and the infants'."

"Do they all have to be separated?" asked Alice, approaching the woman, curious now.

"No. If they're fortunate, we'll be able to locate the men who violated them. And, if the sperm donors seem moral, we'll try to convince them that the right thing to do would be to marry the mother and make the family whole." With her white gloved hand, she traced the chair rail that circled the room, examined the residue, and shook her head. "Needs a thorough dusting."

"How often does that happen? Finding the father, I mean. Not dust on the chair rail."

"Just occasionally. Usually we can't locate the man. He's gone on to his next conquest. Or the ones we do find have terrible potential for being good husbands and fathers. Sometimes, if the mothers are proficient at domestic skills, they can be hired out to families to help support the child. Their babies are fostered out, but they can visit them on their days off. "

Mrs. Vunk walked toward one of the tall windows. She removed a clean handkerchief from her purse, moistened it with spittle, and rubbed briskly at some nearly invisible spots on the pane. "In those cases, the mother and child are able to form an almost natural relationship. Without a husband and father, of course."

"That would be hard. But the mother could at least see her baby sometimes."

"Yes. Those are the happiest situations. It's the ones who can't cook or sew or clean that have the hardest time." She picked up a chart that dangled from a bassinet frame and scanned it. "They're the ones who break down when their babies are brought in for a feeding. They know that as soon as the child is weaned to a bottle, they'll probably never see it again."

"How awful," Hilda responded. "Why do they do it?"

The question was tantamount to putting a needle down on a phonograph disk. Mrs. Vunk's well practiced sermon explained how most of the residents had learned to live just for the moment; they had little concern about tomorrow, let alone about their immortal souls. Their own mothers had failed to guide them morally and to teach them housekeeping skills. And when a young man was the first person who seemed care about such a girl and plied her with spirituous liquors or other mind-altering concoctions, she fell under his spell.

Daily prayers, hymn singing, lessons in the womanly arts, and strict discipline at the Door of Hope brought some of the fallen girls back to the fold. A few, who would not conform and tried to escape from the house, were arrested. They would be confined in a home for delinquent girls and women when they were finally apprehended. Those who managed to evade the law would undoubtedly have neglected their babies as they had been neglected. They would abandon the infant, sell themselves into prostitution, and become enslaved by alcohol and drugs.

"It is our sincere belief that when the amendment prohibiting the sale of liquor, wine, and beer passes in every state, the need for our institution will disappear."

The matron extracted a watch case from her purse and opened it. "Well, young women, I must go and visit the mothers now. I'm not too happy about the condition of this Nursery, however. I expect to see it sparkling the next time I visit. Do you understand? We take special care of our girls at the Door of Hope."

"Yes, Mrs. Vunk. We've been so short staffed, what with the war and all. But I'll make sure the cleaners put this room high on their task list," said Alice. And the lady marched out, this time through the door to the Maternity Ward rather than the one to the main corridor.

"What did you think of her?" Hilda asked Alice, who was running a clean diaper along the chair rail.

"At least she's saving the girls from lives of prostitution and addiction."

"But saving them for what kind of life? How could a mother ever forgive herself for giving up her own baby? And what about the friend I told you about last December? She and her beau had set a date, reserved the church, and announced their decision to get married when his draft number was called. Then he was killed in France. She was pregnant, and her father disowned her; he believed what she'd done was evil. The Door of Hope was the only place she could go."

Hilda extracted a broom from the closet next to the corridor doorway and began to sweep dust bunnies from under bassinets.

Alice was still skeptical. "But Mrs. Vunk is saving these girls from a life of sin. The Door of Hope's Lady Managers used to tell us about their success stories at our Christian Endeavor meetings. The babies are adopted into good families where their futures will be secure. The mothers are found housekeeping positions in well-off Christian households; their services ensure their room and board. We'd take up a collection, and whenever the Door of Hope needed more bedding and nightgowns, we'd spend our meetings hemming the sheets and sewing the garments. It's called benevolence. It's our Christian duty."

Hilda paused and leaned on her broom. "But it wasn't all the girls' fault. Mrs. Vunk made it clear that the single young mothers are her prisoners. But most of the time the men who promised them the world are free to chase after their own pleasures."

Hilda herded her "bunnies" into a dust pan while Alice took a mop from the closet, moistened it in the sink, and damp mopped the remaining particles on the floor. "It sure is complicated," she concluded. "Maybe someday we'll find a better way to solve this situation."

Alice rinsed and wrung out the mop. "I'm glad you stood up to her, though. It's hard being the nurse in charge of a ward now. Some people, like Mrs. Vunk, are so pushy and bossy." She returned to freshening mattresses and laying clean bedding. "I'm not sure how I'd feel about giving up a baby after nine months of waiting. I'm not even sure if I ever want to marry."

Hilda was examining the windows. "I'll have to tell the maintenance man to wash these again. But I can't find any other 'spot' on this one. She must have the eyes of an eagle." She turned toward Alice. "Not marry? What about that soldier? The one who broke into our line in the parade last May? Didn't you keep company with him once when he was on furlough?"

"Yes, once. And we had a nice afternoon. Still. . . .When I think about how steady my father was, how reliable. My Mama and the rest of us could always depend on him."

"We're kind of opposites, you and I. That's what I like best about Charlie! He's unpredictable! When the war started, he went right down to the Navy recruiting office and signed up. Didn't ask his folks; didn't even ask me. Just did it. 'It's an adventure,' he told me. 'Can't resist an adventure like this!'"

Alice was stowing the used bedding in a laundry cart. "Breaking into the parade like that so impulsive. Then again, Alphonso's kind of like my Dad. He's devoted to his mama. She's been sick, you know. In and out of this hospital a lot. I go to see her whenever she's here." She paused, remembering.

"And when this war's over, he'll have a good job at one of the big men's wear stores downtown." She sighed. "At least he's safe now, training other recruits right nearby. Where's your Charlie?"

"I don't know. They won't let him tell me in his letters. I think it's somewhere in the Mediterranean, though. Not in the North Atlantic where U-boats are using American ships for target practice."

Alice began replenishing supplies at the changing tables. "What did he do before he joined?"

"He's a steel worker. Worked in lots of factories here before the War. Charlie's big and strong. He used to prize fight to make a little money on the side. He'll give me lots of good, healthy babies. That's what I want...a handful of them. And he's a family man. Close to his brothers and sisters, and he has dozens of cousins."

Hilda took off her nurses' cap and tied a clean diaper around her red mane. Then, wrapping the broom head in another diaper, she began swiping at the cobwebs in the corners of the ceiling.

Alice rolled the laundry cart toward the doors to the main corridor. "I hadn't really thought about getting married and raising a family. I'm not too keen on becoming a nurse, either. It was just a way to learn a skill I could support myself with. When the war started, the only jobs single women could get were teacher, stenographer, telephone operator, or nurse. Now, though, factories are hiring us to do the jobs men used to do. I could even be a trolley car conductor or wear bloomers and work in the munitions factory at Symington."

"Then why nursing, if you're still not sure?"

"Being in the training school meant free room and board for three years. There's only fourteen thousand dollars left in the Denny estate. My third of that would last me just a few years. When it ran out, I'd have no income and no skills to earn a living."

Alice had put a new tin of talcum powder on the last changing table, and Hilda had removed her head covering and was stowing the broom back in its closet when the Probationers began to bring the newborns, satisfied and asleep now, back into the nursery.

The luncheon crowd at Duffy-Powers cafeteria had thinned considerably by 1:30. Sophia Palmer, District Director of Red Cross nurse recruitment, checked her time piece against the wall clock. She had chosen a table behind a column, but one that gave her a sightline to the main entrance.

The restaurant was still sporting the patriotic décor it had installed over a year ago. The decorating scheme was showing its age, though, repeated launderings having faded the bright red table cloths, countless patrons having worn the nap of the navy blue upholstery to a shiny, gray-blue hue, and accidents and cigar smoke having dulled the once brilliant white walls.

She had arrived a little early, and she was sure that the women she had invited to join her would be prompt. This meeting needed to take place on neutral ground —not in her office which was always busy with Red Cross workers— or in either of the hospitals where her two friends worked.

Rather than her official Red Cross uniform, she wore a loose-fitting, forest green suit, something she might have chosen for a day of shopping. On an empty chair next to her she had laid a large white paper bag labeled "Sibley, Lindsay, and Curr Co." to reinforce that impression. She had asked her friends to dress accordingly and to carry similar shopping containers. Her objective was to give the appearance of three friends meeting for refreshment after a strenuous morning of trying on new clothes.

The steel-haired woman searched through her large handbag, making sure she had brought everything she needed. Yes, they were there, the notebook and pencil and the letter she had received from Emma, which had prompted this meeting.

The letter had come two weeks ago, one of several arriving from France. But this one from Emma Jones, RN, wasn't like the others, written by nurses who were serving in field hospitals near the front. Emma had been chosen to superintend a hospital in Paris where sick American nurses and doctors were being cared for.

An influenza-like illness was decimating the ranks of medical personnel in the field, the nurse wrote, and the victims were being evacuated to Emma's hospital. The letter warned that the disease was highly contagious; it was decimating the allied troops. The microbes, she was sure, were airborne; anyone who came near an infected person was almost sure to contract it. And it was deadly. Some of the patients, who appeared to be on the way to recovery, spiked an even higher temperature. An alarming number of them died, drowning in the fluid that filled their own lungs.

Sophia had contacted officials in Washington. What should communities do to prepare for the day the disease arrived on American shores? But the only response she had received was a directive to launch yet another drive to recruit nurses for army training camps. No alert about an impending epidemic with the power to paralyze an entire community was issued. It was time, she decided, for local healthcare personnel to anticipate what political officials and military leaders were ignoring, or refusing to acknowledge.

General Hospital's Superintendent, Mary Keith, entered the restaurant first, carrying a large flowery hat box. After scanning the room, she nodded toward Sophia and hurried to the table. They immediately engaged in animated talk about current fashions and the relentless rise of the cost of living.

A few minutes later, Maude Johnston, Superintendent of the Homeopathic Hospital, entered with a shirt box labeled "Burke, FitzSimons, Hone Co."

"A bargain," she announced. "For my brother," and she lifted the lid to display a selection of men's shirts. "Madras with detachable soft collars. A dollar thirty-nine apiece or three for only four dollars." Her fellow "shoppers" admired the fine fabric and the pastel colors.

After the waitress took their orders, brought back tall glasses of iced tea, and returned to the kitchen, Sophia began the real conversation. "I invited Sister Clementine from St. Mary's, but she couldn't come on her own. They have to travel in pairs, you know."

Her companions nodded. "And being a man," the older woman went on, "I'm certain that Dr. Lewis from the Hahnemann wouldn't agree with what I'm proposing we do. He and I have had disagreements in the past several years, and he doesn't do anything that his medical board members might question." The younger women smiled, knowingly.

"What's the reason for the *sub rosa* meeting, Sophia?" Mary asked. "Is this a conspiracy?" The hospital administrators exchanged mischievous grins.

"No, not really. But perhaps related to one," their mentor answered. She removed a sheaf of envelopes from her large purse. "Have you been getting mail from nurses who went overseas, like I have?" Her listeners nodded.

"I've heard from Jessica Heal," said Maude. "Her unit has established a hospital in an abandoned hotel and are operating from dawn to dusk. The boys are so happy to have nurses from home taking care of them." She stirred a teaspoon of sugar into her iced tea.

"Mary Laird from our staff wrote a similar message," Mary reported. "I so envy them their youth and stamina. They're doing so much good."

"Most of the letters I've received have the same kind of news," Sophia agreed. "But this one from Emma Jones has been bothering me." She paused for emphasis. "In a few weeks Rochester may be on its own battle front."

Her protégés sat up straight, totally attentive to their mentor's words. "Emma warned me that this year's influenza strain lasts longer than the usual grippe, and the victims are much weaker when they recover. In fact, if they get out of bed as soon as the fever is gone, many of them are stricken with pneumonia. And there's an unusually high mortality rate with this one."

"I've been seeing tiny references to a Spanish influenza every now and then in the newspapers this summer," Mary remembered. "They're all buried in tiny items at the bottom of the first page where no one will read them. It's almost as if someone's trying to hide the information. I asked Dr. Roby about it last week. He said it was only propaganda."

"I asked him about it, too," said Sophia. "He insisted that, since the Army has no major training camps near Rochester, the disease won't come here, or if it does come, it'll infect only the usual number of victims." Frowning, her listeners looked at each other.

"When I asked him about it," Maude added, "he said it wasn't his concern at this point. Influenza isn't a reportable disease like TB and diphtheria. He'll worry about it when it gets here. Right now he's focused on tuberculosis."

"That's probably why our newspapers have been minimizing the threat," Sophia reasoned. "Early last July the *New York Times* reported that a ship carrying Spanish influenza victims was quarantined in the harbor and ships arriving from Europe are being fumigated. But we have no way of isolating the travelers who may bring it here.

"No, Spanish influenza is real," she continued. "And it's very contagious. Emma says it has spread to French civilians, overtaken whole sections of the city. The victims are in the prime of life, not the usual children and oldsters. In some neighborhoods all the bakers are sick, so there's no bread. So many rail men have come down with it that Paris's transit system is totally disrupted. Operators are sick, and the telephone companies can't handle the traffic. Even worse, funeral directors can't keep up with the burials."

All three women were silent for a moment.

"Our local officials don't seem to be worried about what may be coming," Sophia continued. "It's understandable, though; they've got a lot on their plate right now." She punctuated each of her points with a tap of her spoon on the table cloth. "They're concerned that the city won't look good if it doesn't meet Rochester's thirty-one million dollar quota for the Liberty Loan drive. They're worried about the election in November; will the new women voters challenge the city's solid Republican vote? And then they've got the temperance issue. How can they resolve that with so many breweries and saloons in Rochester? Will the bar men all have to go out of business?"

She paused to organize her thoughts. When she spoke again, her voice was assertive: "We ladies need to focus on the issue that threatens to upset everyone's plans. That's why I asked you to meet with me today. Did you bring notebooks with you as I asked?"

The Hospital Superintendents each extracted notepads and fountain pens from their purses. As a team they anticipated what would happen if – or when– the deadly disease began to spread in their home town.

By the time the wait staff began setting the tables for the evening diners, each woman had a long list of things that had to be done almost immediately. They had answered at least a dozen "What if…" questions. What if the entire city had to shut down – the schools, the courts, the churches, the industries? If the hospital staffs got sick, where would the larger community's most critical cases go? Who could best work with Rochester's huge immigrant population, to gain their trust, to explain what to do in their native languages? Who would canvass the city's transient population for victims – in the flop houses on Front Street, in the dozens of hotels, in the hundreds of rooming houses and apartment buildings? What might be done for children whose parents became too sick to take care of them?

If the hospitals could not handle the demand, they decided, then Sophia and her staff would advise city leaders to open emergency hospitals. Maude suggested the YWCA, already equipped with sleeping accommodations for women visiting the city and a huge cafeteria. Mary remembered that the settlement houses, highly respected now in the immigrant neighborhoods they served, could be fitted with cots, bedding, and supplies for patients too sick to be cared for at home.

"If the schools close, the teachers might be willing to help out," Sophia added. "And I'll ask our volunteers to switch from knitting sweaters, hats, and mittens for soldiers to sewing surgical gowns and face masks for nursing assistants and orderlies. If we're creative, I think Rochester can survive the crisis when it arrives."

Whitely's Aunt just finished a dress for her & it has a black velvet sleeveless coat & also a striped silk one. She also bought her new pumps so she'll be all flossied out. She bought a blue crepe kimono embroidered [with] butterflies yesterday and its real pretty.

Chapter 10

Had a dandy time at the picnic yesterday. Austin, Bong ... went with me. It was at lower Maplewood....The girls seemed to enjoy it & I was glad they could go for A[ustin] and B[ong] are total strangers here and don't know anyone so consequently have no place to go on their 3 to 7.

"Remember to keep your face mask on whenever you're in this ward, Bong," Norma warned. She led her classmate to a table next to one of the twelve beds in the long room. "We have only two patients here now. That's why I've been able to handle these boys on my own, with the night nurse, of course. But three more are coming today, and we expect others as the weeks go on. As many as twenty, Miss Keith told me. They're very contagious, and we have to be especially careful. Getting tuberculosis would ruin our chances of graduating on time. Maybe destroy our chances of ever graduating."

"I'll try very hard not to do wrong," her companion replied, her eyebrows narrowing into a frown. "There's nothing uglier than a sick Bong." She removed a notebook and pencil from her apron pocket to write down the special procedures as Norma reviewed them.

"You'll like the patients, though. I worked in a male TB ward like this last summer. As sick as the men are, they'll still flirt with us." She pointed to a bedside table. "Most of the instruments we use are the usual ones – thermometer and alcohol for sterilizing– and you'll need to wear a stethoscope and your time piece to check their respiration."

She lifted a metal basin. "This one's the only different one. The disease is in their lungs, and it makes them cough a lot. They expel the mucus into these. We need to empty and sterilize them at least every half hour when the men are here in the ward."

"Empty basins whenever they spit." Bong spoke the instructions as she jotted them in the note pad. "Looks like we won't have time to sit."

"Always protect yourself." The Canadian held her hands up, reddened fingers splayed apart. "Every time you empty a receptacle, wash and rinse your hands and thoroughly brush under your fingernails. You won't end this service with soft, lovely skin, but you'll stay healthy."

Bong continued aloud as she wrote the next note. "'Empty, then sterilize basins and pans. Brush under nails and scrub your hands.'"

"Mostly we just do general nursing – temps, bedpans, medications, meal trays, and the like. But we need to keep the patients quiet. They'll want to get up and walk around, even the weakest ones. But total rest and lots of fresh air, gallons of water, and heaps of vegetables are the only medications we have at this point. It's a terrible disease; it saps the energy out of every young man who gets it."

Bong looked up from her notes. "Can't we give them an occasional treat? Something that's meaty, salty, or sweet?"

Norma stopped fluffing a pillow. "No! They'll try to bribe you, so be careful. I was helping one of them write a letter home a couple of days ago, and he nearly cried when I told him I would not smuggle in some cigarettes." She sighed. "I can't understand why we think it's patriotic to donate money for cigarettes for the boys overseas. Smoking might calm battlefront anxiety, as they claim, but the men get so dependent on the disgusting things. I hate to think of the day when women start smoking. But I know it's coming."

Both young women looked toward the door, distracted by voices approaching in the corridor outside the ward. They resumed their chores as the voices faded.

"Wh-wh-where are the soldiers n-n-now??"

"The Army's sent an orderly to help them get into and out of bed and to wheel them to the fresh-air porch where they spend most of the day. That's when we make beds, prepare their special diets, and enter their vitals in the record book. In the evening we write letters home for them or play cards or just talk with them."

"D-d-do you think they'll laugh at my stutter?"

"No, I'll explain it to them when I introduce you. Actually, I think they'll like it. They love anything that interrupts the boring hospital routine."

Norma put a cautionary hand on Bong's forearm. "Expect a pinch every now and then, though. When they were off duty at night in the training camps, they were surrounded by buddies and laughter . . . and that confounded cigarette smoke. Along with being sick, the men here are lonely."

She nodded toward a neighboring cot. "Why don't you freshen that bed. Then we can go down to the diet kitchen, and I'll show you how to prepare tonight's supper."

When they finished straightening the ward, the pupil nurses walked toward the door to the corridor.

"Whe-whe-when will the new patients come?"

"We expect the next lot within a week. They'll be on a special rail car from Camp Dix. That's where most of the Rochester boys went for basic training. There may be a few from the smaller upstate camps, like Madison Barracks and Camp Syracuse, but for the most part they're coming in from New Jersey."

GERMAN RETREAT CONTINUES

Hmmm. Well that's good news for a change, Mary Keith mused as she read the headline. *Maybe the war will be over soon. And I'll have a full hospital staff again.* The Superintendent's eyes skimmed through the rest of page one. *Nothing about an epidemic or la grippe, as the French call it. Let's see what else is happening.* She turned to the women's fashions page.

FALL HATS SELECTED TO "SET OFF" SIMPLE FROCKS

Society women must have enormous closet shelves to be able to store all of their new hats. I wouldn't be caught dead wearing any of them except maybe the "new silk turban that imitates fancy straw." Why on earth would someone want to make fine fabric like silk look like straw? she wondered.

Mary loved Sundays when her supervisory duties were light and she had the leisure to read through the thirty-odd pages of the *Democrat and*

Chronicle. She turned to the local news. *Only two accidents brought here yesterday and one to St. Mary's. Pretty calm for a Saturday.*

She checked the help wanted ads. Yes, the ones for a laundress and a kitchen assistant she'd asked Emma to place were there. Maude Johnston over at the Homeopathic was looking for help, too, she noticed. You just couldn't keep good workers nowadays; the factories offered them better pay, and most of the hospital's new hires disappeared a couple of weeks after starting their jobs. *I must ask Emma to order a want ad for a competent bookkeeper and cashier. I just can't do everything around here.*

She glanced through the grainy images on the photo page. As usual they showed uniformed men in trenches, in tanks, on horseback, lying on stretchers attended by male medics, and only one politician – a man, of course. *Two months left before we women can vote. Maybe after we get the hang of politics, the newspaper photos will have different subjects.* She turned the page and smiled: no deaths listed at the General, and only one at the Homeopathic. Again, unusual. The weekends, especially Saturday nights, were normally pretty busy in all of the hospitals.

Here's something, she thought, and folded the pages back to read the whole article. The Fuel Administration was claiming that people who owned automobiles were wasting valuable gasoline in Sunday outings. Washington was considering banning the use of the vehicles except in emergencies and for essential deliveries. *That'll keep hospital traffic down on weekends, if they follow through. I wonder how they'll enforce it. Special licenses maybe?*

Her examination ended on the business page's persistent sour note. Prices of essential items were still going up. Balancing the hospital's books would continue to plague her.

Putting aside the newspaper, she said a silent prayer. *Oh, Lord, please let us end this war soon so that Eunice will come back. I miss her so. And I miss her mathematical magic almost as much as I miss her companionship.*

Mary prepared a cup of tea in her kitchenette, returned to the sitting room, and sat at her desk. Thinking hard, she began to jot down the points she wanted to make at the hospital staff's general meeting this afternoon. Everyone needed to know about the precautions and preparations she and Sophia and Maude had planned at their meeting on Friday. If the General was going to stay afloat through the coming wave of influenza, everyone, from the kitchen and maintenance staff to the head nurses, would have to pitch in.

In the past year and a half, Intermediate pupil Florence Austin had earned the respect of the hospital's kitchen staff. She had been one of the special diet instructor's star pupils. Intuitively she knew how to combine tired old ingredients with seasonings that coaxed out surprising new flavors. She had a talent for transforming bland ingredients into mouth-watering dishes.

The General's cook, Mrs. Weston, was especially fond of Florence. Glowing special diet patients' evaluations had begun to appear ever since the older woman had asked Austin to share her recipes. She'd even started to include some of the tastier special dishes on the regular hospital menus.

So whenever Intermediate pupil asked for permission to use the small room off the main dining room for a meeting with Austin's six closest classmates, Mrs. Weston was happy to oblige. "And," she usually offered, "let me know what you'd like to serve to your friends. I'll make a dish on the side just for your meeting."

Austin had arranged for such a gathering to follow Superintendent Keith's assembly of the full staff. She and Susan, who were both off duty and had attended the general convocation, set the circular table and waited for their friends to arrive. Bong and Norma would not be able to be at this gathering since they were still on TB duty in the Contagious Disease Annex. Alice, Emily, and Hilda were just coming off regular ward duty. At least those three could be caught up on the administrator's announcements.

The trio entered the room, chatting about the day's experiences and their plans for the coming week. When they saw the serious expressions on their hostesses' faces, however, they took seats at the table and waited quietly. They watched Austin bring a huge bowl of shrimp salad and Susan carry two pitchers of lemonade through the swinging door from the kitchen. The salad bowl was passed around with each pupil spooning a mound on her plate. The pitcher of lemonade followed. Ice cubes clanked against the glass as each young woman poured.

"M-m-m-m. Your recipe, Austin?" asked Hilda, savoring a forkful of the salad.

"Yes. It's the touch of lemon balm that gives it that extra tang, I think. That and scallion tops rather than ordinary onions."

"They add color, too," Alice noted.

"How do you do that?" asked Emily.

"What?"

"Reserve this room? Or get Mrs. Weston to make special treats for our meetings?"

"As long as our patients give the menus rave reviews and I conjure up new recipes for her, she's very grateful."

"Wish I had a creative mind like that. I'd ask her to make all sorts of new things. Every one of them tasting like chocolate."

" You'd soon get tired of chocolate all the time, Emie," Hilda said.

"So, what was the general meeting about?" asked Alice.

Susan had taken notes. Using them, she reviewed the Superintendent's warning that a dangerous epidemic called Spanish influenza had begun to appear along the country's eastern coast. It had started in a military training camp near Boston and infected 1,000 recruits in a single week. Officials were trying to confine the disease to the camps, but other cases were now being reported among civilians in port cities like New York and Philadelphia. The victims became powerless to do anything but lie in bed.

Susan's listeners paid close attention to her. Miss Keith, she continued, had said that there were high rates of mortality, especially since the illness often turned into a type of pneumonia for which there was no cure. And its victims were mostly youngish adults rather than the elderly and little children, the typical influenza targets

Sympathetic as always, Hilda spoke up. "Those poor people. Having just plain old seasonal flu makes you miserable, but after a week or so, you begin feeling better. Knowing she has this new kind could destroy a person's will to live."

Emily interrupted, her fork poised in mid air. "How will the hospital handle it? The TB soldiers are filling the Contagious Pavilion. You can't expose our regular patients to influenza without their getting it. It'd race through the wards like a raging inferno."

Susan consulted her notes again. Miss Keith had asked the surgeons to cancel elective surgeries. No tonsillectomies and adenoidectomies will be performed. Only emergency patients and obstetrical deliveries will be admitted, and of course, only the critically ill influenza victims. As far as it is possible, the remaining patients will be isolated from them. And, though families won't like it, no visitors will be allowed in the wards.

The bowl of shrimp salad went around the table again, its contents shrinking as it stopped at every plate.

Susan continued, "Miss Keith thinks eventually the General will have far more influenza patients than any other kind. She estimates that the disease will arrive here in the coming week, and it'll race through Rochester like it is through the largest East Coast cities. When it gets here, all of our classes will be suspended." Her listeners looked at each other and smiled. Relief from stuffy physicians' lectures sounded like a vacation.

At this point Austin took over: "She thinks that the hospital staff will be especially vulnerable because we'll be first to contact the most seriously ill patients. But she's hoping that those of us who had influenza in the past might have some immunity. They'll be assigned to care for the earliest cases. Neither Susan nor I have ever been sick with the 'grippe.' Have any of you?"

Alice, Emily, and Hilda all nodded "yes."

"Whether we've had it or not, starting tomorrow, all of us will need to wear face masks whenever we're in the hospital buildings. When influenza patients start coming in, we'll need to wear surgical gowns and special head gear. The hospital will do everything possible to keep the staff from contracting the disease. Those of us who do get it will receive the hospital's best care."

Susan resumed, "A ward in East Hall is being set aside for any victims among the hospital workforce. As more employees get sick, she'll reserve additional wards for us."

Austin interposed as Susan poured herself more lemonade. "The hospital's interns and resident physicians will act as our physicians if we get sick. That is if the interns and residents don't all come down with it too."

Again, Susan consulted her notes. "Miss Keith says that the hospital staff will come first. We can't help the sickest people in the community if we all get sick ourselves. When the wards are full of patients, the admissions clerk will have to refer new cases to other hospitals."

Alice shrugged her shoulders. "What other hospitals? They'll probably be full too."

Austin continued. "I'm just coming to that. Miss Keith has met with Miss Johnston from the Homeopathic and Miss Palmer from the Red Cross. If the hospitals are all filled to capacity, Miss Palmer's going to pressure Dr. Roby and other city officials to open emergency hospitals around town. In the meantime, she's quietly contacting the YWCA and the settlement centers, asking them to cooperate. And her volunteer seamstresses are sewing surgical gowns, hair coverings, and face masks for us right now."

"But if pupils get sick, like they expect, where will they get the nurses to care for them?" Emily asked. "There are barely enough nurses in the city now."

"For this crisis we'll have to accept help from anyone who can give it. Miss Palmer will appeal to every woman who has had any nursing preparation at all. Even the ones who have only learned elementary skills in first aid classes," Austin continued. "If the high schools close, we may get help from the more courageous of their students. At any rate, we'll probably be seeing all sorts of civilian volunteers in the corridors."

By this time, the salad bowl was empty, and only a few melting slivers of ice lay at the bottom of the tumblers. The five friends sat in silence for a few minutes. Then they began to clear the remnants of Austin's "party" and return them to the kitchen.

"In a way, this might be fun," Emily said, mischief sparking in her eyes. "The Spanish influenza's not here yet, and we don't know how bad it will get, but when it arrives, the regimentation around here will relax. No telling how many of the senseless rules we have to follow I'll be able to bend."

On Monday, September 22, 1918, Alice knew it was raining even before she opened her eyes. She could hear the heavy drops splashing against the window panes. Reluctantly she rose on one elbow and looked toward to Norma's bed. She could barely see the silhouette of a blanket-covered mound. It didn't move.

"Time to rise and shine, Norma." The coldness of the floor as her feet touched it brought her to full alertness. She slid her toes into slippers and went to the light switch on the wall. "Come on, Norma, we have to get up." She looked at the clock on the nightstand. "Uniform inspection is in a half hour."

The mound remained still, but it groaned. Alice approached it and shook the lump that she guessed was a shoulder.

"Stop it, Alice!" The voice was filled with agony. "My head's bursting!" The mound trembled. "And I can't stop shivering!"

Alice grabbed her face mask from the dresser, tied it across her nose and mouth, threw on her bathrobe, and sped to the door. "I'll be back! Don't move!"

"I can't move," came the weak reply.

Nearly twenty-four hours later, a light rap on Alice's dorm room door woke her. Hilda, still in her nightgown, her copper hair hanging in tangled strands from nape to shoulders, opened the door, peeked in, and switched on the overhead light.

"What should I do, Alice?"

Alice turned over and blinked, first against the bright light and then at her clock. "Three-thirty? You must be joking, Hilda." The empty bed opposite her own reminded her that Norma wasn't there. She was in the new influenza ward on the third floor of East Hall.

"Bong won't budge! She just lies in the bed groaning. Then she throws the covers off, but in a minute or two, she starts shivering and covers up again."

"You go back and stay with her, Hilda. Make her as comfortable as possible. Be sure to put on your face mask as soon as you get to your room, though. I'll go downstairs and telephone for an orderly or a porter. She's got Spanish influenza like Norma, I'll bet. Both of them probably picked it up in the TB Ward in the Annex. A soldier probably brought it in."

"Thanks." Norma rushed away, and Alice put on her slippers and bathrobe. For the second morning in two days, adrenalin was boosting her anxiety. *Wonder what Lady Emergency will wake me up with tomorrow*, she thought as she tiptoed down to the first floor, being careful not to disturb the pupils asleep in the rooms along her path.

The following morning, Madam Emergency ignored Alice entirely, but she wasn't disappointed. The day was routine, except for a trip with Hilda to the third floor in East Hall, where Miss Keith had reserved beds for female members of the household who came down with influenza. Dr. Powell, the intern on duty, assured her that Norma and Bong were very sick patients, but their cases weren't critical yet. If they rested and obeyed doctors' orders, the young women would probably recover in two weeks or so.

"So far their cases are pretty typical," the young physician said. "But, tell me, why does the red head always pause before she answers my questions? And then her responses always come out in a rhyme?"

"If you distract her or don't give her time to think up a rhyme, you'll find out," Hilda said.

As the two friends walked back to the main building, she admitted to Alice, "I thought it would be fun to let him puzzle Bong out for himself. He's cute and she's lovable. There may be a match there."

Dame Emergency made her next visit to Alice on the fourth day following Norma's influenza attack. She was in the Surgical Building's post-op work room, counting pills into little cups when Susan exploded through the workroom door.

"Guess who's here," Susan demanded, breathless, her voice muffled by the face mask.

"Who?"

"I just went over to visit Bong and Norma at the end of my lunch break, and they were wheeling him in." She frowned. "You can't tell who anyone is over there except the patients. Everyone's all bundled up in long gowns and caps. The only clues that tell who you're talking to is their shoes and their voice. But the voices are muffled by these face masks."

"Well, tell me. Who's the special person?"

"It's that brazen young man that broke into our marching line in the parade last May. What was his name? Alfred? Alonzo? Wasn't he something, though."

A spasm somewhere in her chest surprised Alice. *Am I coming down with Spanish influenza? No, an elevated heartbeat isn't on the list of symptoms: high fever, chills, headache, dry cough, and the inability to do anything but collapse in bed.* She was still standing, and her body was relaxed. She returned to dropping pills into medication cups.

"Alphonso?" she asked, her face warmed by a flush that was rising in her neck.

"Yes, that's what his name is. But he's sick. Awful sick."

Again, the quick contraction in her rib cage. "Where did you see him?"

"I was just going into East Hall to see Norma and Bong when they wheeled him in ahead of me. They took him to the men's influenza ward they're just setting up. I think he was being transferred from the TB isolation ward."

"Darn!" Alice said, and she began to recount the pills in each cup. "I lost count."

"Well, got to go back on duty. Can't be late," Susan said. And she quickly exited the workroom.

Alice finished portioning the medications. She glanced at her new time piece. *Three more hours before I'm off duty. Then I'll go over to East Hall to visit Norma and Bong. I can snoop around to find out where they've put Alphonso then.* She lifted the tray of pill cups and took them out to the patients who were slowly emerging from their anesthesia-induced comas.

Susan was right. You can't tell who anyone is all bundled up like we are. That's good. No one will notice that I don't belong here. When a Senior pupil had relieved Alice at the end of her post-op ward duty, she had hurried over to East Hall. Robed in a surgical gown, her nose and mouth covered by a mask, and her upswept brown hair turbaned in white terrycloth, she was just as indistinguishable as the other staff members. *This must be what heaven's like,* she thought. *All the spirits in white, floating around and speaking in hushed voices. Just eyes and muffled voices. –Or maybe this is hell.*

She looked in on Norma and Bong intending to cheer them up. With help, Norma was able to sit against her pillows now, and to keep down a bland diet, but she complained about the tasteless food and the fierce headache that was still plaguing her. Bong, on the other hand, was still prostrate. She wasn't groaning any more, but she wasn't saying anything yet either, not even stuttering. Her body heaved now and then, prompted by a dry cough. Clear liquids were all she could handle at this point.

Alice moistened Bong's lips with water and rinsed her forehead with a cool face cloth. Telling her friends about her frenetic routine did not cheered the patients up, especially when Alice ended her visit claiming she'd have liked to be able stay in bed all day like they were doing. They both rolled their eyes. They knew she was lying.

She descended to the first floor where she'd learned workmen were quickly equipping a special ward for male victims of the epidemic. Unmade hospital beds lined both walls, but workmen were still assembling cots in an extra row that ran down the center of the long room. Their obvious attempts to work quietly were useless. The clatter and clang of the metal bed sections assaulted Alice's ears.

Just down the main hall from the ward was a darkened room used to isolate mumps and measles patients for whom, some medical authorities believed, bright lighting could lead to other, more serious conditions. The door was slightly ajar and hushed voices drifted from the dark interior into the corridor. Alice paused, inched the door open a bit farther and peeked into the gloom.

Two figures flanked the bed, a somewhat portly woman seated at one side and a male figure standing next to the other side of the bed. He was reading aloud from a small book in his hand. His baritone tones were chant-like, unintelligible to Alice since they were in a foreign language. *Italian? Latin?* She guessed.

The door's hinges creaked as she nudged it further. The seated woman looked toward the back-lit intruder. "Alice?" she guessed after a moment and stood up.

Tiny slivers of light, filtering into the room through the slats of Venetian blinds, obscured the dim features of the occupants. When Alice's eyes finally adjusted to the dimness, she was able distinguish Mrs. Privitera.

Then she knew. The man standing in the shadows wore a slender purple stole draped around his neck. He was a priest; the words he was uttering were Latin. Until a few moments ago, she realized, the form in the bed had been Alphonso.

He looked at peace. The startlingly brilliant blue eyes were closed. It was as if their color had leached into his cheeks, for they had a bluish cast. For the third time, her heart tugged at her abdomen, and tears stung her eyes.

"Oh, dear," said Mrs. Privitera advancing toward the newcomer. "He didn't want you to know. First the TB, and then the influenza. He didn't want you to get either of them. He was so sick."

The older woman wrapped her arms around Alice and held her close. "But he wanted me to tell you how much he admired you, how many plans he'd made, his dreams for your futures together after this war is over."

Leaning her head on the older woman's soft shoulder, Alice wept freely as she had the day her brother Will phoned to tell her that Mama Sarah had passed away. This time, though, she felt the small comfort that comes from sharing her grief with Alphonso's mother, whose tears were now dampening her own shoulder.

8:00 [a.m.] *is the earliest I've come on and* 9:45 [p.m.] *the latest so far and, believe me, it's an experience I'll never forget. So far we've had 4 deaths since Sunday .... Several of the nurses are sick.... We wear gowns, masks and towels closely wrapped on our heads.*

Fri. night an entire family of 8 came with the flu. I have the [toddler] *and 10 months old baby. The father and 5 kids are in S*[urgical Ward]. *Poor things, I don't believe they had enough to keep body and soul together..*

Chapter 11

West Hall was opened Sun p.m. for "flu" patients exclusively and I was alone there with 9 patients till 4 o'clock when they sent a [graduate] *nurse. Of course we have more* [sick] *nurses and patients now but are working under difficulties due to a shortage of everything.... Nothing was said about the epidemic in this a.m.'s paper and I think 1,000 cases were mentioned yesterday.*

The next month and a half flew by in a blur for the pupils of the General Hospital's Training School for Nurses. Duty assignments for those who remained healthy expanded beyond their usual twelve hours. The couple of half days off every week disappeared.

Every girl who came down with the illness was sick for two weeks or more. When they recuperated sufficiently, they took over the duty hours of pupils who caught the disease later. For everyone, returning to work too soon could be deadly.

As the first members of the household to become sick, Norma, Bong, and Head Nurse North had the women's influenza ward on Three/East to themselves for nearly a week. Thereafter fellow staff members began to fill bed after bed in East Hall. When Austin joined them a week and a half later, the trickle of patients from the household became a steady stream.

It was a flood when Susan fell ill on October 8. By that time, Bong and Emily had been discharged and were back in their dorm rooms regaining their strength. Alice, Emily, and Hilda visited the contagious ward every day.

Her classmates were saddened when young Josephine Hearn, a Senior pupil, died on October 15th, at the height of the *grippe's* hospital invasion. But those who were sick were too miserable and those who were healthy were too overwhelmed by work to allow for a prolonged mourning period. Josephine's simple memorial had to be repeated in the nurses' residence so that the pupils who were working during the earlier service could attend the second one. A young life, filled with promise and potential, obliterated before it had a chance to emerge.

Without Bong's rhyming, the healthy pupils had to depend on Emily for distractions. One evening she shocked everyone when, after taking a dead mouse out of her apron pocket, she dangled it by its tail at the dinner table. "Look what I found in my desk drawer," she explained.

A chorus of "Get rid of it!" "Get that thing out of here!" "Ugh!" prompted her to rush from the dining room and dispose of the creature outside.

A few days later, Hilda noticed that Emily's tightly curled hairdo, normally imprisoned atop her head by a strong net, had shrunk. "What made you decide to do that?" she asked. "It's strictly against the rules to cut our hair. You could be expelled!"

"Who'll notice? The towel turbans hide our heads," the young pupil explained. "As long as the epidemic lasts and we have to wear those things, I can style my hair however I like it." She ran her fingers through the caramel-colored poodle's coat that now hugged her skull. "It'll grow back. Besides, it feels so good not to have that mop weighing me down. And I get a few more minutes in bed every morning now that I don't have to heap it on top of my head. It's a ridiculous rule!"

For a moment Emily smiled to herself. Then she looked directly at her friends, her eyes alive with mischief. "As a matter of fact, I haven't worn my corset since they required us to become mummies in surgical gowns. Talk about feeling free!"

"Better not tell Susan until she's better. You know how she is about the rules," warned Alice.

One afternoon, Emily confided to Alice on their break. "I've got a new job," she whispered.

"Doing what?"

"Well, the election's coming up in a couple of weeks. And since the epidemic won't let the gubernatorial candidates come to Rochester to speak beforehand, the Democratic ward leaders are hiring girls like me to go door to door to pass out electioneering flyers. I do it every chance I can get. Women can vote for the first time, and the boys on the battle front can't vote at all, so no one knows which way the election'll go. The Democrats think they can challenge rigid Republican Rochester."

Alice's head shook in wonder, and her eyes rose to the ceiling. "What next?"

"I'm exhausted," Hilda said as she rolled up her sleeves and began wringing the rinse water out of a uniform. Alice had just entered the basement carrying a basket full of soiled clothing. With half of the laundry staff sick and mountains of soiled bed linens generated by the overcrowded wards, the healthy pupils and head nurses had to hand wash their own uniforms now.

"I don't wonder," replied Alice. "You've been on double duty —first in the maternity ward and then in the influenza halls— for almost two days straight." She turned the hot and cold water spigots on and tested the temperature. As her utility tub began to fill, she added a cup of soap chips.

"Will it ever be over?" The clothespin she held between her teeth garbled Hilda's pronunciation. She removed it and pressed it into the rope that stretched across the room, pinning the uniform upside down. "It's been nearly two weeks since Bong and Norma caught it. And every day three or four more of our classmates go on the sick list."

"I try not to think ahead. But epidemics always play themselves out sooner or later. Remember the smallpox scare in 1902? Once enough people were vaccinated, it finally disappeared. Miss Gilman says they're trying to develop a vaccine that will work against Spanish flu."

"I hope they find one soon. I'm not going to be worth much if I don't get some rest." Hilda unfurled another uniform and pinned its hem to the line. "By the way, we were so busy that I didn't get to tell you how sorry I was when Alphonso died. You were kind of sweet on him, weren't you." It was a statement, not a question.

Alice gently rubbed an apron against the washboard. "Kind of," she said after a pause.

"Had you planned anything about seeing each other after the war?"

"No. Not really. But I thought maybe we might. We're from different backgrounds, you know. But he wasn't like most of the Italian boys I've met. He was a thinker. And he had real ambitions." Alice's voice was strained, like fingers were wrapping around her throat. She leaned farther over the utility tub and scrubbed with more vigor.

Finished with her chore, Hilda packed the Ivory Flakes box into her laundry basket and shifted the load under one arm. She move to Alice's side and put her free arm around her friend's shoulder. "I know you felt more about him than you've let on, Alice. And not being able to attend his funeral on top of it all." Her hand squeezed Alice's shoulder.

Alice's throat closed up tight, and a tear leaked out and splashed into the soapy water. "Sorry. Got to get this done before I go on duty again." Her voice came out strangled.

"Let me know when you're ready to talk about it, okay?" Another squeeze. "When the epidemic is over and we have time to catch up."

At the end of her duty that night, Alice had to drag herself through the tunnel back to the nurses' residence. She was spent, both physically and emotionally.

Wish I had Emily's rebellious spirit, she thought as she removed her corset and undergarments and drew her nightgown over her head. She switched the light off, lay down and, one at a time, mentally ordered the different parts of her body – feet, legs, hands, arms, neck – to relax.

But her brain wouldn't close down by the time she got to her head. *There's so much work. So little I can change. One day I think a patient's getting better, and the next day someone else is in that bed. More often than not, they haven't gone home well; they've gone home to their Maker. And when they do recover, what kind of life will they have? More hunger and sickness and suffering?*

After arguing with herself for ten minutes, she got up, made her way to the writing desk, and switched on the lamp. The stationery and pen and ink were in the drawer right where she had left them last night after she'd written to her sister Bess. The cork slid out of the ink bottle with a small pop.

She spoke the words as she wrote: "Dear Miss Keith." Stopping now and then to consider how to phrase what she was thinking, she continued. "It is with the greatest regret that I write this letter." . . . "I have concluded that neither my physical stamina nor my," . . . "mental temper are suited to the rigors required of a hospital-trained nurse."

She sighed and dipped the pen nib in the ink and rushed to the end. "Therefore, I feel I must withdraw from the General Hospital Training School for Nurses when the current crisis is over."

She signed the letter, folded it, and sealed it in an envelope. It wouldn't do for Norma to see what she'd written yet. She wanted to announce her decision to the members of her group all at once. With her mind now emptied of obsessive thoughts, she switched the lamp off, returned to bed, and fell into a sound sleep.

As Alice neared the hospital's Reception Hall, she could hear excited voices. The words were unfamiliar. Spanish maybe? Italian?

Principal Gilman, shrouded in the now standard white surgical gown, was standing behind the Admissions desk, using it as a barrier against the onslaught of a dozen very angry people.

"No!" she yelled, her voice edged with panic. "You're not allowed to come in like this! You're not even supposed to be together in a group! And where are your face masks? You're going to infect everyone!" She swept one arm toward the main door of the Administration Building. "Go away or I'll call the police!"

The administrator's words only added to the incoherent babbling which now reverberated against the high ceiling.

Alice waited. *Wish I knew another language*, she thought. *Don't want to get near that hornet's nest. I think I'll wait to find out what my next week's work assignment is.*

Just as she was turning to leave, she noticed another person enter the hall through the heavy main door. The figure looked familiar despite the gauze mask that covered half of her facial features: short, a bit plump, a little bosomy, jet black waves of hair falling gracefully to rounded shoulders. *Mrs. Privitera*, Alice thought. *I haven't seen her since Alphonso died. I'll just wait a couple of minutes to say hi.*

Seeing the commotion at the desk, the newcomer approached the group. "*Silenzio!*" the woman yelled. The babbling began to subside. "*Di che si tratta?*" Their voices rose again, but this time their tone was more confused and hurt than angry. Someone actually cared about what they wanted. Every speaker took his or her turn, gesturing with hands and arms to punctuate the words.

The older woman turned toward Miss Gilman and began to translate: "They just want to see Giuseppe Bellavilla. . . . Their son. . . . Her father. . . . His uncle. . . . Their cousin. . . . Her fiancé," she explained, pointing to individuals in the group. "Giuseppe came here two days ago with the Spanish influenza." The visitors watched her closely, silent now, and then they turned their attention back to Miss Gilman

"Please tell them that we can't allow visitors while the epidemic is going on," the administrator said. "It's not safe for the patients. It's not safe for themselves. Especially since they aren't wearing face masks. Good heavens, don't they read the newspapers?"

"No. I'm sorry, Miss. They <u>can't</u> read the newspapers. Even if they knew how to read, there aren't any Italian language newspapers in

Rochester." She turned toward the visitors and explained the situation in their language. Mumbling their disappointment, the group left the Reception Hall.

Mrs. Privitera turned back toward Miss Gilman. "That's why I'm here," she said. "To work. I have to have something to do. The hospital must need somebody like me."

With the sleeve of her surgical gown, Miss Gilman wiped perspiration beads from her forehead and leaned forward. "Of course we need someone like you," she said. "How many days a week can you give us? How many hours a day? How can we get in touch with you? Just someone who speaks Italian would be a godsend, but there are hundreds of other things you can do to help us.

The words flowed from her in a torrent: "The laundry needs people; there's only a skeleton of a staff working in the kitchen; have you had any First Aid training?" She reached under the counter for a form. "Here, please fill this out. Tell us everything you can do." She handed the paper and a pencil to the woman.

"I would be glad to work in the kitchen," Mrs. Privitera said. "Of course, I make mostly pastas. But we have antipasto too, very nourishing. And wonderful *dolces*. If I was working in the kitchen, you could always find me to translate at times like today.

Then she turned her attention to Alice who had approached the pair. With a delighted smile, she encircled the younger woman with her soft, pillow-like arms.

"We'd love to have you here, Mrs. Privitera," the nursing pupil said. "Our menus have been pretty bland since Mrs. Weston's been sick."

"Please call me 'Mama,' Alice. After what we've both been through, I feel like you're a member of my family."

"I wanted so to attend Alphonso's funeral."

"Not to worry. I know you were with us in spirit."

"You'll have to show me where he's buried in Holy Sepulchre when the epidemic is over."

"I will be happy to. And you must join us when we have his memorial Mass."

Mrs. Privitera turned her attention back to Miss Gilman. "I know many other women in my neighborhood who need something to distract them from worrying about their boys in the Army. I'll ask them if they want to volunteer in the hospitals.

Alice guided Mrs. Privitera to a pair of chairs at a small table. There she helped the woman –her new "Mama"– fill out the volunteer form. They both hoped it would help ease Alphonso's mother's grief. And improve the hospital's menus at the same time.

While their relentless routines transformed the pupils into automatons, the hospital's Superintendent felt as if she was walking on a treadmill that speeded up every day. For the two weeks after pupils Whitely and Bong fell ill, cases among the household staff multiplied steadily. Then new flu patients from the neighborhoods surrounding the hospital began to fill newly converted influenza wards until they took over an entire floor.

By October 6th, every bed in East Hall was occupied by influenza victims, and West Hall wards were being prepared for more patients. Half way through October, admissions from the household staff peaked at 49. They and city residents took up nearly every available bed in the hospital. As staff members slowly recovered, new admissions from outside continued to balloon the patient census.

The only regular activity that the Miss Keith could depend on was her early morning meeting with the healthy leaders of the hospital's staff. Each day Principal Gilman reported the number of admissions during the previous twenty-four hours and, as time went on, patients who were being discharged healthy and the number of deaths that had occurred over night.

Then the head nurses would devise work shifts that, while they sometimes extended beyond the usual twelve hours, would be fair to everyone on the roster. A member of the kitchen staff also attended, primarily to report how many of her team were healthy enough to work, but also to plan the grocery order for the day, which depended on the number of sick trays that had to be prepared. Someone from the laundry, always understaffed, reviewed the demands in that department.

After the meeting, Mary would don her surgical gown and head covering and make her rounds in the wards. In a way, she liked the uniform because it made her invisible; she looked like everyone else on the staff. Groups did not stop conversing when she approached them in the corridors, and orderlies demanded that she "Step aside, please," clearing the way for sheet-draped gurneys to pass on their way to the morgue. All business, they treated everyone the same, in their haste, breaking apart teams and pairs hurrying to their next work assignment. The General's Superintendent was just another one of the troops.

One day, though, she doubly appreciated the anonymity that the new hospital garb gave her. When the crisis began, the Board of Lady Managers had surged into the hospital, overseeing procedures, giving the administrators unasked for counsel, and often just getting in the way. On this day, Lady Manager Mrs. Gloucester was making her regular inspection tour of the wards. Wearing only a face mask but still dressed in her fashionable street clothes, the woman was scolding a white-clad attendant severely.

"That is <u>not</u> the way you turn a patient over when you are changing her bed linens!" The voice was strident. "Who ever taught you how to do it that way? Don't you know anything?" She shoved the attendant aside roughly.

"I'm sorry, ma'am. But Miss Reid…." This voice, Mary was sure, had the timid, pleading quality of a Probationer who had been assigned a duty normally reserved for First Year pupils. The young woman had read about the procedure in a textbook and an instructor had demonstrated it, but she had never touched a human being for whom every movement, every touch, even every breath was agony.

"Excuse me, Mrs. Gloucester," the Mary interrupted, the volume of her voice rising to be audible in the ward full of retching and groaning patients."We don't teach our pupils in that tone of voice."

"And just who are you…" the outsider demanded, "…to address me in <u>that</u> tone of voice?" The woman folded her arms in front a corpulent chest. "And how do you know my name?"

"I'm Mary Keith, the Superintendent of this hospital. And I know your name because we attend monthly meetings together. Our masks and gowns make the hospital staff all look alike."

"Well, Miss Keith, I trust you will take over here," said the matron, backing away slightly, but maintaining her superior tone.

"I will definitely do that," the administrator said to the retreating figure. Then she turned to the probationer who had stood by shyly during the exchange. "What's your name, young lady?"

"Agnes Snook, Miss Keith."

"You almost had this right, Miss Snook." Mary patted the younger woman's shoulder. "Here, let me show you what Mrs. Gloucester meant." With exquisite tenderness, she demonstrated the procedure for the pupil. Then they moved on down the line, the probationer gaining confidence with each new bed change.

For the remainder of the morning, Mary lingered in the influenza wards, stepping in to help the duty nurses whenever they needed an extra hand, which was often. While she would never admit that she was eaves dropping, now and then she would linger near small staff or pupil gatherings, listening to conversations that revealed snippets from their personal lives, and sometimes hearing gossip. Exhausted as they were, she gathered, the hospital's workers nevertheless refused to be less than hopeful and to stay committed to their daily challenges.

She spent the remainder of the morning rushing through her administrative tasks, a bit lighter now because the hospital had no room for new patients. Then she would quickly don the surgical gown, face mask and head gear and rejoin the army for afternoon combat in the influenza wards. Her experiences there, in addition to reminding her about the emotional boost she always felt when a patient began a steady recovery, rejuvenated the middle-aged administrator.

But there were some low points, too. Every day around noon, Miss Keith telephoned the General's current population statistics to a clerk at the Department of Health. On a Friday in mid October, Acting Health Officer Roby answered her telephone call personally. "We're short of help here at the Bureau," he explained, responding to her surprise at his voice. "No receptionist. Half of our staff have called in sick today."

For a few moments they exchanged professional observations about the epidemic's progress. "We've passed an ordinance against spitting in public, to begin on Monday," he announced proudly. "And we've ordered that the street cars be fumigated every day and insisted that they run with their windows open."

Mary stamped her foot. "You can't seriously believe that spitting in public is how this disease spreads, Joseph! No one is spitting on the floors of the nurses' residence, I can assure you. Yet thirty-three of our pupils and nursing instructors are sick today. Besides, everyone's wearing gauze masks. They can't spit!" Tethered to her desk by the telephone cord, she couldn't pace off her frustration as usual, so she leaned against the edge and impatiently tapped one foot on the floor.

She decided to reveal what was really on her mind. "Joseph, the Health Bureau's report in this morning's *Democrat* claims that thirty-five Influenza cases are being treated here at the General. Yet, we've admitted nearly twice that number. And, according to your office, there have been only seventeen deaths from the disease in the entire city. But we've reported fifteen flu deaths at this hospital alone. Have only two deaths occurred in the other three hospitals combined? Is the Health Bureau intentionally underreporting the totals?"

There was a pause. "Let me be frank about this, Mary. The real enemy here is panic. The consequences of uncontrolled fear could be devastating to the city and to the country as a whole. Some parents are so scared, they're keeping their children home from school even though they're not sick."

"What do you mean, Joseph? How can downplaying this crisis lessen the pressures the hospitals are under?"

"If people are so afraid that they begin to isolate themselves, they won't go to work, and the factories will be short handed. You know how essential Rochester's products are to winning the war."

She frowned. He sounded like one of those Four-Minute men who were making Liberty Loan speeches on downtown street corners every day.

The city's $31 million goal in the fourth bond drive had been obsessing community leaders for weeks, she recalled.

"Just be patient please, Mary," Dr. Roby went on. "We're going to close the public schools next week. We're asking the factories to stagger their hours so that factory workers and clerical staffs won't intermingle with shoppers on the street cars. That's as close to quarantining the public as a municipal government can get. Running a city of nearly 300,000 is not like being a general in an army where you can order people to do something and they immediately obey."

Impatient with the lecture that was going on far longer than she had wanted, Miss Keith dropped into her desk chair.

Roby cleared his throat, preparing to cap off his sermon. "The city isn't a closed society like a hospital, Mary. We can't just create rules like you can. Next week, though, we're going to tell managers of theaters, dance halls, and bowling alleys –places that cater to crowds just for amusement– that they have to close down. That won't make the owners, their employees, or the performers happy. But Boston is doing it, so we're going to try the idea out."

"What about saloons? People gather there in large groups."

"That's more complicated. Some travelers depend on saloons for their meals. Like hotel guests. They expect to be served alcoholic beverages. Besides, folks will still take streetcars to bars in the surrounding towns. That would spread the flu even farther. Nobody will like what we're doing. But it's got to be done."

Mary frowned. She hadn't thought of that. It'll be uncomfortable for most, but if they had a chance to stop the epidemic's spread, these things were probably necessary.

"We can ask the public to take action with us," the Acting Health Officer went on. "The Protestant Pastors and the Rabbis have volunteered to suspend Sabbath services, and we're hoping that Bishop Hickey will agree to cancel Sunday Mass this week."

That would be drastic, Mary thought. Her Catholic staff members considered missing Sunday Mass a serious sin; they always insisted that they should not be scheduled for duty on that one morning.

"The Chamber of Commerce is our most powerful ally," Roby went on. "They may be able convince the cultural groups and brotherhoods that even more measures, like suspending lectures and regular meetings, are necessary. Eventually, we may even have to police the cemeteries. Only immediate family members will be allowed at funerals. They're doing that in Syracuse. We'll try everything we can think of to stop this disease from spreading."

Despite her annoyance at his paternalistic tone, Mary backed down. The health officer's explanation broadened her perspective. So after a few concluding pleasantries – she wishing that his family remained healthy and he hoping that conditions in the hospitals would improve soon– they said goodbye.

But Mary wanted to discuss the matter further, with a person who could view it from her position. So she telephoned Maude Johnston at the Homeopathic. The receptionist was sorry, but Miss Johnston was not in her office. She was making rounds in that hospital's wards.

Mary spent the forepart of the afternoon helping to rearrange another ward to make room for patient beds that had been clogging the corridor all morning. She was getting the knack of this chore; there'd be a similar situation tomorrow, she knew.

Then she interviewed two applicants for the bookkeeper/cashier position she had advertised earlier in the month. Of course, they were both young males. Generally, women were word –not number– people: stenographers, telephone operators and such. Both of the men she spoke with had some physical problem that had exempted them from the draft. She offered the second candidate the job, hoping that his nervous blinking would not get worse before Eunice returned from France. How she missed her co-worker.

Maybe, she hoped, *there's such confusion of numbers this year that we won't have to publish our monthly statistics. If the Health Bureau can't keep an accurate count of the cases in the city, then how could anyone blame the hospitals for not being able to do it?*

It wasn't until she arrived back in her apartment after dinner that she found time to telephone her counterpart at the Homeopathic Hospital. Having changed into her flannel night dress and bathrobe and prepared a steaming cup of tea, she sat in the easy chair, lifted her slippered feet to the hassock, and found the item she had read in this morning's *Democrat and Chronicle*. Finally, she dialed her friend Maude's private number.

After exchanging a few details about how both hospitals were faring, Mary got to the point. "This morning's paper says that fifteen of your nurses have influenza, Maude. But at the end of the same paragraph, the article says: 'It was said last night that the ailment wasn't influenza.' If your staff don't have the flu, what do they have?"

"They have the flu, Mary. I have no idea who denied that fact. I reported the correct information to the Health Bureau myself."

"I spoke with Dr. Roby at noontime, and he as much as admitted that the powers that be are minimizing the effect this epidemic is having on the hospitals."

Maude agreed. "When I talked with him a couple of days ago, he told me that the newspapers insist on having daily updates from the authorities. Influenza is a seasonal ailment, he told me, like having a cold. Most of the sick people are at home. The State Health Department doesn't require physicians to report flu cases, so they aren't. Quite frankly, I believe that the Health Bureau has no idea of how many actual victims there are in the city. But the newspapers keep hounding him."

She paused. "I realize, though, that he's manipulating our reports. The Homeopathic's fifteen nurses you read about <u>do</u> have the disease, and I think there will be just as many new staff admissions tomorrow."

"Well, I suppose there's nothing we can do about it, Maude. You're probably as busy as we are just finding enough healthy staff to handle the sick people the ambulances are bringing in every day."

"I'm hoping they find a vaccine that works, Mary. Or maybe the disease will just burn itself out, get weaker as time goes on. That's the usual pattern with influenza."

Holding the receiver with her shoulder, Mary refolded the newspaper so she could skim through an adjoining article. "I'm getting really cynical about the situation, Maude. There's another article here that talks about building a new hospital at Edgerton Park to care for soldiers crippled by the war. They estimate that there'll be two thousand of them from this area. If the Spanish influenza isn't over by then…."

"That's what we're here for, Mary, isn't it? Remember the Nightingale pledge we took when we graduated from training school? Our promise to devote our lives to caring for the sick and the injured?"

"I suppose you're right, Maude. This administrative rigmarole is distracting me from our real calling. Thanks for listening to my griping. Talking it through with you has helped me to regain focus."

The hospital administrators wished each other a pleasant evening. An exhausted Mary Keith discarded her tea, now too cold drink, in the kitchenette sink, switched off the den lamp, and went to bed.

But before slipping into a well deserved sleep, the Mary Keith reviewed her day. The conflict with Dr. Roby had been disconcerting. But working as part of the hospital's team, who had often mistaken her as just another nurse, had reminded her how much she loved the profession —its healing and soothing aspects— not the administrative ones.

Sophia Palmer, R. N., leader in the New York State campaign to recognize registered nursing as a *bona fide* profession, was in her glory. Until the influenza crisis, her retirement from hospital superintendency to found and edit the now prestigious *The American Journal of Nursing* had been much too prosaic. Being involved in handling the current life-and-death situation was restoring her vitality. It brought back the sense of purpose she had felt back in the 1890s when she had come to Rochester to take charge of the General Hospital.

During the first week after meeting with Superintendents Keith and Johnston, Sophia telephoned Sister Clementine at St. Mary's and Dr. Lewis at the Hahnemann and reviewed the discussion with them. Then she contacted some acquaintances she could trust to implement their plans discreetly. Two weeks later she waited for the telephone call she intuitively knew would be coming.

"Sophia." The baritone voice revealed some urgency. "Dr. Roby here."

"Hello, Dr. Roby. How are things going down at the Health Bureau?"

"As you might expect, not very well. We're severely short staffed." He sighed. "To make a long story short, Sophia, the Public Safety Department believes that the hospitals will eventually be overcrowded, unable to handle new influenza patients. They're considering transforming the Convention Hall Annex into an emergency hospital to handle the severest cases until the epidemic settles down. Of course, we'll need some nurses to staff the Annex. The building is large, and we'll be able to handle all of the severest cases most efficiently there. Will you please send us a list of registered nurses in the area who can man such a place when and if it is necessary. And, will you consent to direct them?"

Careful to disguise her annoyance at the man's presumptiveness, Miss Palmer replied, "I'm afraid I'll have to decline that honor, Dr. Roby. The Red Cross in Washington has again asked me to comb the area for young women who can take a short course in the emergency training schools they're setting up. They want them for service in the military camps. For me, Washington takes precedence. And, I believe, it probably takes precedence in your situation as well. Can't the Health Bureau draft women into community service?"

His voice revealed frustration, tinged slightly by anxiety. "I don't know what we can do," he said. "The Bureau's being swamped with calls for physicians, and my staff, at least the ones who are still healthy, haven't a minute to spare. I'm about to demand that every doctor in this city report all of their influenza cases every day whether the State Health Department requires it or not."

Now he was complaining. "The newspapers have a voracious appetite for details. They're hounding me about number counts every day. But other than patients admitted to the hospitals, I haven't an inkling about how many sick people there are in Rochester. We may need to open a satellite hospital, but then again, we may not."

Sophia imagined the health official sitting at his desk, blotting sweat beads from his forehead. She smiled briefly at the thought. "Maybe there's a better idea, Dr. Roby."

At first she helped him think through the Convention Hall Annex plan. Yes, they agreed, it was centrally located, and it certainly was big – cavernous as a matter of fact. And the city owned the building, so using it would cost taxpayers nothing. Except, of course, Sophia reminded him when you considered having to remodel the interior: filling in that well that lets sunlight fall from the second-floor skylight down to the main floor, installing additional plumbing for more bathroom facilities and steam pipes for the additional radiators, equipping a kitchen, and countless other updates.

Might there be large, privately owned meeting halls that would be more suitable, she asked him? Any new emergency hospitals would need to separate male patients from females for the sake of efficiency. A few smaller emergency centers could do that. Healthy infants and toddlers whose mothers were sick would be another problem, especially since so many fathers were absent in military training camps or already fighting in France. If and when war widows got sick, where could the youngsters go?

She paused for several seconds to let him digest these new considerations. Impatient for other ideas, Dr. Roby broke the silence, "Yes, go on, please."

"What about the YWCA?" she finally asked, as if the thought had just occurred to her. "Fannie Kollock's been General Secretary there for over a year now. I know she'd be delighted to help out. The building's centrally located and the gymnasium on the main floor would make an ideal emergency hospital. There's a fine cafeteria and a well appointed kitchen, and the gym equipment and swimming pool could help keep children who were on the mend amused. If you had enough civilian volunteers working under a head nurse, that might work."

"Thanks, Sophia. We hadn't thought about that. I'll take your idea back to the Common Council right away."

"Wait a minute, Joseph. Another thing just occurred to me. What about the language problems the hospitals sometimes have? Do you suppose the settlement houses –the one on Baden Street and the Lewis Street Housekeeping Center– might make good satellite hospitals?"

Again she paused, privately counting the seconds to allow the Health Officer to shift his mental gears. "They're in the heart of the immigrant neighborhoods, and they already have staff nurses who can understand Italian and Polish. Nancy Stahl is the registered nurse in charge of the Baden Street Settlement House. It could handle some male patients."

"Hold on a minute," he said. "Let me write this down."

She waited obediently.

"Okay, go ahead."

"Kathryn Weldner is in charge of the Housekeeping Center on Lewis Street. They have a gymnasium too."

"Got that." His mental gears were fully engaged now. "Then, depending on how long this thing goes on, we could open the East Main Street Armory. It's been nearly vacant since Base Hospital 19 left. And State Militia men could act as attendants there."

Sophia imagined she could hear the Health Officer's pencil scratching across his notepad. His mind must be racing now. "The Women's Motor Corps could act as taxi and ambulance drivers."

She heard the faint tapping of his pencil against his teeth. He was calculating. "We're closing the schools Monday, so high school boys will be free, and they could do some of the heavier chores. . . .With fewer transients coming into town, there won't be as many guests in the hotels, so their kitchens might donate light meals." The enthusiasm building in his voice hinted that the doctor wanted time to himself to consider each new idea as it came to him.

"Those are marvelous suggestions, Dr. Roby." Deference to official authority had returned to Sophia's voice. "Why don't you continue working on this on your own. You have a lot to do, I understand."

"Thank you, Sophia. You've stimulated my thinking. Have a pleasant afternoon."

"And may your afternoon go as smoothly as the epidemic will allow, Dr. Roby. Good bye."

A satisfied grin spread across her lips as the Red Cross recruiter replaced the telephone earpiece on its black pedestal.

Sophia checked her reflection in the full-length mirror. Yes, she looked the part: a major preparing to inspect her regiment's operations. Red Cross in Washington wanted a full report, so she had donned her official uniform.

The skirt shows more of my ankles than I'm comfortable with, she thought.

When the tunic's waist button slid smoothly through its hole she was pleasantly surprised. *Used to be pretty snug. A year ago I had to hide the strain with the belt buckle. Meatless Tuesdays and wheatless Wednesdays and sugar restrictions have done wonders for my figure.*

After buckling the belt, she turned to the left and to the right making sure that the tunic top hadn't bunched up in the back. *Pleats and plackets everywhere, and four huge patch pockets. Seems to me like a waste of material. Civilians have to make do with less and less, but military uniforms are covered in excess*, she mused, surprised at her ability to rhyme. She unbuttoned one of the breast pockets and expanded its pleats. *If I could actually use these pockets, I wouldn't need to carry a satchel. But that would make bulges where no one wants to see them. So better not."*

Yes, her silver locks were still snuggly imprisoned in the hairnet, looking for all the world like a skein of yarn waiting for knitting needles to transform it into a sock or a cap or a mitten. She positioned the wide-brimmed hat at a jaunty angle and examined the effect. *No, that won't do. Have to look official today.* Repositioning it and centering its Red Cross, she anchored the felt fedora with a hat pin.

Her first stop was Red Cross headquarters at the corner of East Avenue and Alexander Street. As it had for the past couple of weeks the hushed voices coming from the Work Room sounded unnatural. The sewing and knitting machines filling the room sat silent for a change. Before the influenza had descended on the city, the room hummed with volunteer seamstresses in conversation while their machine motors whirred through hundreds of yards of fabric.

Against one wall of the now nearly empty room, the telephone company had installed a bank of switchboards. Working at them were a half dozen young women, each of their heads embraced by earphones sprouting antennae and each throat circled by a speaker necklace. The operators spoke in hushed voices, plugging and unplugging cords that made geometric patterns against the consoles. A lone woman, clip board and pen in hand, rolled in her wheeled chair back and forth behind the workers, answering their questions and recording observations.

Sophia was curious. But she didn't want to distract the operators or their supervisor, so she silently watched the operation and listened to the messages the telephone team were relaying to their callers:

"Thank you, doctor. We'll call the Health Bureau and relay your report of new cases to them."

"Yes, madam, you can volunteer your roadster and chauffeur by telephoning the Public Health Committee at the Chamber of Commerce."

"I'm certain that the emergency hospitals will appreciate your students' offer, Principal Bennett. Please phone Mrs. Dr. Mulligan who is organizing volunteer teams."

"I'm sorry, Mrs. Natoli, but you'll need to contact your family's physician to ask for help. He will assess your situation and authorize the special services you need. . . .You don't have a physician? . . . . Then if you hold on a minute I'll switch you to the operator that assigns physicians, and she'll find one in your neighborhood."

The Work Room had been transformed into the city's information clearing house. The operators were operating very efficiently.

After jotting notes covering this segment of her official report, she drove to her second stop, the YWCA on Franklin Street. In the vestibule, she met her friend, Fannie Kollock, clad as usual in black bloomers and a loose-fitting, white blouse; a handled jump rope dangled from around her neck. Fannie's face was flushed, and perspiration trails from the moist side burns of her short brown hair led down her to her chin.

The outfit and boyish hairdo would have prompted criticism if Fanny wasn't so well known as a woman's physical fitness advocate. That attitude about how women dressed was changing, though. The girls over at Symington were sporting a new uniform. Bloomers and a short hair style were the required uniform for female workers in the munitions plant.

Fanny reported that everything had been going relatively smoothly since the emergency hospital had opened there a week ago. She was only responsible for maintaining the building and making the facilities available to the workers and volunteers. Nurses Lindsay, Robbins and Vail were out answering the scores of emergency requests for help that came in every day from neighborhood homes. Two additional nurses covered night duty. Most of the patients at the Y had passed the critical point and were on their way to recovery.

After tying on face masks, the two women toured the upper floors, Sophia taking the elevator and Fanny skip-roping her way up the stairs. Mrs. Strong and a couple of the other YW board members were volunteering in the second-floor gym/sick ward that day. A couple of their household servants would keep watch during the night. So far State Militia men had carried in about sixty of the most critically ill women and children. But Fanny was expecting another fifty cots to be set up soon on the fourth floor.

This is going to be a pretty dry report, Sophia thought, *unless something unusual has happened here.* "How is morale among the volunteers?" she asked.

"They have amazing resilience, considering the terrible condition of the victims. The ladies come in every morning with enthusiasm, work almost to exhaustion, and leave in the evening still hoping that the authorities are right." She pantomimed quotation marks in the air: "'There is no cause for alarm.' There's one more thing, though. You could almost call it amusing."

Sophia stopped writing, her pen poised above the notebook. "What is that?"

"Last Thursday, one of the prominent lawyers in town came in and offered his services. It seems that trespassers are afraid of catching the flu and the courts aren't as busy as usual. I didn't know what to do with him, so I took him to the kitchen, gave him an apron, and set him to washing the dishes. When he finished, he said he felt so good about what he had done that he would be back again this week."

Fannie grinned. "He must have passed the word on to some friends because at the beginning of the week a group of professional men — collections agents, bond brokers, architects and the like— came and set up a dish washing club. Now members report morning, noon, and evening. The club has one by-law: if a member misses his assigned time, he must forfeit a ten-cent penalty. The money goes to hire a woman to take his place."

The pair descended to the kitchen in the basement. This facility, Fanny explained, was fully equipped to prepare meals not only for this emergency hospital but also for delivery to homes around the city where mothers were too sick to cook for their families. In the kitchen dietitians from the Mechanics Institute were directing the volunteer cooks.

The two women joined the volunteers who were having lunch. Their conversations reinforced Fannie's assessment of the facility's atmosphere. Invariably, the workers were positive that their efforts would defeat the epidemic.

If the other emergency facilities are like the YW's, Sophia thought as she drove toward the Baden Street Social Settlement House, *I will certainly enjoy writing my final report to Washington.* The store-front Polish bakeries she passed and the Hebrew school two lots away from her destination revealed how culturally diverse this neighborhood had become.

Her interview of Nancy Stahl, the Baden Street dispensary's nurse, went as smoothly as the preceding one. "We opened a week and a half ago with ten male patients. But ever since then we've been steadily approaching our capacity of forty," the younger woman explained.

Despite the severity of the cases, there had been only one death so far. The volunteers here were all male, members of Troop H of the State Guard. When Sophia asked for a distinctive characteristic of the temporary infirmary, Miss Stahl marveled that the soldiers were so willing to follow orders from the nurses. "Before the epidemic, it would have been unthinkable that a strong man dressed in military uniform would respond immediately to a soprano voice telling him to empty a bed pan or change the soiled linens on a cot."

Sophia agreed.

Her third stop took Miss Palmer to the Lewis Street Housekeeping Center, in the heart of the Italian neighborhood within the Jefferson Avenue district. Here, she knew, parents with many *bambinos* were crowded into much-too-small apartments. The disease had afflicted entire families, and the women and children now filled the fifty available beds at the Center. Finding enough nurses to staff the facility had been a problem, mostly because of the language situation. Many of the immigrant women here had not assimilated yet, and communication between patient and nurse would be difficult, if not impossible.

"But a few of the neighborhood women have lived here for several years and are bilingual. They've taken home nursing classes and are responding to the emergency beautifully," Head Nurse Weldner explained.

"The hardest problem the volunteers face is their patients' fear of being in a foreign place without their husbands and other relatives nearby. In the old country, hospitals were where people went to die."

When asked about a distinctive event, the directress replied, "One day a real estate salesman walked in and asked Nurse Carter what he could do. Home purchases and sales have disappeared during the epidemic, so he had time on his hands. I thought for a moment, fetched a mop and a pail, and set him to work on the dispensary floor. When he finished, he was delighted with his work, and now he visits us every few days and takes care of some of the heavier cleaning and maintenance chores."

Miss Palmer drove to her last stop, the First Unitarian Church's Gannett House. With Sunday services and church committee meetings suspended, Pastor Denny had convinced his parishioners that devoting their new parish house to caring for influenza victims was just what the New Testament was calling them to do. It was the most recent emergency hospital to open, and while it had facilities to care for as many as seventy-five patients, only ten were there at present.

At the end of the short tour, Pastor Denny informed Miss Palmer of the generosity of a private family, the Sol Wiles, who had welcomed into their home the children of a mother and father who had died of the disease. Their conversation turned to other survivors in families where death had left children orphans. "Have you looked into the Brewster home on South Fitzhugh Street?" he asked.

"No," she answered.

"The mansion was left untenanted when E. Franklin died last May. His wife had passed in February, God rest her soul. Their daughter, you know, married a politician and lives in Washington now. So the building is vacant. It's spacious, and it would make a wonderful home for orphaned youngsters until relatives and friends can be located to adopt them."

"I'll definitely look into that possibility, Reverend Denny. Thank you for your suggestion."

When she finally arrived at her Brunswick Street home in the late afternoon Sophia collapsed on the sofa and massaged her ankles. She would write her report to the Red Cross in Washington the first thing tomorrow morning. Her superiors, she was positive, would read it with great interest. After that she'd begin searching for and organizing a team to transform the Brewster house into a temporary orphanage.

New beds are brought up frequently but a place is always found for them. We even have patients on the porch...a maternity case in the surgical room. Have patients of all nationalities and walks of life.

Chapter 12

Dear Bess: -
Heard the [city's] *school bells*
ringing here this A.M. Am still with
"Flus" & on account of the emergency
hospitals closing we've been besieged
with patients today but Dr. Roby says
it'll be over in another 10 days. It's just
dreadful seeing entire families wiped
out.

Alice had just enough time to change between her morning assignment in the men's ward and her meeting with Miss Keith. So she hurried back to the nurses home, exchanged her surgical gown for the powder-blue uniform, and anchored the pupil's cap to her top-knot bun with bobby pins. She was glad she hadn't given in to the impulse to cut her dark brown locks short like Emily's.

Her trickster classmate had all the luck. When they finally decided that the only thing the towel turban was useful for was to ward off pediculosis infestation, it had been banished as an official uniform component. Emily hadn't been the only pupil to cut her hair short. The idea caught on with the bolder pupils while the epidemic raged. Now their tresses were just growing back, making it hard to anchor the fragile up-side-down cupcake cap. So a general announcement had been made about all pupils' hairdos; they had to be combed tightly toward the back of the head so that everyone appeared as if they still had long hair.

Before leaving her room, Alice opened the desk drawer and removed the sealed envelope she had placed there a few weeks ago. Whatever Miss Keith wanted to talk with her about wouldn't matter. She intended to withdraw from the school. Of course, she'd miss her classmates, but she just couldn't continue watching helplessly while more sick people, especially her hospital family and closest friends, suffered and died. She would always feel powerless against invisible invaders.

Since Poppa and Momma had passed, she hadn't had time to realize the emotional toll the epidemic was taking. The demands that the disease made on her hadn't given her a moment to weep or to scream in anger at the unfairness of it all, the senseless waste.

Now that the epidemic was waning and she had a minute to think, she decided that nursing was not the right career for her. She could not spend her adult life surrounded by sickness and death.

The sky was cloudless, so she decided to take the sidewalk to the Administration Building rather than going through the subterranean tunnel. The late morning sun, no longer filtered through lush summer foliage, was warm, and she needed only a sweater.

The few leaves that still clung to tree branches shivered in the light breeze. The ones that had fallen to the ground made swishing sounds under each footstep. The scene transmuted into a metaphor in her imagination. The nearly barren trees were remnants of humanity left in the wake of the war and the epidemic. Her classmates were the leaves still holding tightly to the branches. She would soon be one of the dry, dead ones crumbling on the ground. The image was uncomfortable, so she dismissed it and hurried on.

Arriving in the Superintendent's Office anteroom, she hurried to Miss Keith's office door. Folding chairs flanked each side. It looked as if they'd been separated there to discourage interviewees from talking with each other. Emily was sitting in one of them, waiting for her turn.

Alice sat in the empty chair and leaned toward her friend. "Do you know why she wants to meet with us one at a time?" she whispered.

Emily shook her head no. The curls, a little longer than Alice had seen them last, did a kind of dance. *The short bob makes her look a lot cuter*, Alice thought. *Kind of like the mischievous little kid she really is.*

"Probably to scold me for cutting my hair," her friend whispered back. "But Susan's in there now, and she obeys all the rules. So it's probably not a scolding for her."

"Are you still seeing your young Chinese friend? What was his name again? Maybe that's why she wants to talk with you."

"That was Chen. And, no. His family weren't any more enthusiastic about our meetings than mine would have been if I'd told them about him." Emily shrugged her shoulders and spread her forearms apart. "Don't see what all the fuss is about. It was all pretty platonic. I don't think anything would have come of it anyway."

"You can never tell about matters of the heart, Emie. Maybe Miss Keith found out about it, and that's why she wants to see you. To warn you about the impropriety of that kind of a relationship."

The office door opened, and Susan came out, the corners of her lips turned upward in an artificial smile. "It's your turn, Emily," she said. Her classmate got up and entered the Superintendent's office.

"What does she want to see us about, Susan?" Alice whispered.

Susan frowned and pantomimed locking her lips with her fingers. Then she left the anteroom in a hurry.

Alice heard no raised voices through the door during Emily's interview, so she was optimistic that her friend's meeting was going well.

When the younger pupil finally exited, raised eyebrows and shrugged shoulders were the response to Alice's inquiring expression. "Just go in. You'll find out soon enough."

Closing the door behind her, Alice saw Miss Keith sitting behind an uncluttered desk, back straight, hands folded, and mouth smiling as usual.

"Have a seat please, Miss Denny."

The pupil decided to get the unpleasantness over as quickly as possible. Maybe that would cut the meeting short. Before she sat across from the administrator, she drew the envelope out of her apron pocket and handed it to the older woman.

Miss Keith frowned, but using a letter opener, she slit the envelope, withdrew and unfolded the stationery, and read the terse note in silence. Her expression did not change. Then she leaned over, opened a lower desk drawer, and withdrew a manila folder. She removed a stack of about a half dozen sheets of typewritten paper and, stretching across the desk, handed them to Alice.

"Read these please, Alice. They're all resignations and intentions to retire I've written over the past fifteen years."

Alice glanced through the small collection. Indeed, they were all tersely phrased, three-paragraph formal letters. The salutations of most of them addressed Mr. Henry Danforth, Esq., the hospital's long-serving Board of Directors President. Two had been written to Board of Lady Managers presidents.

"I wrote the first one in 1903. It is the one that came closest to actually being read by the person it was addressed to. It concerns what I consider my greatest failure. A pupil nurse, very much like you, Alice, was unable to prevent a mentally imbalanced woman from jumping to her death from the hospital's third floor window.

"I was completely focused on my own concerns – only the second year as Superintendent at the General – and I was learning my job. I failed to empathize with the young student nurse who must have been going through her own personal agony. Fortunately, she did finish her training, and now she has a career as a visiting nurse.

"But her success was no thanks to me. I should have made personal contact with her to help guide her through that traumatic experience. Since that time, I've tried not to make that mistake again. That's why I'm holding individual meetings with all of you pupils now that the epidemic is beginning to come under control. We've all experienced traumatic experiences in the past month and a half."

Alice looked up, admiration for the woman, who had steered the General Hospital through dozens of crises for more than fifteen years, clear in her eyes. She leafed through the remaining letters.

"A couple of those letters were just threats to emphasize my stance on proposed Board policy changes that I firmly opposed. I wrote a couple of them to discourage actions of the Lady Managers that I believed would undermine my authority as Superintendent."

The tears in Alice's eyes were threatening to spill over; she didn't notice that Miss Keith had moved from behind her desk. She looked up as the older woman drew a chair opposite hers and sat in it.

"You'd better take these before I get them wet," the pupil nurse said. With one hand she held out the sheets of paper; with the other she brushed a fugitive tear from her cheek.

Mary put the letters on her lap. She reached for both of Alice's hands and looked directly into her eyes. "The point is, Alice, I never delivered any of these letters. I've kept them as reminders of the challenges I've faced – and of the things I've learned about myself over the past decade and a half." She paused.

"Since last January you've been confronted by personal losses that many young women would consider to be insurmountable challenges."

Alice shifted uncomfortably. For months she had resisted thinking about those events.

"Last winter you came here to ask me for time off when your mother died, and again this spring for her interment service. It was then I began to realize how close she and you must have been.

"But you carried on. Your studies and your work have been outstanding, and your positive attitude has buoyed up the spirits of your classmates." The Superintendent leaned back and smiled. "You've been a distinct asset to this training school, you know.

"Then four of your best friends contracted this deadly sickness, and like everyone, you were in terror that you would lose them. Your duties have been sending you all around the hospital, at all hours of the day and night. And sometimes you've come back to find that a patient you were caring for had died and the ones who remained were just as sick as, or sicker than, they'd been the day before."

The memories breached the dam, releasing a flood of tears. Alice drew a handkerchief from her apron pocket. Miss Keith's right hand reached toward the back of the young woman's neck.

"Alice, I beg you to please take your letter back to your room, at least for a few days. The epidemic is beginning to weaken. We're discharging more recovered flu patients than we are admitting now. Your duty hours will be back to normal next week.

"When you go on duty then, please focus on the patients we're able to help, not just the dying ones. Surely, there'll be more fatalities, but fewer every day."

She drew Alice's head to her own shoulder, as a mother would. "I know you will make a wonderful nurse."

After a minute, Alice lifted her head, dried her cheeks and blew her nose, and then stowed the soggy handkerchief in her pocket. "All right, Miss Keith. I'll wait and think about what you've said. But I can't promise you anything."

Miss Keith went back to her desk and held out Alice's withdrawal letter and its envelope. The pupil put it back in her apron pocket.

"One more thing, Alice," said Miss Keith as she escorted the young woman to her office door.

"Yes?"

"Those half dozen friends of yours. Miss Gilman and I couldn't help but notice how close you all are. I know you're not a clique; you don't exclude any of the other pupils. But you're an unusual team. You support each other, and you brighten the spirits of everyone who works with you.

"We're tired of referring to you as 'those Intermediate pupils,' and having to change the name every time you move to the next level. In a couple of months, it'll be those Senior pupils. But, I must admit it's usually with pleasure and only seldom with aggravation. Will you please put your heads together and suggest a better name we can use for the group?"

Alice managed a smile. "I'll talk to the girls about it, Miss Keith. We don't all think alike, but more often than not, we eventually reach agreement."

Mary Keith ushered the interviewee to her office door. She waited a minute before inviting Hilda, her next appointment, in for their chat. With fingers crossed, she watched her new protégé, exit from the anteroom. The silly, cupcake-shaped cap now bobbled crookedly to one side, anchored by a single bobby pin.

The round table had already been set when Austin entered the little dining room that adjoined the nurses' cafeteria. As she had with other small gatherings, Mrs. Weston agreed to allow the group to enjoy their dessert in privacy for this special occasion. Seven place settings – dessert plate, fork, napkin, and tumbler – circled the rim of the round table. Two pitchers of deep amber cider perspired in the center.

It was Ernestine Bong's twenty-first birthday party, and the hostess placed a basket filled with good-wish notes at one place. Then she began filling the tumblers with cider. The real anniversary of Bong's natal day had happened a month ago, but the birthday girl had been recuperating in her dormitory bed on October 6th, and Austin herself had been a patient in one of the influenza wards, unable to move without her head exploding in pain. She'd been in no condition to plan for a party.

Led by the carrot-haired honoree, five of the friends entered the room, chatting and giggling as they came. Emily, as usual, was holding forth about the election on November 5th. The new women voters had showed the men that they were a political force to be reckoned with. And for weeks they'd practiced with the voting machine levers, so they hadn't been "all thumbs" as some of the men had expected.

"You just wait," the young suffragist said. "In two years women'll be able to vote for President, not just local and state candidates. Wish I'd been old enough to do it this time. It must have felt like when a woman switched on her first electric light." Her arms gestured a wide explosion. "Suddenly! The power to light up an entire room, without having to ask a man for permission."

"But Emie," argued Susan, "weren't you on the Democrats' side? And didn't the Republicans win?"

"That was inevitable in Republican Rochester," came the answer. "But the votes from the soldiers in the training camps haven't all been counted yet. And the governor's race is still really close. I know Mr. Al Smith is going to win over that stuffy old Governor Whitman. Want to bet?" She put her hand out to seal the proposed verbal wager. There were no takers.

Susan's lips tightened into a circle, and she wrinkled her nose. "It's not proper for a lady to bet," she objected.

Austin led Bong to the place of honor. "Everyone's written you a birthday wish, Bong. You can read them now or wait until later."

"I go on duty tonight at ten. I'd rather wait and read them then." She looked around at the group, counting. "We're not all here, but I'll count again." Finishing the recount she wondered. "Six of us present, but where is Ben?"

At the sound of her adopted name, Alice pushed open the swinging door to the kitchen and entered with a huge platter holding a pyramid of rolled pastries.

"Cannoli!" Norma and Hilda exclaimed. Each of the pupil nurses chose a chair.

"Cannoli? What's that?" Susan complained, her nose still wrinkled.

"They're Italian pastries," Alice explained. Smiling, she circled the table, offering the dessert to each guest. "Take two if you want. Mrs. ...or rather Mama...Privitera insisted on making lots of them. They can't hold candles for Bong to make a wish on, but they're as good as cake and there's a delicious filling inside them."

"Is she still volunteering here?" Emily wanted to know.

"Yes. When we had room for regular patients again, rather than just influenza ones, she was afraid the hospital wouldn't need her any more. She's loved helping out here so much. Felt like she was doing something valuable. Miss Keith has just hired her to come in a couple of times a week to help in the kitchen and to share her recipes. " Emily filled her tumbler with cider and passed the pitcher.

"They're the best meals I ever ate." Bong took two of the pastries. "In the past month I've gained way too much weight." Then a third sweet tube joined the first pair. "But 'cause it's my birthday, an extra I'll take. Cannolis won't last long, like our Christmas fruit cake."

Frowning, Susan looked at the sugar-dusted cylinder on her plate. "How do you eat it? They look crisp. This one'll crumble as soon as my fork touches it."

"They're finger food, Susan. Just pick it up and bite into one end." Norma reached her hand toward her own serving.

"Wait a minute. We have to sing 'Happy Birthday' to Bong," interrupted the hostess. And the septet sang a lusty version, with Austin's voice off key as usual.

"So, what's on our agenda tonight, Austin?" Norma asked around the mouthful of the cannoli she had bitten into as soon as the serenade ended.

"How 'bout all going around and telling about the saddest thing we saw in the hospital?" Susan suggested. "Pass me that platter, will you, Hilda? These are really good." She wiped a dab of the sweet cheese filling from the corner of her mouth.

The other party guests responded immediately:

"Too depressing!"

"Good heavens, no!"

"Why on earth would we want to do that?"

Those who had full mouths merely groaned.

"Miss Keith called us all in for a private talk last week," Alice said. "You wouldn't tell me what she told you when you came out of her office, Susan." She looked at each of her other classmates. "And none of you have said anything about your interviews either. So, what did she say to you?"

Susan pouted for a moment. "She thanked me for working so hard after I got over the influenza. And then she told me I will make a good nurse if I loosen up a little –don't tell other people what to do or how to think all the time."

"She thanked me, too," said Norma. "And she congratulated me on learning to get along with different people, more than just Canadians. I'm glad I decided to do that after my other countrymen – or rather country women– graduated last spring."

"Me too," Emily added. "But not the part about getting along. She said I'm probably too quick to break traditions. Said my impulsiveness might eventually get me into deep trouble. I think she was remembering that day we ran the suffragist pennant up the flagpole."Her tawny eyebrows met in a frown. "At least, I hope that's what she was referring to."

"Do you suppose she knows about Chen? Or your new hairdo? Or your electioneering for the Democrats? Or not wearing the official corset?" asked Alice.

"How would she ever know that?"

Alice felt a warm flush rise from her neck to her cheeks, remembering her own interview. "She knew a lot of personal things about me. Was I ever surprised."

"Talk about being surprised," Hilda added."After thanking me for being on duty all those extra hours without complaining, she asked me about my boy friend, Charley. Where he was, and when I thought he'd be discharged and we could get married. How'd she find out about all of that?"

It was the birthday girl's turn. She brushed a small dusting of confectioner sugar off her apron's bodice and put a half-eaten fourth cannoli back on her plate. "She said she was sorry that I'd gotten sick. And she wanted us to name our little clique."

"No!" Alice protested. "She told me they don't think of us as a clique. We don't exclude anyone."

"You know what I meant by that word this time. It's the only word I could use to rhyme."

Austin took her turn next. "Like you, Susan, she sympathized with me for getting the flu. Then she thanked me for organizing the high school volunteers into teams. Thought I'd end up as an administrator, maybe in a hospital or as a Red Cross recruiter. And yes, she mentioned adopting a name for us. And you're right, Alice. She said we weren't a clique, just a very close-knit team." She turned to her classmate whose pink cheeks were now becoming brighter. "So, Ben, confess. What did she say to you?"

"She encouraged me to bring up choosing a name for our group, too." Alice's halting response made it clear she was demurring.

"Come on, now, speak up."

"Well," came the reluctant response, "I had brought a letter with me, and she asked me not to leave it with her. To take it back to my room and think about it."

"And? What was in the letter?"

The words finally burst through Alice's privacy fortress. "My intention to withdraw from the school. I was exhausted when I wrote it a couple of weeks ago. There was sickness and death all around me. I just couldn't see any end to it. And I thought I couldn't spend the rest of my working days just trying to keep dying people alive."

The young women stopped chewing and sipping. One by one they left their places and gathered around their classmate.

"You can't mean it, Alice!"

"You're too smart to do anything else. I couldn't have gotten this far without your tutoring," Norma protested.

"And you're too good a nurse! I'd want anyone who's even remotely like you on my team."

"What else will you do? Now that the war's over, they're forcing women workers back into domestic work to make room for the soldiers coming back." This from Emily.

"You ought to go into teaching, Alice. You'd keep those youngsters in line," Susan advised.

When the comforters began to give Alice some room to speak, she stood up and withdrew an envelope from her pocket. "So I did think about it for awhile. And I remembered how I'd miss all of you if I did withdraw. That helped me shake off my self pity. This is the letter." She tore the envelope in half, then in half again and again. Everyone applauded.

When they had retrieved their places at the table, Austin took over the meeting again. "Well, now. Since Miss Keith would like us to adopt a name, what should we call ourselves?"

"How about Seven Nursing Sisters?"

"Nope, too many syllables."

"That'd make us sound like we're a religious order."

"The Magnificent Seven?"

"We're good, but we're not 'magnificent' yet."

"The Naughty Nurses?" Another suggestion from Emily, her eyes sparkling with mischief.

"No!". . . ."No!"

"Wait a minute. How about looking ahead? It shouldn't just be about what we are now, but who we want to be." Austin said. "Something that has to do with our goal. A symbol?" She raised one hand to the top of her head. "Like graduate nurses' caps. That's my goal anyway —to get rid of these ridiculous upside-down cupcakes we have to wear."

"M-m-mine, too. That'll be the day; it'll be so grand, when we all can wear the black velvet band."

"That's it!" Hilda broke in. "'Band' can mean a team of talented and capable people, like a musical group. But for nurses the 'band' is the black ribbon that identifies the training school they attended."

The vote was unanimous, and Austin was elected to make an appointment with the hospital's Superintendent. It would have to be a time, they insisted, when everyone was off duty. The entire membership of "Black Velvet Band" wanted to announce their official name all together. Like a christening.

Sophia Palmer winced as the heat from the oven door rose to her cheeks. But the smell that was filling her small kitchen was so tempting. By the time her guests arrived, the aroma would have flooded the entire first floor. She basted the turkey one last time. The grease flowed smoothly around the bird's breast and legs, making them shiny again. It sizzled as it reached the farther edges of the pan where it blended with the other caramel-colored drippings.

As she minced the giblets for the gravy, the Red Cross recruiter remembered how she had always loved the spicy atmosphere of Thanksgiving. This year's holiday was even more welcome than past ones had been. The war in Europe was over! A little over two weeks ago the aggressors had surrendered. The doctors and nurses would be returning in a few months, veterans now.

And the influenza epidemic was slowly coming under control. The general hospitals were no longer bursting at the seams with critical cases. Beginning with the Gannett House, the emergency hospitals had closed one by one, their recovering patients transferred to the General, the

Homeopathic, St. Mary's, and the Hahnemann. Although there were still spikes in serious flu cases, the infection seemed to be exhausting itself, weakening. And death notices were trending downward.

The hostess smiled to herself as she remembered her disappointment of a year and a half ago. Then, she'd been too old to sign up for duty in the training camps or for service in overseas hospitals. In the past two months, though, she'd met more challenges than she'd experienced in her five-year tenure as a hospital superintendent. More than in the battle with Albany politicians to establish trained nursing as a recognized profession. Now, she realized, she'd be content to return to the mundane, but predictable, tasks she'd taken on in her retirement.

The doorbell rang just as she replaced the tasty bits in the pot they'd been simmering in. She wiped her hands on her apron and walked to the foyer to welcome the guests.

"Happy Thanksgiving!" Mary Keith and Maude Johnston greeted her in unison.

Sophia took a tray covered with waxed paper from Superintendent Keith. "Looks interesting, Mary. What is it?"

"Antipasto," her guest answered as she breathed in deeply. "Mmmm. Smells good in here." She stowed her coat and hat in the front closet .

"It's Italian. Means 'before the spaghetti.' Actually it's a meal all by itself, a mix of tastes and textures that'll surprise your tongue. Wonderful salad greens, marinated olives, cheeses, and bites of dried meats in an olive oil and vinegar bath. And every now and then an anchovy, a little explosion of flavor. This wonderful Italian woman on our kitchen staff showed me how to make it.

"Let me take that, Maude. And just find a hanger for your coat and hang it next to mine." She took her companion's offering, a deep basket covered by a towel. Lifting a corner of the cover, she breathed in again "What's in here?"

"Dinner rolls," Maude said, shutting the clothespress door. "And an apple pie. Still warm from the oven." The Homeopathic Hospital's administrator looked down the hall toward a kitchen brightened by sunlight. "I love your house, Sophia. And the neighborhood's so neat. What made you move here?"

"Thanks for bringing such delicacies, ladies." The hostess handed the tray back to Mary and led the trio toward the kitchen. "I decided I should live close to Red Cross headquarters when we got so busy there. This little Cape Cod suited my needs perfectly. The turkey's done. All that's left to do is make the gravy. Then we can sit down to the feast."

Half way down the hall a pocket door archway led into a small, simply furnished dining room. They paused to admire the room, which was dominated by a circular table. Around its circumference were three formal place settings. In its center was a raffia cornucopia that spilled real apples and grapes onto the white table cloth.

"Wine goblets, Sophia?" Mary asked. "I thought there wouldn't be a drop left in Rochester. Washington hasn't lifted the wartime restrictions on distilling, wine making, and brewing yet. Where'd you get the spirits?"

"The nurses with the 19th General all pitched in and sent me a case of French wines. Luckily, it survived the ocean voyage. But a stipulation came with the gift. I'll tell you about that later."

"I for one hope the government doesn't lift the restrictions," interrupted Maude. "The hospitals will be far less crowded when there's no more alcohol, not even the two-and-a-half percent beer. There'll be fewer accident victims run over by inebriated drivers, fewer wives beaten by their husbands, fewer malnourished children whose fathers imbibe their paychecks every week."

"Sorry, Maude. I forgot you were a member of WCTU. I do wish you could join us in a Thanksgiving toast," Sophia apologized. "You, Mary?"

"No, I'm not a teetotaler, Sophia. I hope it's red. I think of red wine as medicinal. A sip in the evening relaxes me, especially after days like the ones we've just been through."

"It's a claret, Mary. And yes, I think of it as a tonic – thins the blood, calms the nerves, but only in very small doses. I've been hoarding the gift for occasions like this.

"But I agree with you, too, Maude. I don't believe that the war-time regulations will be lifted in spite of the armistice. We'll most likely continue to have at least a partial prohibition until all the States agree on a Constitutional Amendment."

Removing one of the wine glasses, she placed it in the china cabinet. "Just put the tray there on the sideboard, Mary. And you can put the basket there too, Maude. We'll pass them around when we sit down."

The three women moved to the aromatic room at the end of the hallway. "Mary, the cranberry sauce is in the ice box. And the butter on that counter must be room temperature by now, Maude. Will you please put them on the table?"

The guests busied themselves carrying condiments and serving utensils to the table in the dining room while Sophia made the gravy and poured it into a boat.

"I think we're ready," the hostess said. She turned off the oven, opened its door, and extracted the *entré*, its gleaming skin a crisp, toasty-brown now. Then she transferred the plump bird to a serving platter. "Why don't you put your pie into the oven, Maude. Then it'll be warm by the time we're ready for it."

The trio processed to the table, Mary carrying a generous mound of mashed potatoes and the gravy boat, Maude with a tureen of golden yams, and Sophia bearing the roasted turkey, nestled among steaming scoops of dressing.

When they were seated and she was adding slices of breast meat to the limbs on another platter, Sophia said, "Rather than beginning this meal with a Thanksgiving prayer, why don't we start by recalling some of the experiences we've been through in the past few months that make this the most memorable Thanksgiving of our lives. Will you start us off, Mary?"

Mary filled half of each remaining goblet with claret from a carafe. She picked up her goblet, carefully inspecting its deep red color; then thrusting her nose into the glass, she inhaled its aroma. She raised her goblet toward the hostess.

"My first thank you goes to you, Sophia, for thinking that we were so special that you wanted to share this meal with us. And this wonderful tincture of grapes."

She turned to Maude. "And thank you, Maude. I remember the day I was most discouraged. You reminded me that I needed to pay attention to those who depend on my expertise, not focus on my frustration with people who weren't considering the practical aspects of the health crisis. In other words, I'm most thankful for loyal friends and colleagues like you both, who work with me as a team."

Sophia raised her wine glass. "Hear! Hear!" The wine enthusiasts sipped the crimson nectar. Maude sipped water from her larger tumbler. "I second the motion!"

Sophia passed the meat platter to Maude, Mary passed the antipasto to Sophia, and Maude passed the dinner rolls to Mary. "You're next," nominated the hostess, nodding toward Maude.

"Like Mary, my sincerest thanks go to each of you, my friends. Without your counsel, I wouldn't have survived the past several months. Frankly, ever since I became Superintendent of the Homeopathic, I've been at a real disadvantage. I'm a local girl, trained in the hospital I now superintend. As you may suspect, the group of benevolent women who founded it have kept a very firm hand on the running of our institution.

"That is, they have until the recent crisis. Until now, they've thought of me as a kind of servant, someone to carry out the Lady Managers' policies, transmit their demands to the hospital staff, and make sure that those policies were executed."

She glanced at her dinner partners. "Our working together has shown them – and me – that I have administrative capabilities beyond their own. Now that we're allowed to meet in groups again, I can hear the change in their voices. They respect me, almost as an equal, because I had the foresight they lacked during the epidemic. Thank you both for welcoming me into this outstanding team."

The response was unanimous:"You're very welcome!" "We're delighted to have you on our team!" "You've indeed been a distinct asset!"

Conversation during the remainder of the main meal was sparse. They speculated about whether the celebrations that took place when the end of the war was announced would cause a new surge in new influenza cases. War weary civilians had poured onto the streets, waving flags, hugging and kissing each other, singing patriotic songs. All without wearing the gauze face masks. For the most part, the women savored each bite, recalling now and then about how the scarcity of turkeys and other delicacies the previous Thanksgiving had driven prices to a point where only the well-heeled could afford a traditional dinner.

Finally satisfied, they folded their napkins and placed them next to empty dinner plates.

"So, now it's your turn, Sophia. What makes this Thanksgiving your most memorable one?"

"I'd rather wait 'til we cut into Maude's apple pie and have coffee if it's all right with you. There's some vanilla ice cream in the ice box if you'd like to top the pie off."

The diners agreed and cleared the table. Then Mary set out china cups and saucers and dessert plates. Sophia brought in the ice cream and a scoop while Maude carved generous wedges of the pie she'd extracted from the warm oven.

"All right, Sophia, is your most memorable Thanksgiving event related to the 'stipulation' that the 19th General nurses made when they sent you the wine?" Mary scooped a generous ball of ice cream onto her pie crust where it began to melt immediately.

Sophia cut into her wedge and savored the dessert. "M-m-m-m! Wonderful flavor, Maude. Just the right hint of nutmeg."

She turned back to Mary. "Your guess is right. The letter that came with the wine shipment was from Margaret Scarry. She came to me early on when Base Hospital 19 was starting to organize. She wanted to volunteer with them, but I discouraged her because I knew you needed her at the General, Mary.

"Then when Washington ordered the unit to double in size last winter and the National Red Cross told me I had to find more nurses, I authorized Margaret's leave of absence, allowing her to join the Base Hospital. So she got her wish."

"I remember Nurse Scarry," said Mary. "She used to be an instructor of our probation classes. Not a very patient one, as I recall."

"Well, she and the others are doing a great deal of good where they are now. But that's beside the point. Her letter told me that the case of wine was a bribe. Because they were overseas, the military nurses wouldn't be able to participate in the election on November 5th. They asked me to be sure to cast my vote – not for any specific candidate, but just to vote. If I did, I'd be acting as their surrogate voice."

"And were you able to?" asked Maude.

"Yes. Before one of my emergency hospital inspections last October I made time to register with the other first-time women voters. My polling place was the Frank Parker School, just a little way off from my usual route to the office. I took the same detour on Voting Day." She nodded to each of her guests. "Were you able to find the time? I realize that the registration days and the election happened at the peak of the epidemic. The hospitals were swamped."

"Luckily, my polling place was the Methodist Church on Monroe, just around the corner and a block away from the Homeopathic. I was able to slip away both times during lunch breaks," answered Maude. "And I made sure that my staff and the pupils who were old enough could take a few minutes to cast their ballots."

Mary reported next. "We were indeed very busy, Sophia, but Alice Gilman and I covered for each other. We both were able to register and vote at the Vocational School, just across King Street from Madison Park. Alice Gilman went early in the morning on November 5th, and I followed that afternoon. And Miss Smith scheduled times when our staff and pupils could sneak out for a few minutes to vote.

"The day was cool but clear, a perfect day for a brisk walk. So I cut through the Park and returned to the hospital by way of Madison Street. I remember feeling a warm glow as I passed the Anthony house. I could imagine Susan smiling down on those of us who were finally fulfilling her dream."

"I'm sure she was," said Maude. She put her last morsel of pie into her mouth and leaned back in her chair, full and content.

Sophia spooned the remaining dollop of ice cream from her plate into her coffee and stirred it. "By voting day, I was finally getting some time to breathe –and to think," Sophia continued.

"The epidemic was on the wane. In fact, we were about to close the emergency hospital at Gannett House. The city officials lifted the closing restrictions just in time, on Voting Day eve. That allowed us to assemble to cast our ballots." She sipped her coffee, blotted her lips, and leaned back as Maude had.

"It occurred to me one night last week that we've been waging a war ourselves. Only a quiet one," the hostess continued.

"That's right." Mary replaced her empty cup on its saucer. "I've been thinking along those same lines."

Maude began to stack her china and silver and stood up. "Why don't we explore your analogy while we do the dishes?" she suggested.

The trio cleared the table and, while Sophia washed, her guests towel dried the china, taking each piece back to the dining room table and carefully stacking them.

"So – to the analogy. Like the Army, a year and a half ago, I began enlisting nurses for the Red Cross. My first recruits were for duty overseas. Then nine months ago I had to find more nurses to serve in the military training camps. Finally, in the past two months I've been drafting any women who were willing to fight against the epidemic to volunteer here in Rochester."

"In a way, Maude and I have been recruiting too," Mary chimed in. "We've been encouraging high school girls to enroll in our training schools, even Canadian girls. And we've been instructing college women to take post-graduate courses that will qualify them for careers as registered nurses."

Maude nodded. "But our enemy, the Spanish influenza, was invisible. The scientists couldn't identify the deadly invader in their labs, so they haven't been able to create a vaccine against it."

She carried the goblet she'd been drying to the dining room, speaking as she went. "Our weapons were simple. Sputum cups, not rifles." Then they took turns, adding to a litany Maude had started.

"Bed pans, not bayonets."

"Clean sheets and pillowcases, not mud filled trenches."

"Morphine, not mortars."

"Ambulances and volunteered limousines, not airplanes and tanks."

"Gauze masks, not gas masks."

"And our troops wore surgical gowns, not khaki uniforms."

The stacks of soiled dishes next to the sink diminished steadily as towers of gleaming china rose on the dining room table. They had progressed to the serving plates and bowls now, installing them in kitchen cupboards and on pantry shelves.

Sophia continued. "We had no generals, colonels, or captains. Just Red Cross department heads, hospital administrators, and registered nurses. Our infantry were pupil nurses, volunteer housewives, furloughed teachers and high school students, church parishioners, and retired professionals."

She filled the sink again with hot water and began plunging the pots and pans into the frothing suds. "But there probably won't be newspaper photographs of our casualties, like there always are of men who fell in battle or died of influenza. How many of your nurses died of Spanish influenza, Maude? I lost two volunteer housewives in the Y. W. C. A. emergency wards."

"One of our head nurses," added Maude. "But another one of our graduates caught it in one of the training camps and died there."

"And at the General, Mary?"

"Only one. A student nurse, but a very promising one. So young," Mary sighed.

The litany went on:

"No purple hearts for the hundreds of hospital nurses and staff members who were deathly ill."

"No Distinguished Service Crosses for the ones killed in the line of duty, either here or overseas."

"No detailed newspaper columns praising them for giving their lives for their country. Just a single mention in the Death Notices column."

"And there definitely won't be grand monuments to memorialize them."

Sophia rinsed the roasting pan and put it on the drain board. "You can let that air dry, Mary." She emptied and scoured the sink and dried her hands on a towel.

"Maybe we're being too negative here. I don't think monuments or medals are why we do what needs to be done. Let's just be thankful we made a difference in the crisis." She reached for her companions' hands. "Thank you, God, for that opportunity."

"Amen!" the guests agreed. Then they retired to the sitting room for lighter conversation.

"I'll wager that 1918 will be marked as a very important pivotal year of this century," Mary began.

Maude continued. "And that careers for women will become unlimited, our opportunities expanded as the twentieth century goes on. "Who knows what we women can do when we're given the opportunity to do it?"

The litany took over again:

"Board of Directors members?"

"Executives in important companies?"

"Airplane pilots?"

"Olympic champions?"

"Recognized scientists?"

"Powerful legislators?"

"Foreign diplomats?"

"President of the United States?"

Epilogue

The Settings

Black Velvet Band covers a period that included the initial steps in the transformation of early hospitals from benevolent institutions into modern health systems based on the business model. Before 1918 hospitals were funded primarily by private benefactors and wise investments made by boards of directors, augmented by proceeds from social fund raising events. In addition, local governments compensated the institutions with frugal reimbursements for the care of charity patients; private patient fees subsidized those who could not afford the full cost of their care, and church and fraternal groups sponsored free beds for patients with limited means of support.

One of the most valuable financial resources for a hospital was the establishment of a school of nursing. While they were in training, students gained practical experience while performing increasingly important patient care duties. Compensated by meager allowances and free room and board, their service allowed a hospital to maintain a minimum staff of paid head nurses and instructors, thereby limiting an institution's operating costs.

St. Mary's Hospital, established in a renovated stable in 1857, was the first institution to accept patients in Rochester. Operated by a handful of religious sisters, it served the city's impoverished sick during the first few years. During the Civil War years, its patient census swelled to included Union Army casualties. St. Mary's established a training school for nurses in 1893, continuing to operate under the direction of religious nuns until the late 1990s when it joined Park Ridge Hospital to form the Unity Health System. Documents related to St. Mary's Hospital are housed in the Rochester Medical Museum and Archives, Rochester, N. Y.

The General Hospital referred to in *Black Velvet Band* is based on the historic Rochester City Hospital, which was renamed General Hospital in 1911. Opened in 1864, the early hospital was located on West Main Street. In the 1950s a second, more modern branch was built to serve the northeast area of the city. For a few years thereafter, residents called the new campus Northside Hospital. The two institutions coexisted for ten years, after which the older location was sold to the City of Rochester and the newer institution inherited the name, Rochester General Hospital. Rochester City/Rochester General Hospital's Training School for Nurses began preparing nurses in the profession in 1881; its last class graduated in 1964. Documents related to Rochester General's history are preserved in the Rochester Medical Museum and Archives, Rochester, NY.

Like St. Mary's and Rochester City hospitals, the Homeopathic Hospital arose from the benevolent spirit of its founders. The institution retained its ideological identity until the spring of 1926 when it adopted allopathic or regular medical practices along with a new name, The Genesee Hospital. This facility continued to operate as an independent institution until 1994 when it affiliated with Rochester General Hospital. The campus on Alexander Street ceased operation as a general hospital in 2001. The training school for nurses was established in 1889, the year of the hospital's founding, and it graduated its last class in 1978. Documents related to both its nurse training school and the Hospital's history are preserved in The Rochester Medical Museum and Archives, Rochester, NY.

St. Mary's Hospital established a training school for nurses in 1893. The institution continued to operate under the direction of an order of nuns until the late 1990s when it joined Park Ridge Hospital to form the Unity Health System. Documents related to St. Mary's Hospital are housed in the Rochester Medical Museum and Archives, Rochester, NY.

The Hahnemann Hospital was established by a group of homeopathic physicians in 1889. Renamed Highland Hospital in the fall of 1921, the institution became a unit of the Strong Health System. Documents related to Highland Hospital may be found in the Rare Books and Special Collections division at The University of Rochester.

The Villain

The convergence of three issues in the United States in 1917 and 1918—the curtailment of manufacture, sale, and transportation of spirituous liquors; the enfranchisement of New York State's women; the participation of all citizens in the country's involvement in World War I—identifies those years one as one of the most tumultuous periods of the twentieth century. The arrival of the deadly 1918 influenza pandemic paralyzed America's major cities and challenged their leaders as no previous epidemic had ever done.

The Spanish influenza epidemic was not the first pandemic to reach America's shores. Early in December 1889 another deadly strain of the disease began to blanket the world, rising first in Russia and spreading westward. However, the results in illness and deaths were less severe than those suffered in the 1918 event, and the latter attack affected communities in far different ways. For one thing, its preferred victims were mostly within the typical influenza flu age range: young children and the elderly. In contrast, the 20th century strain favored healthy young men and women during their most active and productive years.

During the earlier epidemic Americans felt protected by geography at first, but within a few weeks, the disease reached this continent and was quickly spreading. Public health was in its infancy, so quarantining ships from abroad was the only procedure used by coastal and inland waterway authorities to stop the infection's spread. Schools, theaters, and other places of entertainment remained open. Newspaper readers in the 1890s were much more concerned about potential strikes and articles of local interest than they were in the epidemic, so there are few newspaper articles that detail its progress.

The most frequently asked question about the 1918 pandemic is "How many people died?" There can be no definitive answer. Influenza visitations were seasonal, like the common cold, so the disease was not reportable until the epidemic was well underway. Estimates of the mortality rate in the United States can only be guessed at, based mostly on the illness's prevalence among soldier victims in training camps who underwent daily roll calls. Elsewhere, hundreds of thousands of civilians were undoubtedly cared for in their homes by family members and neighbors. In remote, isolated rural areas, cases and deaths may have even gone unreported.

The Spanish influenza's short duration also contributed to its reputation as the "forgotten" pandemic. The disease did linger after the two-month crisis it caused in American urban centers, but in a continually weakening form. Thousands of cases and hundreds of deaths did occur after Armistice Day, November 11, 1918, but the disease was gradually transmuting to its typical course: a short-term malady that caused misery for a few weeks, but from which most victims recovered without complications. In fact, the announcement of Germany's capitulation may have extended the epidemic somewhat, at least in Rochester. Newspaper photographs of bunting-clad, euphoric civilians celebrating the end of wartime anxieties and restrictions – every one of the subjects without the ubiquitous gauze face masks they had worn for the past two months – suggest that those who had not yet been exposed yet might have soon become new victims.

The Heroes

Meeting the particular challenges that the epidemic posed required personal resources and specialized skills beyond the abilities of city officials, hospital board members, and even private physicians. The historic record shows that closing of schools, churches, and places of entertainment failed to retard the spread of the disease. Hospital governing boards, whose concerns were primarily financial, had little, if any, involvement in the day-to-day operation of the institutions they directed. Community leaders, focused as they were on the city's commitment to winning the war through factory production and contributions to successive Liberty Loan drives, had no time for anything else. Physician groups were powerless, particularly because the medical theories they espoused were in competition with each other. In fact, the curtailment of social and cultural gatherings created a vacuum of information about heroes that might later have been gleaned from minutes of meetings that were never held and annual reports that could not be compiled with accuracy.

It would take a unique person to be able to marshal the community's health care resources in meeting the crisis. Such a person:
- would have earned the respect of community leaders in health care affairs;
- would have an authoritative voice in the activities of the American Red Cross in Washington;
- would have been acutely sensitive to the handicaps she was placing on local hospitals every time she recruited the hundreds of area nurses for the military's voracious appetite;
- would have been familiar with existing adjunct health facilities and their staffs and able to facilitate the neighborhood centers' transition into emergency hospitals;
- would have been the person to whom the general hospital administrators could look for guidance;
- would have been able to compromise on her personal conviction that only hospital-trained nurses should be depended on for service in institutions for the care of the sick. This overwhelming health care emergency prompted her to change her mind . . . at least for the duration of the crisis.

Sophia Palmer, R.N. fits those qualifications. Miss Palmer had first gained the community's respect in the 1890s and early twentieth century as the Superintendent of Rochester City Hospital. She had gained the respect of the nursing profession as a leader in the crusade for New York State's recognition of the first, self-regulated profession for women. Nationally, she was known in her profession as the founder and editor of the *American Journal of Nursing*. During World War I, Miss Palmer gained prominence in Washington as the Rochester district's advisor to the National Red Cross, credentials that carried great weight among Rochester's political, financial, and industrial leaders.

It would take persons with intimate familiarity with all hospital departments and personnel to mitigate the chaos that threatened Rochester's major health care institutions. Such persons:
- could anticipate the adjustments needed to meet the approaching crisis, *e.g.* curtailing elective procedures to make room for critical

influenza cases, establishing isolation areas to try to prevent cross infection, scheduling a skeletal team of overworked staff members with impartiality;

-would have gained the confidence of every member of a hospital staff who depended on their leadership;

-would be creative and adaptable when hospital corridors were glutted with suffering and dying patients;

-would model hopefulness when daily death counts consistently reached double digits

-would reflect confidence in the roles that every staff member played in keeping the institution afloat, from the head nurses in the wards to the students in the training schools to the ambulance drivers to the dishwashers and laundresses;

-would be able to overcome their frustration when the military repeatedly siphoned off members of the hospitals' essential staffs, when national and local officials underreported the severity of the situation, and when the epidemic prostrated beloved colleagues and the defenseless young nursing students under her care.

Hospital Superintendents – Mary Keith, R.N., Maude Johnston, R.N., Sister Clementine, and Dr. Edward Lewis fit those roles. Miss Keith remained Superintendent of the General Hospital until July 1923. Miss Johnston continued to direct the Homeopathic Hospital until January 1930. Sister Clementine served at St. Mary's until Sister Gertrude replaced her in 1920. Dr. Lewis's tenure as superintendent of the Hahnemann Hospital lasted only during the year of the epidemic.

There were other heroes as well. Because of their youth, the students in the hospitals' nurse training schools placed their lives daily in great jeopardy. They exposed themselves to the contagion whenever they entered the hospital wards. Seeing the bodies of so many young patients being wheeled to the morgue must have been daunting. Finding a roommate suddenly stricken by the disease would have been frightening. Yet records that survive from one of the schools reveal no withdrawals from the rigorous training programs. Moreover, as Alice Denny's letters show, the students accepted unusually long work shifts despite grueling routines and depressing atmospheres without registering a complaint. Staff members in other positions were equally heroic. Even those who fell ill returned to their posts as soon as they recovered. Furthermore, Alice Denny, R.N. devoted the remainder of her working years to nursing. Although several members of the Black Velvet Band —Bong, Emily, Susan, Hilda, and Norma— eventually married and raised families, Alice and Austin devoted the remainder of their working years to nursing.

Finally, the thousands of civilians who placed their —and sometimes their families' – lives in danger, actively volunteered whenever and wherever they could help. Teachers, idled by school closings canvassed neighborhoods, boarding houses, and residential hotels to find individuals and entire families too sick to summon help. Housewives from all social classes rubbed elbows as well as washboards in emergency hospital kitchens and laundries. Wealthy matrons, used to being chauffeured to shopping trips and social events, transformed their own automobiles into delivery vehicles, ferried nurses to residences where they were needed, and delivered nourishing broths to victims stricken in their homes. Private families welcomed children, made orphans by the epidemic, into their own homes. With only factories and mercantile establishments open for business, white-collar professionals drove desperately needed nurses to stricken households, transported critically ill patients to hospitals, mopped floors, assembled hospital beds, changed linens, and emptied bed pans. Their only defense against the deadly disease was a flimsy gauze face mask.

The Spanish influenza epidemic of 1918 demonstrated that, when sudden deadly threats have occurred in this country, Americans do put aside our differences. As the stories of the characters in *Black Velvet Band* demonstrate, crises like the epidemic have the ability to bring out the heroic elements in the human spirit.

Chronology of Real-Time Events Referenced in *Black Velvet Band*

Date	Event
4/30/1901	Mary Keith, R. N. named Superintendent of City Hospital, replacing Sophia Palmer, R.N.
9/21/1903	Distraught, depressed Mrs. Cora Pierson jumps from City Hospital's 3rd floor window
1/1/1909	Rochester City Hospital renamed Rochester General Hospital
9/16/1914	William Denny, Alice's father, dies; Denny estate is mainly stock in Cyphers Co., Buffalo
9/2/1916	Major fire at Cyphers Co., destroys factory building
12/21/1916	Dr. John Swan begins recruits men & nurses for Base Hospital 19, anticipating the country's entry in war
1/9/1917	Alice Denny enters General Hospital's Training School for Nurses as a Probationer
2/16/1917	Names of early volunteers for Base Hosp. 19 published; list includes: Mary Laird, Eunice Smith, Margaret Scarry, General Hosp. RNs & Jessica Heal, Homeopathic Hosp. RN
2/20/1917	Cyphers Co. declares bankruptcy, devaluing Denny family estate; causes: over expansion, fires, wartime reduction in overseas orders & U-boat threat toward shipments
3/20/1917	Officers of Cyphers Co. declare personal bankruptcies; Pres. holds Denny family ins. policy
3/31/1917	Daylight Saving Time instituted for first time to conserve fuel
4/6/1917	*Democrat and Chronicle* headline: "President Signs War Resolution"; the U. S. officially enters the European war
6/6/1917	Operation at General Hosp. on 15 mo. toddler Harold Sisson who had swallowed an open safety pin
8/1/1917	Deadly heat wave (92 degrees); factories release afternoon workforces
10/20/1917	Dibble family automobile hit by locomotive; 7 victims sent to Gen. Hosp. & St. Mary's
11/6/1917	NYS's male electorate votes to allow female suffrage in State
11/12/1917	Amer. Nursing Assoc. holds national survey of trained nurses available for military duty; Sophia Palmer RN district director for local nurse recruitment & Red Cross Advisor is placed in charge
12/16/1917	Washington orders Base Hospital 19 to double original size

Date	Event
Jan. 1918	Cold wave freezes Northeast; coal shipments halted; rail traffic stalled; coal "famine"
2/10/1918	Sarah Denny, Alice's mother dies in Buffalo
4/6/1918	Roch.'s third Liberty Loan Parade; largest in city's history; contingents of women marchers
5/19/1918	Sunday, Lilac Day in Rochester
5/20/1918	Base Hospital 19 leaves Rochester, bound for France
5/22/1918	Toddler Mildred Wright seriously injured, hit by automobile, taken to General Hospital
6/16/1918	General Hospital agrees to admit soldiers from training camps who have been become infected with tuberculosis
6/19/1918	Supt. Mary Keith pleads for more medical professionals for service in local hospitals
6/22/1918	General Hospital exonerated of maltreatment charge in Mildred Wright case
7/14/1918	*D & C* first reports Spanish influenza among German troops
8/16/1918	Newspapers report Spanish influenza now in France and England
9/15/1918	1,000 cases of Spanish influenza reported in a single day at Fort Ayers Training Camp, Mass., near Boston
9/22/1918	Norma Whitely, student nurse, falls victim to Spanish influenza at General Hospital
9/23/1918	Ernestine Bong, student nurse, falls victim to Spanish influenza at General Hospital
9/25/1918	Pvt. Alphonso Privitera admitted to General Hospital suffering from Spanish influenza
9/27/1918	Washington cancels draft call; Spanish influenza rampant in all training camps
9/27/1918	Dr. Roby reports two "suspected" cases in city; 6 cases have already been admitted to General Hospital
9/30/1918	Pvt. Alphonso Privitera dies at General Hospital; cause of death: Spanish influenza
Oct. 1918	Political meetings and campaign speeches suspended in Rochester; electioneering limited to handouts & posters
10/2/1918	Florence Austin, student nurse, falls victim to Spanish influenza
10/4/1918	Student nurses Whitely and Bong discharged from contagious ward, "well"
10/7/1918	Dr. Roby reports about 300 cases in city and claims that 17 Homeopathic hospital nurses have "grip," not Span. Infl

Date	Event
10/8/1918	Susan Kelsey, student nurse, falls victim to Spanish influenza
10/9/1918	Dr. Roby: probably more than 1,000 cases in city; 15 cases @ Hahnemann; 18 cases @ St. Mary's; denies 15 nurses have Spanish influenza @ Homeopathic – not influenza, but "grippe" instead
10/9/1918	City officials order schools, theaters, places of entertainment closed for a week
10/10/1918	Josephine Hearn, student nurse, admitted at General Hosp. with Spanish influenza
10/10/1918	Dr. Roby: Infl. now a reportable disease; private funerals only; 68 new cases in 24 hours
10/11,12, 18,19/1918	All persons must register to be able to vote; NYS women qualified to vote in a major election for the first time.
10/11/1918	Dr. Roby: 25 infl. deaths in 9 days; "situation is not alarming"; only emergencies admitted to hospitals; anyone with minimal nursing training requested to volunteer
10/12/1918	Ordinance forbidding spitting in public is being enforced
10/13/1918	Order: churches, saloons, hotel bars, club rooms, soda fountains, ice cream parlors closed
10/14/1918	Dr. Roby: "no real reason why the … epidemic … should be called Spanish Influenza"; student nurse Florence Austin discharged from hospital care "recovered"
10/15/1918	Student nurse Josephine Hearn dies of Spanish influenza at General Hospital
10/15/1918	Dr. Roby: 1,123 new cases reported yesterday; "situation not one for widespread alarm"
10/16/1918	Only ½ of city's physicians are reporting influenza cases; physicians falling ill at home
10/17/1918	3,333 total reported cases in the city; 26 firemen & 8 policemen ill; student Susan Kelsey discharged from hospital care "recovered"
10/18/1918	Closing order extended; women urged to apply as replacements for sick factory workers
10/18/1918	Idled principals, teachers, & students recruited to work in fruit harvest
10/19/1918	NYS Department declares influenza a reportable disease
10/19/1918	No empty beds in any general hospital; YWCA emergency hosp. opened for women & children
10/20/1918	Baden St. Settlement emergency hospital opened for critical male influenza victims

Date	Event
10/21/1918	City Council considers opening emergency hospital at Convention Hall Annex; plan subsequently rejected
10/22/1918	50+ streetcar motormen and trolley barn workers out sick
10/23/1918	7,237 cases reported thus far; [thousands more being treated at home by families]
10/24/1918	Lewis St. Housekeeping Center opened as emergency hospital for critical men & boys
10/25/1918	City closing to continue; education, cultural, social meetings discouraged
10/25/1918	N. Y. Gov. Whitman's scheduled campaign visit cancelled because of epidemic
10/26/1918	Vacant mansions begin to act as orphanages and shelters for children of stricken parents
10/27/1918	Temperatures of new cases not as high; fewer pneumonia cases as complications
10/29/1918	Gannett House @ Unitarian Church opened as convalescent hospital
10/30/1918	State Armory on East Main St. opened for convalescing patients
11/4/1918	City ban on public gatherings lifted
11/5/1918	Voting Day; NYS women first vote in a major election; Al Smith (D) defeats C. Whitman (R)
11/6/1918	Schools reopened; Gannett House emergency hospital closes
11/8/1918	Hospitals have room for critical cases; Baden St. hospital closes
11/11/1918	Armistice Day; World War I ends
11/14/1918	State Armory convalescent hospital closes
11/16/1918	Y. W. C. A. emergency hospital closes
11/19/1918	Lewis Center emergency hospital closes
11/27/1918	Health Bur. tally of epidemic in Roch.: 13,698 reported cases; 785 certified deaths

Images

The Heroes

Sophia F. Palmer, R. N.

Mary L. Keith, R.N.

Maude L. Johnston, R. N.

Images above courtesy of Rochester Medical Museum and Archives

Alice May Denny
in her student uniform, about 1917
Photograph courtesy of John Linfoot

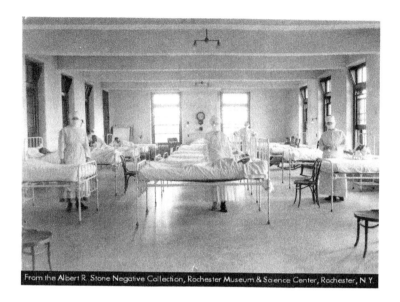

Influenza Wards, Rochester General Hospital, Autumn 1918

From the Albert R. Stone Negative Collection,
Rochester Museum & Science Center, Rochester, NY

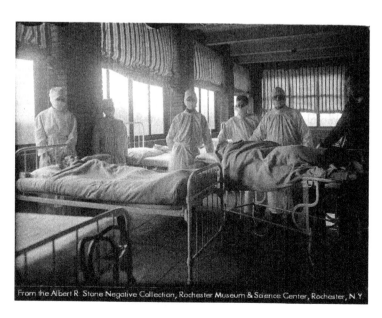

Teresa K. Lehr

Acknowledgments

Twenty years ago, I began researching how the Spanish influenza pandemic of 1918 affected people in various communities across New York State. During my research I gradually realized how few of the historic records that detailed the disease's deadly threat survived. Communities had closed down; meetings had been suspended, which left blank spaces in minute books and among annual reports; officials were preoccupied with generating resources for the country's pursuit of the Great War, so the invasion became a secondary issue.

When I came across the letters written to her sister Bess by student nurse Alice Denny, RGH Class of 1920, and signed "Alice," I knew I had stumbled on a rare, first-hand account of the crisis as it and other events played out during one of America's earliest health care institutions. In the early 1990s, those letters had been donated to the Baker-Cederberg Museum and Archives (currently the Rochester Medical Museum and Archives), the historic repository of Rochester General Hospital. They were a goldmine of information about student life in early residential nurse training schools, the evolution of nursing education, and the local history of Rochester, N. Y. And they recorded personal glimpses into the lives of a hospital's staff during the deadly emergency.

But when serendipity appeared in the form of a genealogical study of the William C. Denny family, that goldmine transformed into a veritable treasure chest. There were other letters, obviously written by the same author but signed "Ben." Not only did the Denny family representative still have those letters, but he and his family were willing to share the information in them with me. I owe John Linwood and other descendants of the Denny family a huge debt of gratitude for recognizing the historic value of the epistolary collection they had preserved for 100 years and more, for the essential role the letters played in helping to flesh out the narrative of *Black Velvet Band*, and for making the priceless historical details included in the Denny correspondence collection available for research.

I am also indebted to local repositories that preserve Rochester's historic documents and make them available for research. RMMA, under the direction of Archivist Kathleen Britton, has been a treasure house of factual information about Rochester City/Rochester General Hospital, the Homeopathic/Genesee Hospital, and St. Mary's Hospital. In addition, the local History Division of Rochester Public Library's in-house and online collections of city directories, period maps, photographs, etc. allowed me to locate the sites and neighborhoods that appear in the novel and to recreate details that contributed to the community's social ambiance.

My consultations with groups and individuals revealed sensitivities that allowed me to give the historical characters personalities. For example,

180

interviews of graduates from Rochester General's and The Genesee Hospital's Schools of Nursing affirmed my suspicion that their shared experiences as students residing together in a female dormitory were a blend of a lot of seriousness with a little bit of silliness. And professionals, like the physician and medical student members of the University of Rochester's Corner Society, advocates for the study of the history of medicine, answered medical and technical questions such as how would a surgeon have removed a swallowed open safety pin from a 15-month old toddler's stomach in 1918.

Writers' groups and other individuals have been invaluable. They read my early drafts carefully, with creative and critical eyes. Observations and suggestions from Word Crafters were particularly insightful and encouraging. The critiques offered me by Night Writers sometimes prompted me to rethink early drafts. And I am further obliged to Rochester City Historian Christine Ridarski, to Sylvia Schenck, RN, Bs, MS, graduate of The Genesee Hospital Class of 1968, and to award-winning story teller, Almeta Whitis, who wrote reviews of their impressions after reading the manuscript.

Finally, I thank long-time neighbor Dave McDowell, whose computer wizardry transformed an embarrassingly pink cover image into one that better reflected historic symbols of the past. And thank you to Dave's wife Fran who loaned him to me one, very cold, January afternoon.

About the Author

Teresa K. (Terry) Lehr has been researching and writing about the history of health care, particularly in Rochester, N.Y., since 1990 when she became Assistant Curator in the Baker-Cederberg Museum and Archives. Ferreting out the unwritten stories she found among the documents in that repository became an obsession which has lasted throughout an eighteen-year hiatus when she served as a full-time lecturer in the Department of English at the College at Brockport, N. Y. and continues in her retirement years.

Upon her retirement in 2011, Terry brought to completion another long-term project, the transcription and abridgment of a collection of Civil War letters, which she had embarked upon with a coeditor colleague in 1994. It was at this juncture that Terry decided that factual history didn't satisfy her enough. She wanted to see the actors move and hear their voices.

So she decided to augment documented information with social context details and with elements that fiction writing involves. Like *Black Velvet Band*, her first history-plus-fiction book, *The Great Tonsil Massacre*, is based on a 1920, 1921 public health project that was promoted and supported by George Eastman and other Rochester industrialists and mercantilists. Most of its characters, however, are imagined creations ordinary people, their emotions, motivations, and reactions affected by the decisions of powerful leaders.

That novella, she would agree, is an example of historical fiction. But because *Black Velvet Band* is tied so tightly to a factual time framework and involves actual historic persons, she calls this new novel a work of fictive history.

Other books published by Teresa K. Lehr include:
- ~ To Serve the Community. (1997) A sesquicentennial history of Rochester General Hospital.
- ~Let the art of Medicine Flourish (2000) A centennial history of the Rochester Academy of Medicine.
- ~ Lighting the Way (2002) A centennial history of St. John's Home.
- ~ For Those Who Shaped Our Heritage (2004) A centennial history of the Fairport Baptist Home.
- ~ Drawn to Tradition, Challenged by Change (2006) A sesquicentennial history of Christ Church, Rochester.
- ~ Emerging Leader (2012) Co-edited with Philip Gerber, PHD. The Civil War Letters of Col. Carter Van Vleck to His Wife.
- ~ The Great Tonsil Massacre (2014). A historical novella.

Reviews

"*Black Velvet Band* is a poignant tale of a young nursing student's experience during one of the most tumultuous periods of the 20th century. Alice Denny's comfortable middle class existence is upset when her father dies unexpectedly, leaving the family with limited income. Alice realizes that she will have to find a way to support herself and chooses one of the few career options open to women in the early 20th century—nursing. The story opens with Alice boarding a trolley on her way to begin her new life in the nurses' training program at Rochester's General Hospital. With the U.S. preparing to enter World War I and shortage of medical personnel to meet both warfront and home front needs, Denny and her classmates would face unprecedented challenges.

"The fictionalized story was inspired by a series of letters that real-life Alice Denny wrote to her sister in 1917 and 1918. Author Terry Lehr weaves together tidbits from Alice's letters, hospital records, newspaper articles, and other sources to create a meticulously researched and richly detailed narrative that invites the reader behind the scenes for a glimpse at an oft-hidden side of the war. The military's demand for trained medical personnel left stateside hospitals short-staffed and placed unusual burdens on student nurses, who were called upon to take the place of graduate nurses who had volunteered to serve the Red Cross overseas, and their supervisors.

"Lehr tells this story from multiple perspectives, including that of Alice and her classmates but also that of nursing supervisor Mary Keith and her colleagues. The author captures the strange combination of emotions—joy, enthusiasm, exhaustion, trauma, and sadness—that the trainees experience while building friendships, sharing dorm rooms, attending classes, studying, and working long shifts in the hospital. But the reader is also treated to a view from the top, as General Hospital's Nursing Supervisor Mary Keith and her colleagues grapple with staff shortages in medical facilities through the city.

"All of their lives take an unexpected turn when Rochester—and the nation—is faced with an unprecedented public health crisis. The 1918 Spanish Influenza epidemic is often overshadowed by the Great War in history textbooks, but the flu was actually much more deadly than the war itself. And herein lays the greatest strength of Lehr's work. By exploring the tragedy of Spanish Influenza through the eyes of the caretakers who treated the victims, and who often became victims themselves, Lehr personalizes the history. Her characters, their voices and emotional reactions, make it real in a way that statistics and most nonfiction accounts cannot. And it is real. Lehr reports the history accurately; there is no exaggeration here, just a thoroughly detailed and honest account of the devastating effect the flu had on Rochester and cities like it through the U.S.—indeed the world.

"*Black Velvet Band* can be read simply as an account of a young woman's coming of age in a period of chaos, trauma, and tragedy—and it will delight those seeking such a story—but it is so much more. It gives voice to the overlooked heroines of World War I and the 1918 Spanish Influenza epidemic and reveals the significant role women played in the early 20th century health care profession."

- Christine Ridarsky, City Historian
    Historical Services Consultant
    Rochester Public Library

"Readers will appreciate the author's passion in telling this story using her creative touch to weave 1918 Influenza Epidemic history in the Rochester, New York area with a compelling tale of how community, hospital, nurse leaders and nursing students implemented plans to combat this critical event.

"As a graduate of one of the nursing school programs and a nursing staff member of two of the hospitals during my career, I felt pride, as a nurse, as the author captured the essence of nursing; chapter–by-chapter.

- Sylvia Schenck, RN, BS, MS
    Class of 1968, The Genesee Hospital (Rochester Homeopathic)
    Hospital School of Nursing

"Once again, Terry Lehr has masterfully shaped a Rochester medical history event into an engrossing read, populated with plausible, relatable characters, including a bevy of young student nurse interns under the tutelage of their dedicated senior nurses, doctors and administrators. We delight in a budding romance as inviting as a springtime stroll through the lilac trees of Highland Park. All of which and more are clothed in an 'edge of your seat' drama of the ravaging mystery and devastating effects of 1918's Influenza Epidemic. From her opening line of 'Here let me help you with that.', Terry Lehr does just that, as her inestimable and well-researched, deft way with a story enhances our knowledge of local history, while propelling us along on a ride that is exhilarating and poignant and, for the most part, true."

- Almeta Whitis, Prize-winning Storyteller

CPSIA information can be obtained
at www.ICGtesting.com
Printed in the USA
BVOW07s2035010318
509472BV00009B/308/P